IN THE foreword to this collection of short stories, W. Somerset Maugham says, "The reader should be satisfied if on closing the book he feels that he has been amused, interested, and moved." Maugham's intention is always primarily to entertain, and in this he is magnificently successful. He eschews the bloody violence so often employed by modern writers to shock the reader's interest. His talent is not obstreperously displayed, so that the reader forgets the author as he reads. His plots are always dramatic, but never forced.

Of these ten stories, "The Lotus Eater" will probably be a particular favorite. It is the story of Thomas Wilson, who seemed the typical manager of a provincial English bank. But at thirty he had bought an annuity for twenty-five years with his small savings, and had gone to Capri to live a life of lazy happiness. Then came the day when his annuity ran out. One of the most amusing stories is certainly "The Three Fat Women of Antibes," quite happy on their diet of fruit juice and anti-  Lena, whispily thin, that nothing ever came to stay. "Gigolette," the story of dove sixty feet into and of the gigolo loved her, is particularly moving. All of them, moving, satirical, or just plain funny, are worthy of the man who has been called the greatest short story writer of our times.

The Mixture As Before

W. SOMERSET MAUGHAM

The Mixture
As Before

THE BOOK LEAGUE OF AMERICA

New York

PRINTED AT THE *Country Life Press*, GARDEN CITY, N. Y., U. S. A.

Foreword

WHEN my last volume of short stories was published *The Times* headed their review of it with the title "The Mixture as Before." This of course was meant in a depreciatory sense, but I did not take it as such and so I have made so bold as to use it for the collection which I am now inviting the public to read. After pursuing the art of fiction for over forty years I have a notion that I know a good deal more about it than most people. In that long period I have seen a number of bright stars creep shyly over the horizon, travel across the sky to burn for a while in midheaven with dazzling effulgence, and then dwindle into an obscurity from which there is little likelihood that they will ever again emerge. The writer has his special communication to make, which when you come to analyze it is the personality with which he is endowed by nature, and during the early years of his activity he is groping in the dark to express it; then, if he is fortunate, he succeeds in doing this and if there is in his personality a certain abundance he may continue for a long time to produce work which is varied and characteristic; but the time comes at last (if he is so imprudent as to live to a ripe age) when, having given what he has to give, his powers seem to fail. He has fashioned all the stories he himself is capable of digging out of the inexhaustible mine which is human nature, and he has created all the characters which can possibly be constituted out of the various sides of his own personality. (For no one, I believe, can create a character from pure observation; if it is to have life it must be at least in some degree a representation of himself: I do not believe Shakespeare could have begotten Hamlet, Brutus and Iago if he had not been himself Iago, Brutus and Hamlet.) A generation has arisen which is strange to him, and it is only by an effort of will that he can understand the interests of a world of which he can now be only an observer. But to understand is not enough; the novelist must feel, and he must not only feel with, he must feel in. It is when he has reached this stage that he finds his readers turning from him in weariness. It is well then if he can bring himself to cease writing books which might just as well have remained unwritten. He is wise to watch warily for the signs which will indicate to him that, having said his say, it behooves him to resign himself to silence. He must be content, he must rejoice even, if a new work which he tenders to the approbation of the public shows no falling off; if, in fact, it can truthfully be called The Mixture as Before.

The writing of stories is very much a matter of luck. They are lying about at every street corner, but the writer may not be there at the moment they are waiting to be picked up or he may be looking at a shop window and pass them unnoticed. He may write them before he has seen all there is in them or he may turn them over in his mind so long that they have lost their freshness. He may not have seen them from the exact standpoint at which they can be written to their best advantage. It is a rare and happy event when he conceives the idea of a story, writes it at the precise moment when it is ripe, and treats it in such a way as to get out of it all it implicitly contains. Then it will be within its limitations perfect. But perfection is seldom achieved. I think a volume of modest dimensions would contain all the short stories which even closely approach it. The reader should be satisfied if in any collection of these short pieces of fiction he finds a general level of competence and on closing the book feels that he has been amused, interested and moved. I have now written between eighty and ninety stories, I shall not write any more; I am quite satisfied if the readers of this collection, should they remember any of those I have written in the past, agree that I have not been overbold in giving it the title I have.

Contents

The Three Fat Women
of Antibes

ONE WAS CALLED Mrs. Richman and she was a widow.
The second was called Mrs. Sutcliffe; she was American and she had divorced two husbands. The third
was called Miss Hickson and she was a spinster. They
were all in the comfortable forties and they were all
well off. Mrs. Sutcliffe had the odd first name of
Arrow. When she was young and slender she had
liked it well enough. It suited her, and the jests it
occasioned, though too often repeated, were very flattering; she was not disinclined to believe that it
suited her character too: it suggested directness,
speed and purpose. She liked it less now that her deli-
cate features had grown muzzy with fat, that her
arms and shoulders were so substantial and her hips
so massive. It was increasingly difficult to find dresses
to make her look as she liked to look. The jests her
name gave rise to now were made behind her back,
and she very well knew that they were far from oblig-

ing. But she was by no means resigned to middle age. She still wore blue to bring out the colour of her eyes and, with the help of art, her fair hair had kept its lustre. What she liked about Beatrice Richman and Frances Hickson was that they were both so much fatter than she, it made her look quite slim; they were both of them older and much inclined to treat her as a little young thing. It was not disagreeable. They were good-natured women, and they chaffed her pleasantly about her beaux; they had both given up the thought of that kind of nonsense, indeed Miss Hickson had never given it a moment's consideration, but they were sympathetic to her flirtations. It was understood that one of these days Arrow would make a third man happy.

"Only you mustn't get any heavier, darling," said Mrs. Richman.

"And for goodness' sake make certain of his bridge," said Miss Hickson.

They saw for her a man of about fifty, but well preserved and of distinguished carriage, an admiral on the retired list and a good golfer, or a widower without encumbrances, but in any case with a sub-stantial income. Arrow listened to them amiably, and kept to herself the fact that this was not at all her idea. It was true that she would have liked to marry again, but her fancy turned to a dark slim Italian with flashing eyes and a sonorous title or to a Spanish don of noble lineage; and not a day more than thirty. There were times when, looking at herself in her mirror, she was certain she did not look any more than that herself.

They were great friends, Miss Hickson, Mrs. Richman and Arrow Sutcliffe. It was their fat that had brought them together and bridge that had cemented their alliance. They had met first at Carlsbad, where they were staying at the same hotel and were treated by the same doctor who used them with the same ruthlessness. Beatrice Richman was enormous. She was a handsome woman, with fine eyes, rouged cheeks and painted lips. She was very well content to be a widow with a handsome fortune. She adored her food. She liked bread and butter, cream, potatoes and suet puddings, and for eleven months of the year ate pretty well everything she had a mind to, and for one month went to Carlsbad to reduce. But every year she grew fatter. She upbraided the doctor, but got no sympathy from him. He pointed out to her various plain and simple facts.

"But if I'm never to eat a thing I like life isn't worth living," she expostulated.

He shrugged his disapproving shoulders. Afterwards she told Miss Hickson that she was beginning to suspect he wasn't so clever as she had thought. Miss Hickson gave a great guffaw. She was that sort of woman. She had a deep bass voice, a large flat sallow face from which twinkled little bright eyes; she walked with a slouch, her hands in her pockets, and when she could do so without exciting attention smoked a long cigar. She dressed as like a man as she could.

"What the deuce should I look like in frills and furbelows?" she said. "When you're as fat as I am you may just as well be comfortable."

She wore tweeds and heavy boots and whenever she could went about bareheaded. But she was as strong as an ox and boasted that few men could drive a longer ball than she. She was plain of speech, and she could swear more variously than a stevedore. Though her name was Frances she preferred to be called Frank. Masterful, but with tact, it was her jovial strength of character that held the three together. They drank their waters together, had their baths at the same hour, they took their strenuous walks together, pounded about the tennis court with a professional to make them run, and ate at the same table their sparse and regulated meals. Nothing impaired their good humour but the scales, and when one or other of them weighed as much on one day as she had the day before neither Frank's coarse jokes, the *bonhomie* of Beatrice nor Arrow's pretty kittenish ways sufficed to dispel the gloom. Then drastic measures were resorted to, the culprit went to bed for twenty-four hours and nothing passed her lips but the doctor's famous vegetable soup which tasted like hot water in which a cabbage had been well rinsed.

Never were three women greater friends. They would have been independent of anyone else if they had not needed a fourth at bridge. They were fierce, enthusiastic players, and the moment the day's cure was over they sat down at the bridge table. Arrow, feminine as she was, played the best game of the three, a hard, brilliant game, in which she showed no mercy and never conceded a point or failed to take advantage of a mistake. Beatrice was solid and reliable. Frank was dashing; she was a great theorist, and had all the authorities at the tip of her tongue. They had long arguments over the rival systems. They bombarded one another with Culbertson and Sims. It was obvious that not one of them ever played a card without fifteen good reasons, but it was also obvious from the subsequent conversation that there were fifteen equally good reasons why she should not have played it. Life would have been perfect, even with the prospect of twenty-four hours of that filthy soup when the doctor's rotten (Beatrice) bloody (Frank) lousy (Arrow) scales pretended one hadn't lost an ounce in two days, if only there had not been this constant difficulty of finding someone to play with them who was in their class.

It was for this reason that on the occasion with which this narrative deals Frank invited Lena Finch to come and stay with them at Antibes. They were spending some weeks there on Frank's suggestion. It seemed absurd to her, with her common sense, that immediately the cure was over Beatrice who always lost twenty pounds should by giving way to her ungovernable appetite put it all on again. Beatrice was weak. She needed a person of strong will to watch her diet. She proposed then that on leaving Carlsbad they should take a house at Antibes where they could get plenty of exercise, everyone knew that nothing slimmed you like swimming, and as far as possible could go on with the cure. With a cook of their own they could at least avoid things that were obviously fattening. There was no reason why they should not all lose several pounds more. It seemed a very good idea. Beatrice knew what was good for her, and she could resist temptation well enough if temptation was not put right under her nose. Besides, she liked gambling, and a flutter at the Casino two or three times a week would pass the time very pleasantly. Arrow adored Antibes, and she would be looking her best after a month at Carlsbad. She could just pick and choose among the young Italians, the passionate Spaniards, the gallant Frenchmen and the long-limbed English who sauntered about all day in bathing trunks and gay-coloured dressing gowns. The plan worked very well. They had a grand time. Two days a week they ate nothing but hard-boiled eggs and raw tomatoes, and they mounted the scales every morning with light hearts. Arrow got down to eleven stone and felt just like a girl; Beatrice and Frank by standing in a certain way just avoided the thirteen. The machine they had bought registered kilogrammes, and they got extraordinarily clever at translating these in the twinkling of an eye to pounds and ounces.

But the fourth at bridge continued to be the difficulty. This person played like a foot, the other was so slow that it drove you frantic, one was quarrelsome, another was a bad loser, a third was next door to a crook. It was strange how hard it was to find exactly the player you wanted.

One morning when they were sitting in pyjamas on the terrace overlooking the sea, drinking their tea (without milk or sugar) and eating a rusk prepared by Dr. Hudebert and guaranteed not to be fattening, Frank looked up from her letters.

"Lena Finch is coming down to the Riviera," she said.

"Who's she?" asked Arrow.

"She married a cousin of mine. He died a couple of months ago, and she's just recovering from a nervous breakdown. What about asking her to come here for a fortnight?"

"Does she play bridge?" asked Beatrice.

"You bet your life she does," boomed Frank in her deep voice. "And a damned good game too.

We should be absolutely independent of outsiders."

"How old is she?" asked Arrow.

"Same age as I am."

"That sounds all right."

It was settled. Frank, with her usual decisiveness, stalked out as soon as she had finished her breakfast to send a wire, and three days later Lena Finch arrived. Frank met her at the station. She was in deep but not obtrusive mourning for the recent death of her husband. Frank had not seen her for two years. She kissed her warmly and took a good look at her.

"You're very thin, darling," she said.

Lena smiled bravely.

"I've been through a good deal lately. I've lost a lot of weight."

Frank sighed, but whether from sympathy with her cousin's sad loss, or from envy, was not obvious.

Lena was not, however, unduly depressed, and after a quick bath was quite ready to accompany Frank to Eden Roc. Frank introduced the stranger to her two friends and they sat down in what was known as the Monkey House. It was an enclosure covered with glass overlooking the sea, with a bar at the back, and it was crowded with chattering people in bathing costumes, pyjamas or dressing gowns, who were seated at the tables having drinks. Beatrice's soft heart went out to the lorn widow, and Arrow, seeing that she was pale, quite ordinary to look at and probably forty-eight, was prepared to like her very much. A waiter approached them.

"What will you have, Lena dear?" Frank asked.

"Oh, I don't know, what you all have, a dry Martini or a White Lady."

Arrow and Beatrice gave her a quick look. Everyone knows how fattening cocktails are.

"I daresay you're tired after your journey," said Frank kindly.

She ordered a dry Martini for Lena and a mixed lemon and orange juice for herself and her two friends.

"We find alcohol isn't very good in all this heat," she explained.

"Oh, it never affects me at all," Lena answered airily, "I like cocktails."

Arrow went very slightly pale under her rouge (neither she nor Beatrice ever wet their faces when they bathed, and they thought it absurd of Frank, a woman of her size, to pretend she liked diving), but she said nothing. The conversation was gay and easy, they all said the obvious things with gusto, and presently they strolled back to the villa for luncheon.

In each napkin were two little antifat rusks. Lena gave a bright smile as she put them by the side of her plate.

"May I have some bread?" she asked.

The grossest indecency would not have fallen on the ears of those three women with such a shock. Not one of them had eaten bread for ten years. Even Beatrice, greedy as she was, drew the line there. Frank, the good hostess, recovered herself first.

"Of course, darling," she said, and turning to the butler asked him to bring some.

"And some butter," said Lena in that pleasant easy way of hers.

There was a moment's embarrassed silence.

"I don't know if there's any in the house," said Frank, "but I'll enquire. There may be some in the kitchen."

"I adore bread and butter, don't you?" said Lena, turning to Beatrice.

Beatrice gave a sickly smile and an evasive reply. The butler brought a long crisp roll of French bread. Lena slit it in two and plastered it with the butter which was miraculously produced. A grilled sole was served.

"We eat very simply here," said Frank. "I hope you won't mind."

"Oh, no, I like my food very plain," said Lena as she took some butter and spread it over her fish. "As long as I can have bread and butter and potatoes and cream I'm quite happy."

The three friends exchanged a glance. Frank's great sallow face sagged a little, and she looked with distaste at the dry, insipid sole on her plate. Beatrice came to the rescue.

"It's such a bore, we can't get cream here," she said. "It's one of the things one has to do without on the Riviera."

"What a pity," said Lena.

The rest of the luncheon consisted of lamb cutlets, with the fat carefully removed so that Beatrice should not be led astray, and spinach boiled in water, with stewed pears to end up with. Lena tasted her pears and gave the butler a look of enquiry. That resourceful man understood her at once, and though powdered sugar had never been served at that table before, handed her without a moment's hesitation a bowl of it. She helped herself liberally. The other three pretended not to notice. Coffee was served, and Lena took three lumps of sugar in hers.

"You have a very sweet tooth," said Arrow in a tone which she struggled to keep friendly.

"We think saccharine so much more sweetening," said Frank, as she put a tiny tablet of it into her coffee.

"Disgusting stuff," said Lena.

Beatrice's mouth drooped at the corners, and she gave the lump sugar a yearning look.

"Beatrice!" boomed Frank sternly.

Beatrice stifled a sigh and reached for the saccharine.

Frank was relieved when they could sit down to the bridge table. It was plain to her that Arrow and

Beatrice were upset. She wanted them to like Lena, and she was anxious that Lena should enjoy her fortnight with them. For the first rubber Arrow cut with the newcomer.

"Do you play Vanderbilt or Culbertson?" she asked her.

"I have no conventions," Lena answered in a happy-go-lucky way, "I play by the light of nature."

"I play strict Culbertson," said Arrow acidly.

The three fat women braced themselves to the fray. No conventions indeed! They'd learn her. When it came to bridge even Frank's family feeling was forgotten, and she settled down with the same determination as the others to trim the stranger in their midst. But the light of nature served Lena very well. She had a natural gift for the game and great experience. She played with imagination, quickly, boldly, and with assurance. The other players were in too high a class not to realize very soon that Lena knew what she was about, and since they were all thoroughly good-natured, generous women, they were gradually mollified. This was real bridge. They all enjoyed themselves. Arrow and Beatrice began to feel more kindly towards Lena, and Frank, noticing this, heaved a fat sigh of relief. It was going to be a success.

After a couple of hours they parted, Frank and Beatrice to have a round of golf, and Arrow to take a brisk walk with a young Prince Roccamare whose acquaintance she had lately made. He was very sweet and young and good-looking. Lena said she would rest.

They met again just before dinner.

"I hope you've been all right, Lena dear," said Frank. "I was rather conscience-stricken at leaving you with nothing to do all this time."

"Oh, don't apologize. I had a lovely sleep, and then I went down to Juan and had a cocktail. And d'you know what I discovered? You'll be so pleased. I found a dear little teashop where they've got the most beautiful thick fresh cream. I've ordered half a pint to be sent every day. I thought it would be my little contribution to the household."

Her eyes were shining. She was evidently expecting them to be delighted.

"How very kind of you," said Frank, with a look that sought to quell the indignation that she saw on the faces of her two friends. "But we never eat cream. In this climate it makes one so bilious."

"I shall have to eat it all myself then," said Lena cheerfully.

"Don't you ever think of your figure?" Arrow asked with icy deliberation.

"The doctor said I must eat."

"Did he say you must eat bread and butter and potatoes and cream?"

"Yes. That's what I thought you meant when you said you had simple food."

"You'll get simply enormous," said Beatrice.

Lena laughed gaily.

"No, I shan't. You see, nothing ever makes me fat. I've always eaten everything I wanted to, and it's never had the slightest effect on me."

The stony silence that followed this speech was only broken by the entrance of the butler.

"*Mademoiselle est servie,*" he announced.

They talked the matter over late that night, after Lena had gone to bed, in Frank's room. During the evening they had been furiously cheerful, and they had chaffed one another with a friendliness that would have taken in the keenest observer. But now they dropped the mask. Beatrice was sullen, Arrow was spiteful and Frank was unmanned.

"It's not very nice for me to sit there and see her eat all the things I particularly like," said Beatrice plaintively.

"It's not very nice for any of us," Frank snapped back.

"You should never have asked her here," said Arrow.

"How was I to know?" cried Frank.

"I can't help thinking that if she really cared for her husband she would hardly eat so much," said Beatrice. "He's only been buried two months. I mean, I think you ought to show some respect for the dead."

"Why can't she eat the same as we do?" asked Arrow viciously. "She's a guest."

"Well, you heard what she said. The doctor told her she must eat."

"Then she ought to go to a sanatorium."

"It's more than flesh and blood can stand, Frank," moaned Beatrice.

"If I can stand it you can stand it."

"She's your cousin, she's not our cousin," said Arrow. "I'm not going to sit there for fourteen days and watch that woman make a hog of herself."

"It's so vulgar to attach all this importance to food," Frank boomed, and her voice was deeper than ever. "After all the only thing that counts really is spirit."

"Are you calling *me* vulgar, Frank?" asked Arrow with flashing eyes.

"No, of course she isn't," interrupted Beatrice.

"I wouldn't put it past you to go down in the kitchen when we're all in bed and have a good square meal on the sly."

Frank sprang to her feet.

"How dare you say that, Arrow! I'd never ask anybody to do what I'm not prepared to do myself. Have you known me all these years and do you think me capable of such a mean thing?"

"How is it you never take off any weight then?"

Frank gave a gasp and burst into a flood of tears.

"What a cruel thing to say! I've lost pounds and pounds."

She wept like a child. Her vast body shook, and great tears splashed on her mountainous bosom.

"Darling, I didn't mean it," cried Arrow.

She threw herself on her knees and enveloped what she could of Frank in her own plump arms. She wept, and the mascara ran down her cheeks.

"D'you mean to say I don't look thinner?" Frank sobbed. "After all I've gone through!"

"Yes, dear, of course you do," cried Arrow through her tears. "Everybody's noticed it."

Beatrice, though naturally of a placid disposition, began to cry gently. It was very pathetic. Indeed, it would have been a hard heart that failed to be moved by the sight of Frank, that lion-hearted woman, crying her eyes out. Presently, however, they dried their tears and had a little brandy and water, which every doctor had told them was the least fattening thing they could drink, and then they felt much better. They decided that Lena should have the nourishing food that had been ordered her, and they made a solemn resolution not to let it disturb their equanimity. She was certainly a first-rate bridge player, and after all it was only for a fortnight. They would do whatever they could to make her stay enjoyable. They kissed one another warmly and separated for the night feeling strangely uplifted. Nothing should interfere with the wonderful friendship that had brought so much happiness into their three lives.

But human nature is weak. You must not ask too much of it. They ate grilled fish while Lena ate macaroni sizzling with cheese and butter; they ate grilled cutlets and boiled spinach while Lena ate *pâté de foie gras;* twice a week they ate hard-boiled eggs and raw tomatoes, while Lena ate peas swimming in cream and potatoes cooked in all sorts of delicious ways. The chef was a good chef, and he leapt at the opportunity afforded him to send up one dish more rich, tasty and succulent than the other.

"Poor Jim," sighed Lena, thinking of her husband, "he loved French cooking."

The butler disclosed the fact that he could make half a dozen kinds of cocktail, and Lena informed them that the doctor had recommended her to drink burgundy at luncheon and champagne at dinner. The three fat women persevered. They were gay, chatty and even hilarious (such is the natural gift that women have for deception), but Beatrice grew limp and forlorn, and Arrow's tender blue eyes acquired a steely glint. Frank's deep voice grew more raucous. It was when they played bridge that the strain showed itself. They had always been fond of talking over their hands, but their discussions had been friendly. Now a distinct bitterness crept in, and sometimes one pointed out a mistake to another with quite unnecessary frankness. Discussion turned to argument and argument to altercation. Sometimes the session ended in angry silence. Once Frank accused Arrow of deliberately letting her down. Two or three times Beatrice, the softest of the three, was reduced to tears. On another occasion Arrow flung down her cards and swept out of the room in a pet. Their tempers were getting frayed. Lena was the peacemaker.

"I think it's such a pity to quarrel over bridge," she said. "After all, it's only a game."

It was all very well for her. She had had a square meal and half a bottle of champagne. Besides, she had phenomenal luck. She was winning all their money. The score was put down in a book after each session, and hers mounted up day after day with unfailing regularity. Was there no justice in the world? They began to hate one another. And though they hated her too they could not resist confiding in her. Each of them went to her separately and told her how detestable the others were. Arrow said she was sure it was bad for her to see so much of women so much older than herself. She had a good mind to sacrifice her share of the lease and go to Venice for the rest of the summer. Frank told Lena that with her masculine mind it was too much to expect that she could be satisfied with anyone so frivolous as Arrow and so frankly stupid as Beatrice.

"I must have intellectual conversation," she

boomed. "When you have a brain like mine you've got to consort with your intellectual equals."

Beatrice only wanted peace and quiet.

"Really I hate women," she said. "They're so unreliable; they're so malicious."

By the time Lena's fortnight drew to its close the three fat women were barely on speaking terms. They kept up appearances before Lena, but when she was not there made no pretences. They had got past quarrelling. They ignored one another, and when this was not possible treated each other with icy politeness.

Lena was going to stay with friends on the Italian Riviera, and Frank saw her off by the same train as that by which she had arrived. She was taking away with her a lot of their money.

"I don't know how to thank you," she said, as she got into the carriage. "I've had a wonderful visit."

If there was one thing that Frank Hickson prided herself on more than on being a match for any man it was that she was a gentlewoman, and her reply was perfect in its combination of majesty and graciousness.

"We've all enjoyed having you here, Lena," she said. "It's been a real treat."

But when she turned away from the departing train she heaved such a vast sigh of relief that the platform shook beneath her. She flung back her massive shoulders and strode home to the villa.

"Ouf!" she roared at intervals. "Ouf!"

She changed into her one-piece bathing suit, put on her espadrilles and a man's dressing gown (no nonsense about it) and went to Eden Roc. There was still time for a bathe before luncheon. She passed through the Monkey House, looking about her to say good morning to anyone she knew, for she felt on a sudden at peace with mankind, and then stopped dead still. She could not believe her eyes. Beatrice was sitting at one of the tables, by herself; she wore the pyjamas she had bought at Molyneux's a day or two before, she had a string of pearls round her neck, and Frank's quick eyes saw that she had just had her hair waved; her cheeks, her eyes, her lips were made up. Fat, nay vast, as she was, none could deny that she was an extremely handsome woman. But what was she doing? With the slouching gait of the Neanderthal man which was Frank's characteristic walk she went up to Beatrice. In her black bathing dress Frank looked like the huge cetacean which the Japanese catch in the Torres Straits and which the vulgar call a sea cow.

"Beatrice, what are you doing?" she cried in her deep voice.

It was like the roll of thunder in the distant mountains. Beatrice looked at her coolly.

"Eating," she answered.

"Damn it, I can see you're eating."

In front of Beatrice was a plate of *croissants* and a plate of butter, a pot of strawberry jam, coffee and a jug of cream. Beatrice was spreading butter thick on the delicious hot bread, covering this with jam, and then pouring the thick cream over all.

"You'll kill yourself," said Frank.

"I don't care," mumbled Beatrice with her mouth full.

"You'll put on pounds and pounds."

"Go to hell!"

She actually laughed in Frank's face. My God, how good those *croissants* smelt!

"I'm disappointed in you, Beatrice. I thought you had more character."

"It's your fault. That blasted woman. You would have her down. For a fortnight I've watched her gorge like a hog. It's more than flesh and blood can stand. I'm going to have one square meal if I bust."

The tears welled up to Frank's eyes. Suddenly she felt very weak and womanly. She would have liked a strong man to take her on his knee and pet her and cuddle her and call her little baby names. Speechless, she sank down on a chair by Beatrice's side. A waiter came up. With a pathetic gesture she waved towards the coffee and *croissants*.

"I'll have the same," she sighed.

She listlessly reached out her hand to take a roll, but Beatrice snatched away the plate.

"No, you don't," she said. "You wait till you get your own."

Frank called her a name which ladies seldom apply to one another in affection. In a moment the waiter brought her *croissants*, butter, jam and coffee.

"Where's the cream, you fool?" she roared like a lioness at bay.

She began to eat. She ate gluttonously. The place was beginning to fill up with bathers coming to enjoy a cocktail or two after having done their duty by the sun and the sea. Presently Arrow strolled along with Prince Roccamare. She had on a beautiful silk wrap which she held tightly round her with one hand in order to look as slim as possible, and she bore her head high so that he should not see her double chin. She was laughing gaily. She felt like a girl. He had just told her (in Italian) that her eyes made the blue of the Mediterranean look like pea soup. He left her to go into the men's room to brush his sleek black hair, and they arranged to meet in five minutes for a drink. Arrow walked on to the women's room to put a little more rouge on her cheeks and a little more red on her lips. On her way she caught sight of Frank and Beatrice. She stopped. She could hardly believe her eyes.

"My God!" she cried. "You beasts. You hogs." She seized a chair. "Waiter."

Her appointment went clean out of her head. In the twinkling of an eye the waiter was at her side.

"Bring me what these ladies are having," she ordered.

Frank lifted her great heavy head from her plate. "Bring me some *pâté de foie gras*," she boomed.

"Frank!" cried Beatrice.

"Shut up."

"All right. I'll have some too."

The coffee was brought, and the hot rolls and cream and the *pâté de foie gras*, and they set to. They spread the cream on the *pâté* and they ate it. They devoured great spoonfuls of jam. They crunched the delicious crisp bread voluptuously. What was love to Arrow then? Let the Prince keep his palace in Rome and his castle in the Apennines. They did not speak. What they were about was much too serious. They ate with solemn, ecstatic fervour.

"I haven't eaten potatoes for twenty-five years," said Frank in a far-off brooding tone.

"Waiter," cried Beatrice, "bring fried potatoes for three."

"*Très bien, madame.*"

The potatoes were brought. Not all the perfumes of Arabia smelt so sweet. They ate them with their fingers.

"Bring me a dry Martini," said Arrow.

"You can't have a dry Martini in the middle of a meal, Arrow," said Frank.

"Can't I? You wait and see."

"All right then. Bring me a double dry Martini," said Frank.

"Bring three double dry Martinis," said Beatrice.

They were brought and drunk at a gulp. The women looked at one another and sighed. The misunderstandings of the last fortnight dissolved, and the sincere affection each had for the other welled up again in their hearts. They could hardly believe that they had ever contemplated the possibility of severing a friendship that had brought them so much solid satisfaction. They finished the potatoes.

"I wonder if they've got any chocolate éclairs," said Beatrice.

"Of course they have."

And of course they had. Frank thrust one whole into her huge mouth, swallowed it and seized another, but before she ate it she looked at the other two and plunged a vindictive dagger into the heart of the monstrous Lena.

"You can say what you like, but the truth is she played a damned rotten game of bridge, really."

"Lousy," agreed Arrow.

But Beatrice suddenly thought she would like a meringue.

A Man with a Conscience

St. laurent de maroni is a pretty little place. It is
neat and clean. It has an Hôtel de Ville and a Palais
de Justice of which many a town in France would be
proud. The streets are wide, and the fine trees that
border them give a grateful shade. The houses look as
though they had just had a coat of paint. Many of
them nestle in little gardens, and in the gardens are
palm trees and flame of the forest; cannas flaunt their
bright colours and crotons their variety; the bougain-
villaeas, purple or red, riot profusely, and the elegant
hibiscus offers its gorgeous flowers with a negligence
that seems almost affected. St. Laurent de Maroni is
the centre of the French penal settlements of Guiana,
and a hundred yards from the quay at which you land
is the great gateway of the prison camp. These pretty
little houses in their tropical gardens are the resi-
dences of the prison officials, and if the streets are
neat and clean it is because there is no lack of con-

victs to keep them so. One day, walking with a casual acquaintance, I came upon a young man, in the round straw hat and the pink-and-white stripes of the convict's uniform, who was standing by the roadside with a pick. He was doing nothing.

"Why are you idling?" my companion asked him.

The man gave his shoulders a scornful shrug.

"Look at the blade of grass there," he answered. "I've got twenty years to scratch it away."

St. Laurent de Maroni exists for the group of prison camps of which it is the centre. Such trade as it has depends on them; its shops, kept by Chinese, are there to satisfy the wants of the warders, the doctors and the numerous officials who are connected with the penal settlements. The streets are silent and deserted. You pass a convict with a dispatch case under his arm: he has some job in the administration; or another with a basket: he is a servant in somebody's house. Sometimes you come upon a little group in the charge of a warder; often you see them strolling to or from the prison unguarded. The prison gates are open all day long, and the prisoners freely saunter in and out. If you see a man not in the prison uniform, he is probably a freed man who is condemned to spend a number of years in the colony and who, unable to get work, living on the edge of starvation, is drinking himself to death on the cheap strong rum which is called tafia.

There is a hotel at St. Laurent de Maroni, and here I had my meals. I soon got to know by sight the habitual frequenters. They came in and sat each at his little table, ate their meals in silence and went out again. The hotel was kept by a coloured woman, and the man she lived with, an ex-convict, was the only waiter. But the governor of the colony, who lives at Cayenne, had put at my disposal his own bungalow, and it was there I slept. An old Arab looked after it; he was a devout Mahomedan, and at intervals during the day I heard him say his prayers. To make my bed, keep my rooms tidy and run errands for me, the commandant of the prison had assigned me another convict. Both were serving life sentences for murder; the commandant told me that I could place entire confidence in them; they were as honest as the day, and I could leave anything about without the slightest risk. But I will not conceal from the reader that when I went to bed at night I took the precaution to lock my door and to bolt my shutters. It was foolish, no doubt, but I slept more comfortably.

I had come with letters of introduction, and both the governor of the prison settlements and the commandant of the camp at St. Laurent did everything they could to make my visit agreeable and instructive. I will not here narrate all I heard and saw. I am not a reporter. It is not my business to attack or to defend the system which the French have thought fit to adopt in regard to their criminals. Besides, the system is now condemned; prisoners will soon cease to be sent out to French Guiana, to suffer the illnesses incident to the climate and the work in malarial jungles to which so many are relegated, to endure nameless degradations, to lose hope, to rot, to die. I will only say that I saw no physical cruelty. On the other hand I saw no attempt to make the criminal on the expiration of his sentence a useful citizen. I saw nothing done for his spiritual welfare. I heard nothing of classes that he could attend in order to improve his education, or organized games that might distract his mind. I saw no library where he could get books to read when his day's work was done. I saw a condition of affairs that only the strongest character could hope to surmount. I saw a brutishness that must reduce all but a very few to apathy and despair.

All this has nothing to do with me. It is vain to torment oneself over sufferings that one cannot alleviate. My object here is to tell a story. As I am well aware, one can never know everything there is to be known about human nature. One can be sure only of one thing, and that is that it will never cease to have a surprise in store for you. When I had got over the impression of bewilderment, surprise and horror to which my first visit to the prison camp gave rise, I bethought myself that there were certain matters that I was interested to enquire into. I should inform

the reader that three quarters of the convicts at St.
Laurent de Maroni are there for murder. This is not
official information and it may be that I exaggerate;
every prisoner has a little book in which are set down
his crime, his sentence, his punishments, and whatever else the authorities think necessary to keep note
of; and it was from an examination of a considerable
number of these that I formed my estimate. It gave
me something of a shock to realize that in England
far, far the greater number of these men whom I saw
working in shops, lounging about the verandas of
their dormitories or sauntering through the streets
would have suffered capital punishment. I found
them not at all disinclined to speak of the crime for
which they had been convicted, and in pursuance of
my purpose I spent the better part of one day enquiring into crimes of passion. I wanted to know exactly
what was the motive that had made a man kill his
wife or his girl. I had a notion that jealousy and
wounded honour might not perhaps tell the whole
story. I got some curious replies, and among them
one that was not to my mind lacking in humour. This
was from a man working in the carpenter's shop who
had cut his wife's throat; when I asked him why he
had done it, he answered with a shrug of the shoulders:
"*Manque d'entente.*" His casual tone made the best
translation of this: We didn't get on very well. I could
not help observing that if men in general looked upon

this as an adequate reason for murdering their wives, the mortality in the female sex would be alarming. But after putting a good many questions to a good many men, I arrived at the conclusion that at the bottom of nearly all these crimes was an economic motive; they had killed their wives or mistresses not only from jealousy, because they were unfaithful to them, but also because somehow it affected their pockets. A woman's infidelity was sometimes an occasion of financial loss, and it was this in the end that drove a man to his desperate act; or, himself in need of money to gratify other passions, he murdered because his victim was an obstacle to his exclusive possession of it. I do not conclude that a man never kills his woman because his love is spurned or his honour tarnished. I only offer my observation on these particular cases as a curious sidelight on human nature. I should not venture to deduce from it a general rule.

I spent another day enquiring into the matter of conscience. Moralists have sought to persuade us that it is one of the most powerful agents in human behaviour. Now that reason and pity have agreed to regard hell-fire as a hateful myth, many good men have seen in conscience the chief safeguard that shall induce the human race to walk in the way of righteousness. Shakespeare has told us that it makes cowards of us all. Novelists and playwrights have described for us the pangs that assail the wicked; they have vividly pictured the anguish of a stricken conscience and the sleepless nights it occasions; they have shown it poisoning every pleasure till life is so intolerable that discovery and punishment come as a welcome relief. I had often wondered how much of all this was true. Moralists have an axe to grind; they must draw a moral. They think that if they say a thing often enough people will believe it. They are apt to state that a thing is so when they consider it desirable that it should be. They tell us that the wages of sin is death; we know very well that it is not always. And so far as the authors of fiction are concerned, the playwrights and the novelists, when they get hold of an effective theme they are disposed to make use of it without bothering very much whether it agrees with the facts of life. Certain statements about human nature become, as it were, common property and so are accepted as self-evident. In the same way painters for ages painted shadows black, and it was not till the impressionists looked at them with unprejudiced eyes and painted what they saw that we discovered that shadows were coloured. It had sometimes struck me that perhaps conscience was the expression of a high moral development, so that its influence was strong only in those whose virtue was so shining that they were unlikely to commit any action for which they could seriously reproach themselves. It is generally

accepted that murder is a shocking crime, and it is
the murderer above all other criminals who is supposed to suffer remorse. His victim, we have been
led to believe, haunts his dreams in horrifying nightmares, and the recollection of his dreadful deed tor-
tures his waking hours. I could not miss the opportunity to enquire into the truth of this. I had no
intention of insisting if I encountered reticence or
distress, but I found in none of those with whom I
talked any such thing. Some said that in the same
circumstances they would do as they had done before.
Determinists without knowing it, they seemed to
look upon their action as ordained by a fate over
which they had no control. Some appeared to think
that their crime was committed by someone with
whom they had no connection.

"When one's young, one's foolish," they said, with
a careless gesture or a deprecating smile.

Others told me that if they had known what the
punishment was they would suffer, they would certainly have held their hands. I found in none any
regret for the human being they had violently bereft
of life. It seemed to me that they had no more feeling
for the creature they had killed than if it had been a
pig whose throat they had cut in the way of business.
Far from feeling pity for their victim, they were more
inclined to feel anger because he had been the occasion of their imprisonment in that distant land. In

only one man did I discern anything that might appropriately be called a conscience, and his story was so remarkable that I think it well worth narrating. For in this case it was, so far as I can understand, remorse that was the motive of the crime. I noticed the man's number, which was printed on the chest of the pink-and-white pyjamas of his prison uniform, but I have forgotten it. Anyhow, it is of no consequence. I never knew his name. He did not offer to tell me, and I did not like to ask it. I will call him Jean Charvin.

I met him on my first visit to the camp with the commandant. We were walking through a courtyard round which were cells, not punishment cells, but individual cells which are given to well-behaved prisoners who ask for them. They are sought after by those to whom the promiscuity of the dormitories is odious. Most of them were empty, for their occupants were engaged in their various employments. Jean Charvin was at work in his cell, writing at a small table, and the door was open. The commandant called him, and he came out. I looked into the cell. It contained a fixed hammock, with a dingy mosquito net; by the side of this was a small table on which were his bits and pieces, a shaving mop and a razor, a hairbrush and two or three battered books. On the walls were photographs of persons of respectable appearance and illustrations from picture papers.

He had been sitting on his bed to write, and the table on which he had been writing was covered with papers. They looked like accounts. He was a handsome man, tall, erect and lean, with flashing dark eyes and clean-cut, strong features. The first thing I noticed about him was that he had a fine head of long, naturally waving dark brown hair. This at once made him look different from the rest of the prisoners, whose hair is close-cropped, but cropped so badly, in ridges, that it gives them a sinister look. The commandant spoke to him of some official business, and then as we were leaving added in a friendly way:

"I see your hair is growing well."

Jean Charvin reddened and smiled. His smile was boyish and engaging.

"It'll be some time yet before I get it right again."

The commandant dismissed him, and we went on.

"He's a very decent fellow," he said. "He's in the accountant's department, and he's had leave to let his hair grow. He's delighted."

"What is he here for?" I asked.

"He killed his wife. But he's only got six years. He's clever and a good worker. He'll do well. He comes from a very decent family, and he's had an excellent education."

I thought no more of Jean Charvin, but by chance I met him next day on the road. He was coming towards me. He carried a black dispatch case under

his arm, and except for the pink-and-white stripes of
his uniform and the ugly round straw hat that concealed his handsome head of hair, you might have
taken him for a young lawyer on his way to court.
He walked with a long, leisurely stride, and he had
an easy, you might almost say a gallant, bearing.
He recognized me, and taking off his hat bade me
good morning. I stopped, and for something to say
asked him where he was going. He told me he was
taking some papers from the governor's office to the
bank. There was a pleasing frankness in his face, and
his eyes, his really beautiful eyes, shone with good
will. I supposed that the vigour of his youth was such
that it made life, notwithstanding his position and his
surroundings, more than tolerable, even pleasant.
You would have said that here was a young man
without a care in the world.

"I hear you're going to St. Jean tomorrow," he
said.

"Yes. It appears I must start at dawn."

St. Jean is a camp seventeen kilometres from St.
Laurent, and it is here that are interned the habitual
criminals who have been sentenced to transportation
after repeated terms of imprisonment. They are petty
thieves, confidence men, forgers, tricksters and such-
like; the prisoners of St. Laurent, condemned for
more serious offences, look upon them with contempt.

"You should find it an interesting experience,"

Jean Charvin said, with his frank and engaging smile. "But keep your pocketbook buttoned up, they'd steal the shirt off your back if they had half a chance. They're a dirty lot of scoundrels!"

That afternoon, waiting till the heat of the day was less, I sat on the veranda outside my bedroom and read; I had drawn the jalousies, and it was tolerably cool. My old Arab came up the stairs on his bare feet, and in his halting French told me that there was a man from the commandant who wanted to see me.

"Send him up," I said.

In a moment the man came, and it was Jean Charvin. He told me that the commandant had sent him to give me a message about my excursion next day to St. Jean. When he had delivered it I asked him if he would not sit down and have a cigarette with me. He wore a cheap wrist watch, and he looked at it.

"I have a few minutes to spare. I should be glad to." He sat down and lit the cigarette I offered him. He gave me a smiling look of his soft eyes. "Do you know, this is the first time I've ever been asked to sit down since I was sentenced." He inhaled a long whiff of his cigarette. "Egyptian. I haven't smoked an Egyptian cigarette for three years."

The convicts make their own cigarettes out of a coarse, strong tobacco that is sold in square blue packets. Since one is not allowed to pay them for the services they may render you, but may give them tobacco, I had bought a good many packets of this.

"How does it taste?"

"One gets accustomed to everything, and to tell you the truth, my palate is so vitiated, I prefer the stuff we get here."

"I'll give you a couple of packets."

I went into my room and fetched them. When I returned he was looking at some books that were lying on the table.

"Are you fond of reading?" I asked.

"Very. I think the want of books is what I most suffer from now. The few I can get hold of I'm forced to read over and over again."

To so great a reader as myself no deprivation seems more insupportable than the lack of books.

"I have several French ones in my bag. I'll look them out, and if you care to have them I'll give them to you if you can come along again."

My offer was due only in part to kindness; I wanted to have another chance of a talk with him.

"I should have to show them to the commandant. He would only let me keep them if there was no doubt they couldn't possibly corrupt my morals. But he's a good-natured man, I don't think he'll make any difficulties."

There was a hint of slyness in the smile with which he said this, and I suspected that he had taken the measure of the well-meaning, conscientious chief of the camp and knew pretty well how to get on the right side of him. It would have been unjust to blame him if he exercised tact, and even cunning, to render his lot as tolerable as might be.

"The commandant has a very good opinion of you."

"He's a fine man. I'm very grateful to him, he's done a great deal for me. I'm an accountant by profession and he's put me in the accountant's department. I love figures, it gives me an intense satisfaction to deal with them, they're living things to me, and now that I can handle them all day long I feel myself again."

"And are you glad to have a cell of your own?"

"It's made all the difference. To be herded with fifty men, the scum of the earth, and never to be alone for a minute—it was awful. That was the worst of all. At home, at Le Havre—that is where I lived—I had an apartment, modest of course, but my own, and we had a maid who came in by the day. We lived decently. It made it ten times harder for me than for the rest, most of them, who have never known anything but squalor, filth and promiscuity."

I had asked him about the cell in the hope that I could get him to talk about the life that is led in those vast dormitories in which the men are locked from five in the evening till five next morning. During these twelve hours they are their own masters. A warder can enter, they told me, only at the risk of his life. They have no light after eight o'clock, but from sardine tins, a little oil, and a rag they make lamps by the light of which they can see enough to play cards. They gamble furiously, not for love, but for the money they keep secreted on their bodies; they are unscrupulous, ruthless men, and naturally enough bitter quarrels often arise. They are settled with knives. Often in the morning, when the dormitory is opened, a man is found dead, but no threats, no promises, will induce anyone to betray the slayer. Other things Jean Charvin told me which I cannot narrate. He told me of one young fellow who had come out from France on the same ship with himself and with whom he had made friends. He was a good-looking boy. One day he went to the commandant and asked him if he could have a cell to himself. The commandant asked him why he wanted one. He explained. The commandant looked through his list and told him that at the moment all were occupied, but that as soon as there was a vacancy he should have one. Next morning when the dormitory was opened, he was found dead on his hammock with his belly ripped open to the breastbone.

"They're savage brutes, and if one isn't a brute by the time one arrives only a miracle can save one from becoming as brutal as the rest."

Jean Charvin looked at his watch and got up. He

walked away from me and then, with his charming smile, turned and faced me.

"I must go now. If the commandant gives me permission I will come and get the books you were kind enough to offer me."

In Guiana you do not shake hands with a convict, and a tactful man, taking leave of you, puts himself in such a position that there can be no question of your offering him your hand or of refusing his should he, forgetting for a moment, instinctively tender it. Heaven knows, it would have meant nothing to me to shake hands with Jean Charvin; it gave me a pang to see the care he had taken to spare me embarrassment.

I saw him twice more during my stay at St. Laurent. He told me his story, but I will tell it now in my words rather than in his, for I had to piece it together from what he said at one time and another, and what he left out I have had to supply out of my own imagination. I do not believe it has led me astray. It was as though he had given me three letters out of a number of five-letter words; the chances are that I have guessed most of the words correctly.

Jean Charvin was born and bred in the great seaport of Le Havre. His father had a good post in the customs. Having finished his education, he did his military service and then looked about for a job. Like a great many other young Frenchmen he was pre-

pared to sacrifice the hazardous chance of wealth for
a respectable security. His natural gift for figures
made it easy for him to get a place in the accountant's
department of a large exporting house. His future was
assured. He could look forward to earning a sufficient
income to live in the modest comfort of the class to
which he belonged. He was industrious and well
behaved. Like most young Frenchmen of his generation he was athletic. He swam and played tennis in
summer, and in winter he bicycled. On two evenings
a week to keep himself fit he spent a couple of hours
in a gymnasium. Through his childhood, his ado-
lescence and his young manhood, he lived in the
constant companionship of a boy called, shall we say
for the purposes of this narrative, Henri Renard,
whose father was also an official in the customs. Jean
and Riri went to school together, played together,
worked for their examinations together, spent their
holidays together, for the two families were intimate,
had their first affairs with girls together, partnered
one another in the local tennis tournaments, and did
their military service together. They never quarrelled.
They were never so happy as in one another's society.
They were inseparable. When the time came for them
to start working, they decided that they would go
into the same firm; but that was not so easy; Jean
tried to get Riri a job in the exporting house that had
engaged him, but could not manage it, and it was not

till a year later that Riri got something to do. But by then trade was as bad at Le Havre as everywhere else, and in a few months he found himself once more without employment.

Riri was a light-hearted youth, and he enjoyed his leisure. He danced, bathed and played tennis. It was thus that he made the acquaintance of a girl who had recently come to live at Le Havre. Her father had been a captain in the colonial army, and on his death her mother had returned to Le Havre, which was her native place. Marie-Louise was then eighteen. She had spent almost all her life in Tonkin. This gave her an exotic attraction for the young men who had never been out of France in their lives, and first Riri, then Jean, fell in love with her. Perhaps that was inevitable; it was certainly unfortunate. She was a well-brought-up girl, an only child, and her mother, besides her pension, had a little money of her own. It was evident that she could be pursued only with a view to marriage. Of course Riri, dependent for the while entirely on his father, could not make an offer that there was the least chance of Madame Meurice, Marie-Louise's mother, accepting; but having the whole day to himself he was able to see a great deal more of Marie-Louise than Jean could. Madame Meurice was something of an invalid, so that Marie-Louise had more liberty than most French girls of her age and station. She knew that both Riri and

Jean were in love with her, she liked them both and was pleased by their attentions, but she gave no sign that she was in love with either. It was impossible to tell which she preferred. She was well aware that Riri was not in a position to marry her.

"What did she look like?" I asked Jean Charvin.

"She was small, with a pretty little figure, with large grey eyes, a pale skin and soft, mouse-coloured hair. She was rather like a little mouse. She was not beautiful, but pretty, in a quaint demure way; there was something very appealing about her. She was easy to get on with. She was simple and unaffected. You couldn't help feeling that she was reliable and would make anyone a good wife."

Jean and Riri hid nothing from one another, and Jean made no secret of the fact that he was in love with Marie-Louise, but Riri had met her first, and it was an understood thing between them that Jean should not stand in his way. At length she made her choice. One day Riri waited for Jean to come away from his office and told him that Marie-Louise had consented to marry him. They had arranged that as soon as he got a job his father should go to her mother and make the formal offer. Jean was hard hit. It was not easy to listen with eager sympathy to the plans that the excitable and enchanted Riri made for the future. But he was too much attached to Riri to feel sore with him; he knew how lovable he was, and he could not blame Marie-Louise. He tried with all his might to accept honestly the sacrifice he made on the altar of friendship.

"Why did she choose him rather than you?" I asked.

"He had immense vitality. He was the gayest, most amusing lad you ever met. His high spirits were infectious. You couldn't be dull in his company."

"He had pep," I smiled.

"And an incredible charm."

"Was he good-looking?"

"No, not very. He was shorter than me, slight and wiry; but he had a nice, good-humoured face." Jean Charvin smiled rather pleasantly. "I think without any vanity I can say that I was better-looking than Riri."

But Riri did not get a job. His father, tired of keeping him in idleness, wrote to everyone he could think of, the members of his family and his friends in various parts of France, asking them if they could not find something, however modest, for Riri to do; and at last he got a letter from a cousin in Lyons who was in the silk business to say that his firm were looking for a young man to go out to Phnom-Penh, in Cambodia, where they had a branch, to buy native silk for them. If Riri was willing to take the job he could get it for him.

Though, like all French parents, Riri's hated him

to emigrate, there seemed no help for it, and it was
determined, although the salary was small, that he
must go. He was not disinclined. Cambodia was not
so far from Tonkin, and Marie-Louise must be familiar with the life. She had so often talked of it that
he had come to the conclusion that she would be glad
to go back to the East. To his dismay she told him
that nothing would induce her to. In the first place
she could not desert her mother, whose health was
obviously declining; and then, after having at last
settled down in France, she was determined never
again to leave it. She was sympathetic to Riri, but
resolute. With nothing else in prospect his father
would not hear of his refusing the offer; there was no
help for it, he had to go. Jean hated losing him, but
from the moment Riri told him his bad news, he had
realized with an exulting heart that fate was playing
into his hands. With Riri out of his way for five years
at least and, unless he were incompetent, with the
probability that he would settle in the East for good,
Jean could not doubt that after a while Marie-Louise
would marry him. His circumstances, his settled,
respectable position in Le Havre, where she could be
near her mother, would make her think it very sensible; and when she was no longer under the spell of
Riri's charm there was no reason why her great liking
for him should not turn to love. Life changed for him.
After months of misery he was happy again, and

though he kept them to himself he too now made great plans for the future. There was no need any longer to try not to love Marie-Louise.

Suddenly his hopes were shattered. One of the shipping firms at Le Havre had a vacancy, and it looked as though the application that Riri had quickly made would be favourably considered. A friend in the office told him that it was a certainty. It would settle everything. It was an old and conservative house, and it was well known that when you once got into it you were there for life. Jean Charvin was in despair, and the worst of it was that he had to keep his anguish to himself. One day the director of his own firm sent for him.

When he reached this point Jean stopped. A harassed look came into his eyes.

"I'm going to tell you something now that I've never told to anyone before. I'm an honest man, a man of principle; I'm going to tell you of the only discreditable action I've ever done in my life."

I must remind the reader here that Jean Charvin was wearing the pink-and-white stripes of the convict's uniform, with his number stencilled on his chest, and that he was serving a term of imprisonment for the murder of his wife.

"I couldn't imagine what the director wanted with me. He was sitting at his desk when I went into his office, and he gave me a searching look.

"'I want to ask you a question of great importance,' he said. 'I wish you to treat it as confidential.
I shall of course treat your answer as equally so.'

"I waited. He went on:

"'You've been with us for a considerable time. I
am very well satisfied with you, there is no reason
why you shouldn't reach a very good position in the
firm. I put implicit confidence in you.'

"'Thank you, sir,' I said. 'I will always try to
merit your good opinion.'

"'The question at issue is this. Monsieur Untel
is proposing to engage Henri Renard. He is very
particular about the character of his employees, and
in this case it is essential that he shouldn't make a
mistake. Part of Henri Renard's duties would be to
pay the crews of the firm's ships, and many hundreds
of thousand francs will pass through his hands. I
know that Henri Renard is your great friend and
that your families have always been very intimate.
I put you on your honour to tell me whether Monsieur
Untel would be justified in engaging this young man.'

"I saw at once what the question meant. If Riri
got the job he would stay and marry Marie-Louise, if
he didn't he would go out to Cambodia and I should
marry her. I swear to you it was not I who answered,
it was someone who stood in my shoes and spoke with
my voice, I had nothing to do with the words that
came from my mouth.

"'*Monsieur le directeur*,' I said, 'Henri and I have been friends all our lives. We have never been separated for a week. We went to school together; we shared our pocket money and our mistresses when we were old enough to have them; we did our military service together.'

"'I know. You know him better than anyone in the world. That is why I ask you these questions.'

"'It is not fair, *Monsieur le directeur*. You are asking me to betray my friend. I cannot, and I will not answer your questions.'

"The director gave me a shrewd smile. He thought himself much cleverer than he really was.

"'Your answer does you credit, but it has told me all I wished to know.' Then he smiled kindly. I suppose I was pale, I daresay I was trembling a little. 'Pull yourself together, my dear boy; you're upset and I can understand it. Sometimes in life one is faced by a situation where honesty stands on the one side and loyalty on the other. Of course one mustn't hesitate, but the choice is bitter. I shall not forget your behaviour in this case, and on behalf of Monsieur Untel I thank you.'

"I withdrew. Next morning Riri received a letter informing him that his services were not required, and a month later he sailed for the Far East."

Six months after this Jean Charvin and Marie-Louise were married. The marriage was hastened by the increasing gravity of Madame Meurice's illness. Knowing that she could not live long, she was anxious to see her daughter settled before she died. Jean wrote to Riri telling him the facts, and Riri wrote back warmly congratulating him. He assured him that he need have no compunctions on his behalf; when he had left France he realized that *he* could never marry Marie-Louise, and he was glad that Jean was going to. He was finding consolation at Phnom-Penh. His letter was very cheerful. From the beginning Jean had told himself that Riri, with his mercurial temperament, would soon forget Marie-Louise, and his letter looked as if he had already done so. He had done him no irreparable injury. It was a justification. For if *he* had lost Marie-Louise he would have died; with him it was a matter of life and death.

For a year Jean and Marie-Louise were extremely happy. Madame Meurice died, and Marie-Louise inherited a couple of hundred thousand francs; but with the depression and the unstable currency they decided not to have a child till the economic situation was less uncertain. Marie-Louise was a good and frugal housekeeper. She was an affectionate, amiable and satisfactory wife. She was placid. This before he married her had seemed to Jean a rather charming trait, but as time wore on it was borne in upon him that her placidity came from a certain lack of emotional ardour. It concealed no depth. He had always

thought she was like a little mouse; there was something mouselike in her furtive reticences; she was
oddly serious about trivial matters and could busy
herself indefinitely with things that were of no consequence. She had her own tiny little set of interests
and they left no room in her pretty sleek head for any
others. She sometimes began a novel, but seldom
cared to finish it. Jean was obliged to admit to himself that she was rather dull. The uneasy thought
came to him that perhaps it had not been worth while
to do a dirty trick for her sake. It began to worry him.
He missed Riri. He tried to persuade himself that
what was done was done and that he had really not
been a free agent, but he could not quite still the
prickings of his conscience. He wished now that when
the director of his firm spoke to him he had answered
differently.

Then a terrible thing happened. Riri contracted
typhoid fever and died. It was a frightful shock for
Jean. It was a shock to Marie-Louise too; she paid
Riri's parents the proper visit of condolence, but she
neither ate less heartily nor slept less soundly. Jean
was exasperated by her composure.

"Poor chap, he was always so gay," she said, "he
must have hated dying. But why did he go out there?
I told him the climate was bad; it killed my father,
and I knew what I was talking about."

Jean felt that he had killed him. If he had told the

director all the good he knew of Riri, knew as no one else in the world did, he would have got the post and would now be alive and well.

"I shall never forgive myself," he thought. "I shall never be happy again. Oh, what a fool I was, and what a cad!"

He wept for Riri. Marie-Louise sought to comfort him. She was a kind little thing and she loved him.

"You mustn't take it too hardly. After all you wouldn't have seen him for five years, and you'd have found him so changed that there wouldn't have been anything between you any more. He would have been a stranger to you. I've seen that sort of thing happen so often. You'd have been delighted to see him, and in half an hour you'd have discovered that you had nothing to say to one another."

"I daresay you're right," he sighed.

"He was too scatter-brained ever to have amounted to anything very much. He never had your firmness of character and your clear, solid intellect."

He knew what she was thinking. What would have been her position now if she had followed Riri to Indo-China and found herself at twenty-one a widow with nothing but her own two hundred thousand francs to live on? It was a lucky escape, and she congratulated herself on her good sense. Jean was a husband of whom she could be proud. He was earning good money. Jean was tortured by remorse. What he had suffered before was nothing to what he suffered now. The anguish that the recollection of his treachery caused him was worse than a physical pain gnawing at his vitals. It would assail him suddenly when he was in the middle of his work and twist his heartstrings with a violent pang. His agony was such that he craved for relief, and it was only by an effort of all his will that he prevented himself from making a full confession to Marie-Louise. But he knew how she would take it; she would not be shocked, she would think it rather a clever trick and be even subtly flattered that for her sake he had been guilty of a despicable act. She could not help him. He began to dislike her. For it was for her that he had done the shameful thing, and what was she? An ordinary, commonplace, rather calculating little woman.

"What a fool I've been," he repeated.

He did not even find her pretty any more. He knew now that she was terribly stupid. But of course she was not to blame for that, she was not to blame because he had been false to his friend; and he forced himself to be as sweet and tender to her as he had always been. He did whatever she wanted. She had only to express a wish for him to fulfil it if it was in his power. He tried to pity her, he tried to be tolerant; he told himself that from her own petty standpoint she was a good wife, methodical, saving, and in her manner, dress and appearance, a credit to a respectable young man. All that was true; but it was on her account that Riri had died, and he loathed her. She bored him to distraction. Though he said nothing, though he was kind, amiable and indulgent, he could often have killed her. When he did, however, it was almost without meaning to. It was ten months after Riri's death, and Riri's parents, Monsieur and Madame Renard, gave a party to celebrate the engagement of their daughter. Jean had seen little of them since Riri's death and he did not want to go. But Marie-Louise said they must; he had been Riri's greatest friend and it would be a grave lack of politeness on Jean's part not to attend an important celebration in the family. She had a keen sense of social obligation.

"Besides, it'll be a distraction for you. You've been in poor spirits for so long, a little amusement will do you good. There'll be champagne, won't there? Madame Renard doesn't like spending money, but on an occasion like this she'll have to sacrifice herself."

Marie-Louise chuckled slyly when she thought what a wrench it would be to Madame Renard to unloose her purse strings.

The party had been very gay. It gave Jean a nasty turn when he found that they were using Riri's old room for the women to put their wraps in and the men their coats. There was plenty of champagne. Jean drank a great deal to drown the bitter remorse that tormented him. He wanted to deaden the sound in his ears of Riri's laugh and to shut his eyes to the good humour of his shining glance. It was three o'clock when they got home. Next day was Sunday, so Jean had no work to go to. They slept late. The rest I can tell in Jean Charvin's own words.

"I had a headache when I woke. Marie-Louise was not in bed. She was sitting at the dressing table brushing her hair. I've always been very keen on physical culture, and I was in the habit of doing exercises every morning. I didn't feel very much inclined to do them that morning, but after all that champagne I thought I'd better. I got out of bed and took up my Indian clubs. Our bedroom was fairly large, and there was plenty of room to swing them between the bed and the dressing table where Marie-Louise was sitting. I did my usual exercises. Marie-Louise had started a little while before having her hair cut differently, quite short, and I thought it repulsive. From the back she looked like a boy, and the stubble of cropped hair on her neck made me feel rather sick. She put down her brushes and began to powder her face. She gave a nasty little laugh.

"'What are you laughing at?' I asked.

"'Madame Renard. That was the same dress she wore at our wedding; she'd had it dyed and done over, but it didn't deceive me. I'd have known it anywhere.'

"It was such a stupid remark, it infuriated me. I was seized with rage, and with all my might I hit her over the head with my Indian club. I broke her skull, apparently, and she died two days later in hospital without recovering consciousness."

He paused for a moment. I handed him a cigarette and lit another myself.

"I was glad she did. We could never have lived together again, and it would have been very hard to explain my action."

"Very."

"I was arrested and tried for murder. Of course I swore it was an accident, I said the club had slipped out of my hand, but the medical evidence was against me. The prosecution proved that such an injury as Marie-Louise had suffered could only have been caused by a violent and deliberate blow. Fortunately for me they could find no motive. The public prosecutor tried to make out that I had been jealous of the attentions some man had paid her at the party and that we had quarrelled on that account, but the man he mentioned swore that he had done nothing to arouse my suspicions, and others at the party testified that we had left the best of friends. They found on the dressing table an unpaid dressmaker's bill, and the prosecutor suggested that we had quarrelled about that, but I was able to prove that Marie-Louise paid for her clothes out of her own money, so that the bill could not possibly have been the cause of a dispute. Witnesses came forward and said that I had always been kind to Marie-Louise. We were generally looked upon as a devoted couple. My character was excellent, and my employer spoke in the highest terms of me. I was never in danger of losing my head, and at one moment I thought I had a chance of getting off altogether. In the end I was sentenced to six years. I don't regret what I did, for from that day, all the time I was in prison awaiting my trial, and since, while I've been here, I've ceased to worry about Riri. If I believed in ghosts I'd be inclined to say that Marie-Louise's death has laid Riri's. Anyhow, my conscience is at rest, and after all the torture I suffered I can assure you that everything I've gone through since is worth it; I feel I can now look the world in the face again."

I know that this is a fantastic story; I am by way of being a realist, and in the stories I write I seek verisimilitude. I eschew the bizarre as scrupulously as I avoid the whimsical. If this had been a tale that I was inventing I would certainly have made it more probable. As it is, unless I had heard it with my own ears I am not sure that I should believe it. I do not know whether Jean Charvin told me the truth, and yet the words with which he closed his final visit to me had a convincing ring. I had asked him what were his plans for the future.

"I have friends working for me in France," he answered. "A great many people thought at the time that I was the victim of a grave miscarriage of justice; the director of my firm is convinced that I was unjustly condemned; and I may get a reduction of my sentence. Even if I don't, I think I can count upon getting back to France at the end of my six years. You see, I'm making myself very useful here. The accounts were very badly kept when I took them over, and I've got them in apple-pie order. There have been leakages, and I am convinced that if they'll give me a free hand, I can stop them. The commandant likes me and I'm certain that he'll do everything he can for me. At the worst I shan't be much over thirty when I get back."

"But won't you find it rather difficult to get work?"

"A clever accountant like me, and a man who's honest and industrious, can always get work. Of course I shan't be able to live in Le Havre, but the director of my firm has business connections at Lille and Lyons and Marseilles. He's promised to do something for me. No, I look forward to the years to come with a good deal of confidence. I shall settle down somewhere, and as soon as I'm comfortably fixed up I shall marry. After what I've been through I want a home."

We were sitting in one of the corners of the veranda that surrounded my house in order to get any draught there might be, and on the north side I had left a jalousie undrawn. The strip of sky you saw with a single coconut tree on one side, its green foliage harsh against the blue, looked like an advertisement for a tropical cruise. Jean Charvin's eyes searched the distance as though he sought to see the future.

"But next time I marry," he said thoughtfully, "I shan't marry for love, I shall marry for money."

The Treasure

Richard harenger was a happy man. Notwithstanding what the pessimists, from Ecclesiastes onwards, have said, this is not so rare a thing to find in this unhappy world, but Richard Harenger knew it, and that is a very rare thing indeed. The golden mean which the ancients so highly prized is out of fashion, and those who follow it must put up with polite derision from those who see no merit in self-restraint and no virtue in common sense. Richard Harenger shrugged a polite and amused shoulder. Let others live dangerously, let others burn with a hard gemlike flame, let others stake their fortunes on the turn of a card, walk the tightrope that leads to glory or the grave, or hazard their lives for a cause, a passion or an adventure. He neither envied the fame their exploits brought them nor wasted his pity on them when their efforts ended in disaster.

But it must not be inferred from this that Richard

59

Harenger was a selfish or a callous man. He was
neither. He was considerate and of a generous disposition. He was always ready to oblige a friend, and
he was sufficiently well off to be able to indulge himself in the pleasure of helping others. He had some
money of his own, and he occupied in the Home Office
a position that brought him an adequate stipend. The
work suited him. It was regular, responsible and
pleasant. Every day when he left the office he went
to his club to play bridge for a couple of hours, and
on Saturdays and Sundays he played golf. He went
abroad for his holidays, staying at good hotels, and
visited churches, galleries and museums. He was a
regular first-nighter. He dined out a good deal. His
friends liked him. He was easy to talk to. He was
well read, knowledgeable and amusing. He was besides
of a personable exterior, not remarkably handsome,
but tall, slim and erect of carriage, with a lean, intelligent face; his hair was growing thin, for he was
now approaching the age of fifty, but his brown eyes
retained their smile and his teeth were all his own. He
had from nature a good constitution, and he had
always taken care of himself. There was no reason
in the world why he should not be a happy man, and
if there had been in him a trace of self-complacency
he might have claimed that he deserved to be.

He had the good fortune even to sail safely through
those perilous, unquiet straits of marriage in which

so many wise and good men have made shipwreck. Married for love in the early twenties, his wife and he, after some years of almost perfect felicity, had drifted gradually apart. Neither of them wished to marry anyone else, so there was no question of divorce (which indeed Richard Harenger's situation in the government service made undesirable), but for con- venience' sake, with the help of the family lawyer, they arranged a separation which left them free to lead their lives as each one wished without inter- ference from the other. They parted with mutual expressions of respect and good will.

Richard Harenger sold his house in St. John's Wood and took a flat within convenient walking distance of Whitehall. It had a sitting room which he lined with his books, a dining room into which his Chippendale furniture just fitted, a nice-sized bedroom for himself, and beyond the kitchen a couple of maids' rooms. He brought his cook, whom he had had for many years, from St. John's Wood, but needing no longer so large a staff dismissed the rest of the servants and applied at a registry office for a house-parlourmaid. He knew exactly what he wanted, and he explained his needs to the superintendent of the agency with precision. He wanted a maid who was not too young, first be- cause young women are flighty and secondly because, though he was of mature age and a man of principle, people would talk, the porter and the tradesmen if

nobody else, and both for the sake of his own reputation and that of the young person he considered
that the applicant should have reached years of
discretion. Besides that he wanted a maid who could
clean silver well. He had always had a fancy for old
silver, and it was reasonable to demand that the forks
and spoons that had been used by a woman of quality
under the reign of Queen Anne should be treated with
tenderness and respect. He was of a hospitable nature
and liked to give at least once a week little dinners
of not less than four people and not more than eight.
He could trust his cook to send in a meal that his
guests would take pleasure in eating and he desired
his parlourmaid to wait with neatness and dispatch.
Then he needed a perfect valet. He dressed well, in
a manner that suited his age and condition, and he
liked his clothes to be properly looked after. The
parlourmaid he was looking for must be able to press
trousers and iron a tie, and he was very particular
that his shoes should be well shone. He had small
feet, and he took a good deal of trouble to have well-
cut shoes. He had a large supply, and he insisted that
they should be treed up the moment he took them off.
Finally the flat must be kept clean and tidy. It was
of course understood that any applicant for the post
must be of irreproachable character, sober, honest,
reliable and of a pleasing exterior. In return for this
he was prepared to offer good wages, reasonable

liberty and ample holidays. The superintendent listened without batting an eyelash, and telling him that she was quite sure she could suit him, sent him a string of candidates which proved that she had not paid the smallest attention to a word he said. He saw them all personally. Some were obviously inefficient, some looked fast, some were too old, others too young, some lacked the presence he thought essential; there was not one to whom he was inclined even to give a trial. He was a kindly, polite man, and he declined their services with a smile and a pleasant expression of regret. He did not lose patience. He was prepared to interview house-parlourmaids till he found one who was suitable.

Now it is a funny thing about life, if you refuse to accept anything but the best you very often get it: if you utterly decline to make do with what you can get, then somehow or other you are very likely to get what you want. It is as though Fate said, "This man's a perfect fool, he's asking for perfection," and then just out of her feminine wilfulness flung it in his lap. One day the porter of the flats said to Richard Harenger out of a blue sky:

"I hear you're lookin' for a house-parlourmaid, sir. There's someone I know lookin' for a situation as might do."

"Can you recommend her personally?"

Richard Harenger had the sound opinion that one

servant's recommendation of another was worth much more than that of an employer.

"I can vouch for her respectability. She's been in some very good situations."

"I shall be coming in to dress about seven. If that's convenient to her I could see her then."

"Very good, sir. I'll see that she's told."

He had not been in more than five minutes when the cook, having answered a ring at the front door, came in and told him that the person the porter had spoken to him about had called.

"Show her in," he said.

He turned on some more light so that he could see what the applicant looked like, and getting up, stood with his back to the fireplace. A woman came in and stood just inside the door in a respectful attitude.

"Good evening," he said. "What is your name?"

"Pritchard, sir."

"How old are you?"

"Thirty-five, sir."

"Well, that's a reasonable age."

He gave his cigarette a puff and looked at her reflectively. She was on the tall side, nearly as tall as he, but he guessed that she wore high heels. Her black dress fitted her station. She held herself well. She had good features and a rather high colour.

"Will you take off your hat?" he asked.

She did so, and he saw that she had pale brown

hair. It was neatly and becomingly dressed. She looked strong and healthy. She was neither fat nor thin. In a proper uniform she would look very presentable. She was not inconveniently handsome, but she was certainly a comely, in another class of life you might almost have said a handsome, woman. He proceeded to ask her a number of questions. Her answers were satisfactory. She had left her last place for an adequate reason. She had been trained under a butler and appeared to be well acquainted with her duties. In her last place she had been head parlour-maid of three, but she did not mind undertaking the work of the flat single-handed. She had valeted a gentleman before who had sent her to a tailor's to learn how to press clothes. She was a little shy, but neither timid nor ill at ease. Richard asked her his questions in his amiable, leisurely way, and she answered them with modest composure. He was considerably impressed. He asked her what references she could give. They seemed extremely satisfactory.

"Now look here," he said, "I'm very much inclined to engage you. But I hate changes, I've had my cook for twelve years: if you suit me and the place suits you I hope you'll stay. I mean, I don't want you to come to me in three or four months and say that you're leaving to get married."

"There's not much fear of that, sir. I'm a widow.

I don't believe marriage is much catch for anyone in my position, sir. My husband never did a stroke of work from the day I married him to the day he died, and I had to keep him. What I want now is a good home."

"I'm inclined to agree with you," he smiled. "Marriage is a very good thing, but I think it's a mistake to make a habit of it."

She very properly made no reply to this, but waited for him to announce his decision. She did not seem anxious about it. He reflected that if she was as competent as she appeared she must be well aware that she would have no difficulty in finding a place. He told her what wages he was offering, and these seemed to be satisfactory to her. He gave her the necessary information about the place, but she gave him to understand that she was already apprised of this, and he received the impression, which amused rather than disconcerted him, that she had made certain enquiries about him before applying for the situation. It showed prudence on her part and good sense.

"When would you be able to come in if I engaged you? I haven't got anybody at the moment. The cook's managing as best she can with a char, but I should like to get settled as soon as possible."

"Well, sir, I was going to give myself a week's holiday, but if it's a matter of obliging a gentleman

I don't mind giving that up. I could come in to-morrow if it was convenient."

Richard Harenger gave her his attractive smile.

"I shouldn't like you to do without a holiday that I daresay you've been looking forward to. I can very well go on like this for another week. Go and have your holiday and come to me when it's over."

"Thank you very much, sir. Would it do if I came in tomorrow week?"

"Quite well."

When she left, Richard Harenger felt he had done a good day's work. It looked as though he had found exactly what he was after. He rang for the cook and told her he had engaged a house-parlourmaid at last.

"I think you'll like her, sir," she said. "She came in and 'ad a talk with me this afternoon. I could see at once she knew her duties. And she's not one of them flighty ones."

"We can but try, Mrs. Jeddy. I hope you gave me a good character."

"Well, I said you was particular, sir. I said you was a gentleman as liked things just so."

"I admit that."

"She said she didn't mind that. She said she liked a gentleman as knew what was what. She said there's no satisfaction in doing things proper if nobody notices. I expect you'll find she'll take a rare lot of pride in her work."

"That's what I want her to do. I think we might go farther and fare worse."

"Well, sir, there is that to it, of course. And the proof of the pudding's the eating. But if you ask my opinion I think she's going to be a real treasure."

And that is precisely what Pritchard turned out. No man was ever better served. The way she shone shoes was marvellous, and he set out of a fine morning for his walk to the office with a more jaunty step because you could almost see yourself reflected in them. She looked after his clothes with such attention that his colleagues began to chaff him about being the best-dressed man in the Civil Service. One day, coming home unexpectedly, he found a line of socks and handkerchiefs hung up to dry in the bathroom. He called Pritchard.

"D'you wash my socks and handkerchiefs yourself, Pritchard? I should have thought you had enough to do without that."

"They do ruin them so at the laundry, sir. I prefer to do them at home if you have no objection."

She knew exactly what he should wear on every occasion, and without asking him was aware whether she should put out a dinner jacket and a black tie in the evening or a dress coat and a white one. When he was going to a party where decorations were to be worn he found his neat little row of medals automatically affixed to the lapel of his coat. He soon ceased to choose every morning from his wardrobe the tie he wanted, for he found that she put out for him without fail the one he would have himself selected. Her taste was perfect. He supposed she read his letters, for she always knew what his movements were, and if he had forgotten at what hour he had an engagement he had no need to look in his book, for Pritchard could tell him. She knew exactly what tone to use with persons with whom she conversed on the telephone. Except with tradesmen, with whom she was apt to be peremptory, she was always polite, but there was a distinct difference in her manner if she was addressing one of Mr. Harenger's literary friends or the wife of a Cabinet Minister. She knew by instinct with whom he wished to speak and with whom he didn't. From his sitting room he sometimes heard her with placid sincerity assuring a caller that he was out, and then she would come in and tell him that So-and-so had rung up, but she thought he wouldn't wish to be disturbed.

"Quite right, Pritchard," he smiled.

"I knew she only wanted to bother you about that concert," said Pritchard.

His friends made appointments with him through her, and she would tell him what she had done on his return in the evening.

"Mrs. Soames rang up, sir, and asked if you would lunch with her on Thursday, the eighth, but I said

you were very sorry but you were lunching with Lady
Versinder. Mr. Oakley rang up and asked if you'd go
to a cocktail party at the Savoy next Tuesday at six.
I said you would if you possibly could, but you might
have to go to the dentist's."

"Quite right."

"I thought you could see when the time came, sir."

She kept the flat like a new pin. On one occasion
soon after she entered his service, Richard, coming
back from a holiday, took out a book from his shelves
and at once noticed that it had been dusted. He rang
the bell.

"I forgot to tell you, when I went away, under no
circumstances ever to touch my books. When books
are taken out to be dusted they're never put back in
the right place. I don't mind my books being dirty,
but I hate not being able to find them."

"I'm very sorry, sir," said Pritchard. "I know
some gentlemen are very particular and I took care
to put back every book exactly where I took it from."

Richard Harenger gave his books a glance. So far
as he could see, every one was in its accustomed place.
He smiled.

"I apologize, Pritchard."

"They were in a muck, sir. I mean, you couldn't
open one without getting your hands black with
dust."

She certainly kept his silver as he had never had it

kept before. He felt called upon to give her a special word of praise.

"Most of it's Queen Anne and George I, you know," he explained.

"Yes, I know, sir. When you've got something good like that to look after, it's a pleasure to keep it like it should be."

"You certainly have a knack for it. I never knew a butler who kept his silver as well as you do."

"Men haven't the patience women have," she replied modestly.

As soon as he thought Pritchard had settled down in the place, he resumed the little dinners he was fond of giving once a week. He had already discovered that she knew how to wait at table, but it was with a warm sense of complacency that he realized then how competently she could manage a party. She was quick, silent and watchful. A guest had hardly felt the need of something before Pritchard was at his elbow offering him what he wanted. She soon learned the tastes of his more intimate friends and remembered that one liked water instead of soda with his whisky and that another particularly fancied the knuckle end of a leg of lamb. She knew exactly how cold a hock should be not to ruin its taste and how long claret should have stood in the room to bring out its bouquet. It was a pleasure to see her pour out a bottle of burgundy in such a fashion as not to disturb the grounds. On one

occasion she did not serve the wine Richard had ordered. He somewhat sharply pointed this out to her.

"I opened the bottle, sir, and it was slightly corked.
So I got the Chambertin, as I thought it was safer."

"Quite right, Pritchard."

Presently he left this matter entirely in her hands,
for he discovered that she knew perfectly what wines
his guests would like. Without orders from him she
would provide the best in his cellar and his oldest
brandy if she thought they were the sort of people
who knew what they were drinking. She had no belief
in the palate of women, and when they were of the
party was apt to serve the champagne which had to
be drunk before it went off. She had the English servant's instinctive knowledge of social differences, and
neither rank nor money blinded her to the fact that
someone was not a gentleman, but she had favourites
among his friends, and when someone she particularly
liked was dining, with the air of a cat that has swallowed a canary she would pour out for him a bottle of
a wine that Harenger kept for very special occasions.
It amused him.

"You've got on the right side of Pritchard, old
boy," he exclaimed. "There aren't many people she
gives this wine to."

Pritchard became an institution. She was known
very soon to be the perfect parlourmaid. People envied Harenger the possession of her as they envied

nothing else that he had. She was worth her weight in gold. Her price was above rubies. Richard Harenger beamed with self-complacency when they praised her.

"Good masters make good servants," he said gaily.

One evening, when they were sitting over their port and she had left the room, they were talking about her.

"It'll be an awful blow when she leaves you."

"Why should she leave me? One or two people have tried to get her away from me, but she turned them down. She knows where she's well off."

"She'll get married one of these days."

"I don't think she's that sort."

"She's a good-looking woman."

"Yes, she has quite a decent presence."

"What are you talking about? She's a very handsome creature. In another class of life she'd be a well-known society beauty with her photograph in all the papers."

At that moment Pritchard came in with the coffee. Richard Harenger looked at her. After seeing her every day, off and on, for four years it was now, my word, how time flies, he had really forgotten what she looked like. She did not seem to have changed much since he had first seen her. She was no stouter than then, she still had the high colour, and her regular features bore the same expression which was at once intent and vacuous. The black uniform suited her. She left the room.

"She's a paragon, and there's no doubt about it."

"I know she is," answered Harenger. "She's perfection. I should be lost without her. And the strange thing is that I don't very much like her."

"Why not?"

"I think she bores me a little. You see, she has no conversation. I've often tried to talk to her. She answers when I speak to her, but that's all. In four years she's never volunteered a remark of her own. I know absolutely nothing about her. I don't know if she likes me or if she's completely indifferent to me. She's an automaton. I respect her, I appreciate her, I trust her. She has every quality in the world, and I've often wondered why it is that with all that I'm so completely indifferent to her. I think it must be that she is entirely devoid of charm."

They left it at that.

Two or three days after this, since it was Pritchard's night out and he had no engagement, Richard Harenger dined by himself at his club. A page boy came to him and told him that they had just rung up from his flat to say that he had gone out without his keys and should they be brought along to him in a taxi? He put his hand to his pocket. It was a fact. By a singular chance he had forgotten to replace them when he had changed into a blue serge suit before coming out to dinner. His intention had been to play bridge, but it was an off night at the club, and there seemed little chance of a decent game; it occurred to him that it would be a good opportunity to see a picture that he had heard talked about, so he sent back the message by the page that he would call for the keys himself in half an hour.

He rang at the door of his flat, and it was opened by Pritchard. She had the keys in her hand.

"What are you doing here, Pritchard?" he asked. "It's your night out, isn't it?"

"Yes, sir. But I didn't care about going, so I told Mrs. Jeddy she could go instead."

"You ought to get out when you have the chance," he said, with his usual thoughtfulness. "It's not good for you to be cooped up here all the time."

"I get out now and then on an errand, but I haven't been out in the evening for the last month."

"Why on earth not?"

"Well, it's not very cheerful going out by yourself, and somehow I don't know anyone just now that I'm particularly keen on going out with."

"You ought to have a bit of fun now and then. It's good for you."

"I've got out of the habit of it somehow."

"Look here, I'm just going to the cinema. Would you like to come along with me?"

He spoke in kindliness, on the spur of the moment,

and the moment he had said the words half regretted them.

"Yes, sir, I'd like to," said Pritchard.

"Run along then and put on a hat."

"I shan't be a minute."

She disappeared, and he went into the sitting room and lit a cigarette. He was a little amused at what he was doing, and pleased, too; it was nice to be able to make someone happy with so little trouble to himself. It was characteristic of Pritchard that she had shown neither surprise nor hesitation. She kept him waiting about five minutes, and when she came back he noticed that she had changed her dress. She wore a blue frock in what he supposed was artificial silk, a small black hat with a blue brooch on it, and a silver fox round her neck. He was a trifle relieved to see that she looked neither shabby nor showy. It would never occur to anyone who happened to see them that this was a distinguished official in the Home Office taking his housemaid to the pictures.

"I'm sorry to have kept you waiting, sir."

"It doesn't matter at all," he said graciously.

He opened the front door for her, and she went out before him. He remembered the familiar anecdote of Louis XIV and the courtier and appreciated the fact that she had not hesitated to precede him. The cinema for which they were bound was at no great distance from Mr. Harenger's flat, and they walked there. He talked about the weather and the state of the roads and Adolf Hitler. Pritchard made suitable replies. They arrived just as Mickey the Mouse was starting, and this put them in a good humour. During the four years she had been in his service Richard Harenger had hardly ever seen Pritchard even smile, and now it diverted him vastly to hear her peal upon peal of joyous laughter. He enjoyed her pleasure. Then the principal attraction was thrown on the screen. It was a good picture, and they both watched it with breathless excitement. Taking his cigarette case out to help himself, he automatically offered it to Pritchard.

"Thank you, sir," she said, taking one.

He lit it for her. Her eyes were on the screen and she was almost unconscious of his action. When the picture was finished they streamed out with the crowd into the street. They walked back towards the flat. It was a fine starry night.

"Did you like it?" he said.

"Like anything, sir. It was a real treat."

A thought occurred to him.

"By the way, did you have any supper tonight?"

"No, sir, I didn't have time."

"Aren't you starving?"

"I'll have a bit of bread and cheese when I get in and I'll make meself a cup of cocoa."

"That sounds rather grim." There was a feeling of

gaiety in the air, and the people who poured past them, one way and another, seemed filled with a pleasant elation. In for a penny, in for a pound, he said to himself. "Look here, would you like to come and have a bit of supper with me somewhere?"

"If you'd like to, sir."

"Come on."

He hailed a cab. He was feeling very philanthropic and it was not a feeling that he disliked at all. He told the driver to go to a restaurant in Oxford Street which was gay, but at which he was confident there was no chance of meeting anyone he knew. There was an orchestra, and people danced. It would amuse Pritchard to see them. When they sat down a waiter came up to them.

"They've got a set supper here," he said, thinking that was what she would like. "I suggest we have that. What would you like to drink? A little white wine?"

"What I really fancy is a glass of ginger beer," she said.

Richard Harenger ordered himself a whisky and soda. She ate the supper with hearty appetite, and though Harenger was not hungry, to put her at her ease he ate too. The picture they had just seen gave them something to talk about. It was quite true what they had said the other night, Pritchard was not a bad-looking woman, and even if someone had seen them together he would not have minded. It would make rather a good story for his friends when he told them how he had taken the incomparable Pritchard to the cinema and then afterwards to supper. Pritchard was looking at the dancers with a faint smile on her lips.

"Do you like dancing?" he said.

"I used to be a rare one for it when I was a girl. I never danced much after I was married. My husband was a bit shorter than me, and somehow I never think it looks well unless the gentleman's taller, if you know what I mean. I suppose I shall be getting too old for it soon."

Richard was certainly taller than his parlourmaid. They would look all right. He was fond of dancing and he danced well. But he hesitated. He did not want to embarrass Pritchard by asking her to dance with him. It was better not to go too far perhaps. And yet what did it matter? It was a drab life she led. She was so sensible, if she thought it a mistake he was pretty sure she would find a decent excuse.

"Would you like to take a turn, Pritchard?" he said, as the band struck up again.

"I'm terribly out of practice, sir."

"What does that matter?"

"If you don't mind, sir," she answered coolly, rising from her seat.

She was not in the least shy. She was only afraid

that she would not be able to follow his step. They moved on to the floor. He found she danced very well.

"Why, you dance perfectly, Pritchard," he said.

"It's coming back to me."

Although she was a big woman, she was light on her feet, and she had a natural sense of rhythm. She was very pleasant to dance with. He gave a glance at the mirrors that lined the walls, and he could not help reflecting that they looked very well together. Their eyes met in the mirror; he wondered whether she was thinking that, too. They had two more dances, and then Richard Harenger suggested that they should go. He paid the bill and they walked out. He noticed that she threaded her way through the crowd without a trace of self-consciousness. They got into a taxi and in ten minutes were at home.

"I'll go up the back way, sir," said Pritchard.

"There's no need to do that. Come up in the lift with me."

He took her up, giving the night porter an icy glance, so that he should not think it strange that he came back at that somewhat late hour with his parlourmaid, and with his latchkey let her into the flat.

"Well, good night, sir," she said. "Thank you very much. It's been a real treat for me."

"Thank *you*, Pritchard. I should have had a very dull evening by myself. I hope you've enjoyed your outing."

"That I have, sir, more than I can say."

It had been a success. Richard Harenger was satisfied with himself. It was a kindly thing for him to have done. It was a very agreeable sensation to give anyone so much real pleasure. His benevolence warmed him and for a moment he felt a great love in his heart for the whole human race.

"Good night, Pritchard," he said, and because he felt happy and good he put his arm round her waist and kissed her on the lips.

Her lips were very soft. They lingered on his, and she returned his kiss. It was the warm, hearty embrace of a healthy woman in the prime of life. He found it very pleasant, and he held her to him a little more closely. She put her arms round his neck.

.   .   .   .   .

As a general rule he did not wake till Pritchard came in with his letters, but next morning he woke at half past seven. He had a curious sensation that he did not recognize. He was accustomed to sleep with two pillows under his head, and he suddenly grew aware of the fact that he had only one. Then he remembered and with a start looked round. The other pillow was beside his own. Thank God, no sleeping head rested there, but it was plain that one had. His heart sank. He broke out into a cold sweat.

"My God, what a fool I've been!" he cried out loud.

How could he have done anything so stupid? What on earth had come over him? He was the last man to play about with servant girls. What a disgraceful thing to do! At his age and in his position. He had not heard Pritchard slip away. He must have been asleep. It wasn't even as if he'd liked her very much. She wasn't his type. And as he had said the other night, she rather bored him. Even now he only knew her as Pritchard. He had no notion what her first name was. What madness! And what was to happen now? The position was impossible. It was obvious he couldn't keep her, and yet to send her away for what was his fault as much as hers seemed shockingly unfair. How idiotic to lose the best parlourmaid a man ever had just for an hour's folly!

"It's that damned kindness of heart of mine," he groaned.

He would never find anyone else to look after his clothes so admirably or clean the silver so well. She knew all his friends' telephone numbers, and she understood wine. But of course she must go. She must see for herself that after what had happened things could never be the same. He would make her a handsome present and give her an excellent reference. At any minute she would be coming in now. Would she be arch, would she be familiar? Or would she put on airs? Perhaps even she wouldn't trouble to come in with his letters. It would be awful if he had to ring the bell and Mrs. Jeddy came in and said: "Pritch-ard's not up yet, sir, she's having a lie in after last night."

"What a fool I've been! What a contemptible cad!"

There was a knock at the door. He was sick with anxiety.

"Come in."

Richard Harenger was a very unhappy man.

Pritchard came in as the clock struck. She wore the print dress she was in the habit of wearing during the early part of the day.

"Good morning, sir," she said.

"Good morning."

She drew the curtains and handed him his letters and the papers. Her face was impassive. She looked exactly as she always looked. Her movements had the same competent deliberation that they always had. She neither avoided Richard's glance nor sought it.

"Will you wear your grey, sir? It came back from the tailor's yesterday."

"Yes."

He pretended to read his letters, but he watched her from under his eyelashes. Her back was turned to him. She took his vest and drawers and folded them over a chair. She took the studs out of the shirt he had worn the day before and studded a clean one. She put out some clean socks for him and placed them on the seat of a chair with the suspenders to match by the side. Then she put out his grey suit and attached the braces to the back buttons of the trousers. She opened his wardrobe and after a moment's reflection chose a tie to go with the suit. She collected on her arm the suit of the day before and picked up the shoes.

"Will you have breakfast now, sir, or will you have your bath first?"

"I'll have breakfast now," he said.

"Very good, sir."

With her slow quiet movements, unruffled, she left the room. Her face bore that rather serious, deferential, vacuous look it always bore. What had happened might have been a dream. Nothing in Pritchard's demeanour suggested that she had the smallest recollection of the night before. He gave a sigh of relief. It was going to be all right. She need not go, she need not go. Pritchard was the perfect parlourmaid. He knew that never by word nor gesture would she ever refer to the fact that for a moment their relations had been other than those of master and servant. Richard Harenger was a very happy man.

The Lotus Eater

MOST PEOPLE, the vast majority in fact, lead the lives that circumstances have thrust upon them, and though some repine, looking upon themselves as round pegs in square holes, and think that if things had been different they might have made a much better showing, the greater part accept their lot, if not with serenity, at all events with resignation. They are like tramcars travelling for ever on the selfsame rails. They go backwards and forwards, backwards and forwards, inevitably, till they can go no longer and then are sold as scrap iron. It is not often that you find a man who has boldly taken the course of his life into his own hands. When you do, it is worth while having a good look at him.

That was why I was curious to meet Thomas Wilson. It was an interesting and a bold thing he had done. Of course the end was not yet, and until the experiment was concluded it was impossible to call it successful. But from what I had heard it seemed he must be an odd sort of fellow, and I thought I should like to know him. I had been told he was reserved, but I had a notion that with patience and tact I could persuade him to confide in me. I wanted to hear the facts from his own lips. People exaggerate, they love to romanticize, and I was quite prepared to discover that his story was not nearly so singular as I had been led to believe.

And this impression was confirmed when at last I made his acquaintance. It was on the Piazza in Capri, where I was spending the month of August at a friend's villa, and a little before sunset, when most of the inhabitants, native and foreign, gather together to chat with their friends in the cool of the evening. There is a terrace that overlooks the Bay of Naples, and when the sun sinks slowly into the sea the island of Ischia is silhouetted against a blaze of splendour. It is one of the most lovely sights in the world. I was standing there with my friend and host watching it, when suddenly he said:

"Look, there's Wilson."

"Where?"

"The man sitting on the parapet, with his back to us. He's got a blue shirt on."

I saw an undistinguished back and a small head of grey hair short and rather thin.

"I wish he'd turn round," I said.

"He will presently."

"Ask him to come and have a drink with us at Morgano's."

"All right."

The instant of overwhelming beauty had passed and the sun, like the top of an orange, was dipping into a wine-red sea. We turned round and, leaning our backs against the parapet, looked at the people who were sauntering to and fro. They were all talking their heads off, and the cheerful noise was exhilarating. Then the church bell, rather cracked, but with a fine resonant note, began to ring. The Piazza at Capri, with its clock tower over the footpath that leads up from the harbour, with the church up a flight of steps, is a perfect setting for an opera by Donizetti, and you felt that the voluble crowd might at any moment break out into a rattling chorus. It was charming and unreal.

I was so intent on the scene that I had not noticed Wilson get off the parapet and come towards us. As he passed us, my friend stopped him.

"Hulloa, Wilson, I haven't seen you bathing the last few days."

"I've been bathing on the other side for a change."

My friend then introduced me. Wilson shook hands with me politely, but with indifference; a great many strangers come to Capri for a few days, or a few weeks, and I had no doubt he was constantly meeting

people who came and went; and then my friend asked
him to come along and have a drink with us.

"I was just going back to supper," he said.

"Can't it wait?" I asked.

"I suppose it can," he smiled.

Though his teeth were not very good, his smile was
attractive. It was gentle and kindly. He was dressed
in a blue cotton shirt and a pair of grey trousers,
much creased and none too clean, of a thin canvas,
and on his feet he wore a pair of very old espadrilles.
The get-up was picturesque, and very suitable to the
place and the weather, but it did not at all go with his
face. It was a lined, long face, deeply sunburned, thin-
lipped, with small grey eyes rather close together and
tight, neat features. The grey hair was carefully
brushed. It was not a plain face—indeed in his youth
Wilson might have been good-looking—but a prim
one. He wore the blue shirt open at the neck, and the
grey canvas trousers, not as though they belonged to
him, but as though, shipwrecked in his pyjamas, he
had been fitted out with odd garments by com-
passionate strangers. Notwithstanding this careless
attire he looked like the manager of a branch office in
an insurance company, who should by rights be wearing a black coat with pepper and salt trousers, a white
collar and an unobjectionable tie. I could very well
see myself going to him to claim the insurance money
when I had lost a watch, and being rather discon-

certed, while I answered the questions he put to me, by his obvious impression, for all his politeness, that people who made such claims were either fools or knaves.

Moving off, we strolled across the Piazza and down the street till we came to Morgano's. We sat in the garden. Around us people were talking in Russian, German, Italian and English. We ordered drinks. Donna Lucia, the host's wife, waddled up and in her low, sweet voice passed the time of day with us. Though middle-aged now and portly, she had still traces of the wonderful beauty that, thirty years before, had driven artists to paint so many bad portraits of her. Her eyes, large and liquid, were the eyes of Hera, and her smile was affectionate and gracious. We three gossiped for a while, for there is always a scandal of one sort or another in Capri to make a topic of conversation, but nothing was said of particular interest, and in a little while Wilson got up and left us. Soon afterwards we strolled up to my friend's villa to dine. On the way he asked me what I had thought of Wilson.

"Nothing," I said. "I don't believe there's a word of truth in your story."

"Why not?"

"He isn't the sort of man to do that sort of thing."

"How does anyone know what anyone is capable of?"

"I should put him down as an absolutely normal man of business who's retired on a comfortable income from gilt-edged securities. I think your story's just the ordinary Capri tittle-tattle."

"Have it your own way," said my friend.

We were in the habit of bathing at a beach called the Baths of Tiberius. We took a fly down the road to a certain point and then wandered through lemon groves and vineyards, noisy with cicadas and heavy with the hot smell of the sun, till we came to the top of the cliff down which a steep winding path led to the sea. A day or two later, just before we got down, my friend said:

"Oh, there's Wilson back again."

We scrunched over the beach, the only drawback to the bathing-place being that it was shingle and not sand, and as we came along Wilson saw us and waved. He was standing up, a pipe in his mouth, and he wore nothing but a pair of trunks. His body was dark brown, thin but not emaciated, and, considering his wrinkled face and grey hair, youthful. Hot from our walk, we undressed quickly and plunged at once into the water. Six feet from the shore it was thirty feet deep, but so clear that you could see the bottom. It was warm, yet invigorating.

When I got out, Wilson was lying on his belly, with a towel under him, reading a book. I lit a cigarette and sat down beside him.

"Had a nice swim?" he asked.

He put his pipe inside his book to mark the place and, closing it, put it down on the pebbles beside him. He was evidently willing to talk.

"Lovely," I said. "It's the best bathing in the world."

"Of course people think those were the baths of Tiberius." He waved his hand towards a shapeless mass of masonry that stood half in the water and half out. "But that's all rot. It was just one of his villas, you know."

I did. But it is just as well to let people tell you things when they want to. It disposes them kindly towards you if you suffer them to impart information. Wilson gave a chuckle.

"Funny old fellow, Tiberius. Pity they're saying now there's not a word of truth in all those stories about him."

He began to tell me all about Tiberius. Well, I had read my Suetonius too, and I had read histories of the Early Roman Empire, so there was nothing very new to me in what he said. But I observed that he was not ill-read. I remarked on it.

"Oh, well, when I settled down here I was naturally interested, and I have plenty of time for reading. When you live in a place like this, with all its associations, it seems to make history so actual. You might almost be living in historical times yourself."

I should remark here that this was in 1913. The world was an easy, comfortable place, and no one could have imagined that anything might happen seriously to disturb the serenity of existence.

"How long have you been here?" I asked.

"Fifteen years." He gave the blue and placid sea a glance, and a strangely tender smile hovered on his thin lips. "I fell in love with the place at first sight. You've heard, I daresay, of the mythical German who came here on the Naples boat just for lunch and a look at the Blue Grotto and stayed forty years; well, I can't say I exactly did that, but it's come to the same thing in the end. Only it won't be forty years in my case. Twenty-five. Still, that's better than a poke in the eye with a sharp stick."

I waited for him to go on. For what he had just said looked indeed as though there might be something after all in the singular story I had heard. But at that moment my friend came dripping out of the water very proud of himself because he had swum a mile, and the conversation turned to other things.

After that I met Wilson several times, either in the Piazza or on the beach. He was amiable and polite. He was always pleased to have a talk and I found out that he knew not only every inch of the island but also the adjacent mainland. He had read a great deal on all sorts of subjects, but his speciality was the history of Rome, and on this he was very well informed.

He seemed to have little imagination and to be of no more than average intelligence. He laughed a good deal, but with restraint, and his sense of humour was tickled by simple jokes. A commonplace man. I did not forget the odd remark he had made during the first short chat we had had by ourselves, but he never so much as approached the topic again. One day on our return from the beach, dismissing the cab at the Piazza, my friend and I told the driver to be ready to take us up to Anacapri at five. We were going to climb Monte Solaro, dine at a tavern we favoured, and walk down in the moonlight. For it was full moon, and the views by night were lovely. Wilson was standing by while we gave the cabman instructions, for we had given him a lift to save him the hot dusty walk, and more from politeness than for any other reason I asked him if he would care to join us.

"It's my party," I said.

"I'll come with pleasure," he answered.

But when the time came to set out, my friend was not feeling well, he thought he had stayed too long in the water, and would not face the long and tiring walk. So I went alone with Wilson. We climbed the mountain, admired the spacious view, and got back to the inn as night was falling, hot, hungry and thirsty. We had ordered our dinner beforehand. The food was good, for Antonio was an excellent cook, and the wine came from his own vineyard. It was so light that you felt you could drink it like water, and we finished the first bottle with our macaroni. By the time we had finished the second we felt that there was nothing much wrong with life. We sat in a little garden under a great vine laden with grapes. The air was exquisitely soft. The night was still, and we were alone. The maid brought us *bel paese* cheese and a plate of figs. I ordered coffee and strega, which is the best liqueur they make in Italy. Wilson would not have a cigar, but lit his pipe.

"We've got plenty of time before we need start," he said. "The moon won't be over the hill for another hour."

"Moon or no moon," I said briskly, "of course we've got plenty of time. That's one of the delights of Capri, that there's never any hurry."

"Leisure," he said. "If people only knew! It's the most priceless thing a man can have and they're such fools they don't even know it's something to aim at. Work? They work for work's sake. They haven't got the brains to realize that the only object of work is to obtain leisure."

Wine has the effect on some people of making them indulge in general reflections. These remarks were true, but no one could have claimed that they were original. I did not say anything, but struck a match to light my cigar.

"It was full moon the first time I came to Capri,"

he went on reflectively. "It might be the same moon as tonight."

"It was, you know," I smiled.

He grinned. The only light in the garden was what came from an oil lamp that hung over our heads. It had been scanty to eat by, but it was good now for confidences.

"I didn't mean that. I mean, it might be yesterday. Fifteen years it is, and when I look back it seems like a month. I'd never been to Italy before. I came for my summer holiday. I went to Naples by boat from Marseilles, and I had a look round—Pompeii, you know, and Paestum and one or two places like that; then I came here for a week. I liked the look of the place right away, from the sea, I mean, as I watched it come closer and closer; and then when we got into the little boats from the steamer and landed at the quay, with all that crowd of jabbering people who wanted to take your luggage, and the hotel touts, and the tumble-down houses on the Marina and the walk up to the hotel, and dining on the terrace—well, it just got me. That's the truth. I didn't know if I was standing on my head or my heels. I'd never drunk Capri wine before, but I'd heard of it; I think I must have got a bit tight. I sat on that terrace after they'd all gone to bed and watched the moon over the sea, and there was Vesuvius with a great red plume of smoke rising up from it. Of course I know now that wine I drank was ink, Capri wine my eye, but I thought it all right then. But it wasn't the wine that made me drunk, it was the shape of the island and those jabbering people, the moon and the sea and the oleander in the hotel garden. I'd never seen an oleander before."

It was a long speech, and it had made him thirsty. He took up his glass, but it was empty. I asked him if he would have another strega.

"It's sickly stuff. Let's have a bottle of wine. That's sound, that is, pure juice of the grape and can't hurt anyone."

I ordered more wine, and when it came filled the glasses. He took a long drink and after a sigh of pleasure went on.

"Next day I found my way to the bathing place we go to. Not bad bathing, I thought. Then I wandered about the island. As luck would have it, there was a *festa* up at the Punta di Timberio, and I ran straight into the middle of it. An image of the Virgin and priests, acolytes swinging censers, and a whole crowd of jolly, laughing, excited people, a lot of them all dressed up. I ran across an Englishman there and asked him what it was all about. 'Oh, it's the feast of the Assumption,' he said. 'At least that's what the Catholic Church says it is, but that's just their hanky-panky. It's the festival of Venus. Pagan, you know. Aphrodite rising from the sea and all that.' It gave me quite a funny feeling to hear him. It seemed to take one a long way back, if you know what I mean. After that I went down one night to have a look at the Faraglioni by moonlight. If the fates had wanted me to go on being a bank manager they oughtn't to have let me take that walk."

"You were a bank manager, were you?" I asked. I had been wrong about him, but not far wrong.

"Yes. I was manager of the Crawford Street branch of the York and City. It was convenient for me because I lived up Hendon way. I could get from door to door in thirty-seven minutes."

He puffed at his pipe and relit it.

"That was my last night, that was. I'd got to be back at the bank on Monday morning. When I looked at those two great rocks sticking out of the water, with the moon above them, and all the little lights of the fishermen in their boats catching cuttlefish, all so peaceful and beautiful, I said to myself, well, after all, why should I go back? It wasn't as if I had anyone dependent on me. My wife had died of bronchial pneumonia four years before, and the kid went to live with her grandmother, my wife's mother. She was an old fool, she didn't look after the kid properly and she got blood poisoning, they amputated her leg, but they couldn't save her and she died, poor little thing."

"How terrible," I said.

"Yes, I was cut up at the time, though of course

not so much as if the kid had been living with me, but I daresay it was a mercy. Not much chance for a girl with only one leg. I was sorry about my wife, too. We got on very well together. Though I don't know if it would have continued. She was the sort of woman who was always bothering about what other people'd think. She didn't like travelling. Eastbourne was her idea of a holiday. D'you know, I'd never crossed the channel till after her death."

"But I suppose you've got other relations, haven't you?"

"None. I was an only child. My father had a brother, but he went to Australia before I was born. I don't think anyone could easily be more alone in the world than I am. There wasn't any reason I could see why I shouldn't do exactly what I wanted. I was thirty-four at that time."

He had told me he had been on the island for fifteen years. That would make him forty-nine. Just about the age I should have given him.

"I'd been working since I was seventeen. All I had to look forward to was doing the same old thing day after day till I retired on my pension. I said to myself, 'Is it worth it? What's wrong with chucking it all up and spending the rest of my life down here?' It was the most beautiful place I'd ever seen. But I'd had a business training, I was cautious by nature. 'No,' I said, 'I won't be carried away like this, I'll go tomorrow like I said I would and think it over. Perhaps when I get back to London I'll think quite differently.' Damned fool, wasn't I? I lost a whole year that way."

"You didn't change your mind, then?"

"You bet I didn't. All the time I was working I kept thinking of the bathing here and the vineyards and the walks over the hills and the moon and the sea, and the Piazza in the evening when everyone walks about for a bit of a chat after the day's work is over. There was only one thing that bothered me; I wasn't sure if I was justified in not working like everybody else did. Then I read a sort of history book, by a man called Marion Crawford it was, and there was a story about Sybaris and Crotona. There were two cities; and in Sybaris they just enjoyed life and had a good time, and in Crotona they were hardy and industrious and all that. And one day the men of Crotona came over and wiped Sybaris out, and then after a while a lot of other fellows came over from somewhere else and wiped Crotona out. Nothing remains of Sybaris, not a stone, and all that's left of Crotona is just one column. That settled the matter for me."

"Oh?"

"It came to the same in the end, didn't it? And when you look back now, who were the mugs?"

I did not reply, and he went on.

"The money was rather a bother. The bank didn't pension one off till after thirty years' service, but if you retired before that they gave you a gratuity. With that and what I'd got for the sale of my house and the little I'd managed to save, I just hadn't enough to buy an annuity to last the rest of my life. It would have been silly to sacrifice everything so as to lead a pleasant life and not have a sufficient income to make it pleasant. I wanted to have a little place of my own, a servant to look after me, enough to buy tobacco, decent food, books now and then, and something over for emergencies. I knew pretty well how much I needed. I found I had just enough to buy an annuity for twenty-five years."

"You were thirty-five at the time?"

"Yes. It would carry me on till I was sixty. After all, no one can be certain of living longer than that; a lot of men die in their fifties, and by the time a man's sixty he's had the best of life."

"On the other hand no one can be sure of dying at sixty," I said.

"Well, I don't know. It depends on himself, doesn't it?"

"In your place I should have stayed on at the bank till I was entitled to my pension."

"I should have been forty-seven then. I shouldn't have been too old to enjoy my life here, I'm older than that now and I enjoy it as much as I ever did, but I should have been too old to experience the particular pleasure of a young man. You know, you can have just as good a time at fifty as you can at thirty, but it's not the same sort of good time. I wanted to live the perfect life while I still had the energy and the spirit to make the most of it. Twenty-five years seemed a long time to me, and twenty-five years of happiness seemed worth paying something pretty substantial for. I'd made up my mind to wait a year, and I waited a year. Then I sent in my resignation, and as soon as they paid me my gratuity I bought the annuity and came on here."

"An annuity for twenty-five years?"

"That's right."

"Have you never regretted?"

"Never. I've had my money's worth already. And I've got ten years more. Don't you think after twenty-five years of perfect happiness one ought to be satisfied to call it a day?"

"Perhaps."

He did not say in so many words what he would do then, but his intention was clear. It was pretty much the story my friend had told me, but it sounded different when I heard it from his own lips. I stole a glance at him. There was nothing about him that was not ordinary. No one, looking at that neat, prim face, could have thought him capable of an unconventional action. I did not blame him. It was his own life that he had arranged in this strange manner, and I did not see why he should not do what he liked with it. Still, I could not prevent the little shiver that ran down my spine.

"Getting chilly?" he smiled. "We might as well start walking down. The moon'll be up by now."

Before we parted, Wilson asked me if I would like to go and see his house one day; and two or three days later, finding out where he lived, I strolled up to see him. It was a peasant's cottage, well away from the town, in a vineyard, with a view of the sea. By the side of the door grew a great oleander in full flower. There were only two small rooms, a tiny kitchen and a lean-to in which firewood could be kept. The bedroom was furnished like a monk's cell, but the sitting room, smelling agreeably of tobacco, was comfortable enough, with two large armchairs that he had brought from England, a large roll-top desk, a cottage piano and crowded bookshelves. On the walls were framed engravings of pictures by G. F. Watts and Lord Leighton. Wilson told me that the house belonged to the owner of the vineyard who lived in another cottage higher up the hill, and his wife came in every day to do the rooms and the cooking. He had found the place on his first visit to Capri, and taking it on his return for good had been there ever since. Seeing the piano and music open on it, I asked him if he would play.

"I'm no good, you know, but I've always been fond of music, and I get a lot of fun out of strumming."

He sat down at the piano and played one of the movements from a Beethoven sonata. He did not play very well. I looked at his music, Schumann and Schubert, Beethoven, Bach and Chopin. On the table on which he had his meals was a greasy pack of cards. I asked him if he played patience.

"A lot."

From what I saw of him then and from what I heard from other people I made for myself what I think must have been a fairly accurate picture of the life he had led for the last fifteen years. It was certainly a very harmless one. He bathed; he walked a great deal, and he seemed never to lose his sense of the beauty of the island which he knew so intimately; he played the piano and he played patience; he read. When he was asked to a party he went and, though a trifle dull, was agreeable. He was not affronted if he was neglected. He liked people, but with an aloofness that prevented intimacy. He lived thriftily, but with sufficient comfort. He never owed a penny. I imagine he had never been a man whom sex had greatly troubled, and if in his younger days he had had now and then a passing affair with a visitor to the island whose head was turned by the atmosphere, his emotion, while it lasted, remained, I am pretty sure, well under his control. I think he was determined that nothing should interfere with his independence of spirit. His only passion was for the beauty of nature, and he sought felicity in the simple and natural things that life offers to everyone. You may say that it was a grossly selfish existence. It was. He was of no use to anybody, but on the other hand he did nobody any harm. His only object was his own happiness, and it looked as though he had attained it. Very few people know where to look for happiness; fewer still find it. I don't know whether he was a fool or a wise man. He was certainly a man who knew his own mind. The odd thing about him to me was that he was so immensely commonplace. I should never have given him a second thought but for what I knew, that on a certain day, ten years from then, unless a chance illness cut the thread before, he must deliberately take leave of the world he loved so well. I wondered whether it was the thought of this, never quite absent from his mind, that gave him the peculiar zest with which he enjoyed every moment of the day.

I should do him an injustice if I omitted to state that he was not at all in the habit of talking about himself. I think the friend I was staying with was the only person in whom he had confided. I believe he told me the story only because he suspected I already knew it, and on the evening on which he told it me he had drunk a good deal of wine.

My visit drew to a close, and I left the island. The

year after, war broke out. A number of things happened to me, so that the course of my life was greatly
altered, and it was thirteen years before I went to
Capri again. My friend had been back some time, but
he was no longer so well off, and had moved into a
house that had no room for me; so I was putting up
at the hotel. He came to meet me at the boat, and we
dined together. During dinner I asked him where
exactly his house was.

"You know it," he answered. "It's the little place
Wilson had. I've built on a room and made it quite
nice."

With so many other things to occupy my mind, I
had not given Wilson a thought for years; but now,
with a little shock, I remembered. The ten years he
had before him when I made his acquaintance must
have elapsed long ago.

"Did he commit suicide as he said he would?"

"It's rather a grim story."

Wilson's plan was all right. There was only one
flaw in it, and this, I suppose, he could not have fore-
seen. It had never occurred to him that after twenty-
five years of complete happiness, in this quiet back-
water, with nothing in the world to disturb his serenity, his character would gradually lose its strength.
The will needs obstacles in order to exercise its power;
when it is never thwarted, when no effort is needed to
achieve one's desires, because one has placed one's

desires only in the things that can be obtained by stretching out one's hand, the will grows impotent. If you walk on a level all the time, the muscles you need to climb a mountain will atrophy. These observations are trite, but there they are. When Wilson's annuity expired he had no longer the resolution to make the end which was the price he had agreed to pay for that long period of happy tranquillity. I do not think, as far as I could gather, both from what my friend told me and afterwards from others, that he wanted courage. It was just that he couldn't make up his mind. He put it off from day to day.

He had lived on the island for so long and had always settled his accounts so punctually, that it was easy for him to get credit; never having borrowed money before, he found a number of people who were willing to lend him small sums when now he asked for them. He had paid his rent regularly for so many years that his landlord, whose wife Assunta still acted as his servant, was content to let things slide for several months. Everyone believed him when he said that a relative had died and that he was temporarily embarrassed because, owing to legal formalities, he could not for some time get the money that was due to him. He managed to hang on after this fashion for something over a year. Then he could get no more credit from the local tradesmen, and there was no one to lend him any more money. His landlord gave him notice to leave the house unless he paid up the arrears of rent before a certain date.

The day before this he went into his tiny bedroom, closed the door and the window, drew the curtain and lit a brazier of charcoal. Next morning when Assunta came to make his breakfast she found him insensible but still alive. The room was draughty, and though he had done this and that to keep out the fresh air he had not done it very thoroughly. It almost looked as though at the last moment, and desperate though his situation was, he had suffered from a certain infirmity of purpose. Wilson was taken to the hospital, and though very ill for some time he at last recovered. But as a result either of the charcoal poisoning or of the shock, he was no longer in complete possession of his faculties. He was not insane, at all events not insane enough to be put in an asylum, but he was quite obviously no longer in his right mind.

"I went to see him," said my friend. "I tried to get him to talk, but he kept looking at me in a funny sort of way, as though he couldn't quite make out where he'd seen me before. He looked rather awful lying there in bed, with a week's growth of grey beard on his chin; but except for that funny look in his eyes he seemed quite normal."

"What funny look in his eyes?"

"I don't know exactly how to describe it. Puzzled. It's an absurd comparison, but suppose you threw a stone up into the air and it didn't come down but just stayed there . . ."

"It would be rather bewildering," I smiled.

"Well, that's the sort of look he had."

It was difficult to know what to do with him. He had no money and no means of getting any. His effects were sold, but for too little to pay what he owed. He was English, and the Italian authorities did not wish to make themselves responsible for him. The British consul in Naples had no funds to deal with the case. He could of course be sent back to England, but no one seemed to know what could be done with him when he got there. Then Assunta, the servant, said that he had been a good master and a good tenant, and as long as he had the money had paid his way; he could sleep in the woodshed in the cottage in which she and her husband lived, and he could share their meals. This was suggested to him. It was difficult to know whether he understood or not. When Assunta came to take him from the hospital, he went with her without remark. He seemed to have no longer a will of his own.

She had been keeping him now for two years.

"It's not very comfortable, you know," said my friend. "They've rigged him up a ramshackle bed and given him a couple of blankets, but there's no window, and it's icy cold in winter and like an oven in summer. And the food's pretty rough. You know how these peasants eat: macaroni on Sundays and meat once in a blue moon."

"What does he do with himself all the time?"

"He wanders about the hills. I've tried to see him two or three times, but it's no good; when he sees you coming he runs like a hare. Assunta comes down to have a chat with me now and then, and I give her a bit of money so that she can buy him tobacco, but God knows if he ever gets it."

"Do they treat him all right?" I asked.

"I'm sure Assunta's kind enough. She treats him like a child. I'm afraid her husband's not very nice to him. He grudges the cost of his keep. I don't believe he's cruel or anything like that, but I think he's a bit sharp with him. He makes him fetch water and clean the cowshed and that sort of thing."

"It sounds pretty rotten," I said.

"He brought it on himself. After all, he's only got what he deserved."

"I think on the whole we all get what we deserve," I said. "But that doesn't prevent its being rather horrible."

Two or three days later my friend and I were taking a walk. We were strolling along a narrow path through an olive grove.

"There's Wilson," said my friend suddenly. "Don't look, you'll only frighten him. Go straight on."

I walked with my eyes on the path, but out of the

corners of them I saw a man hiding behind an olive tree. He did not move as we approached, but I felt that he was watching us. As soon as we had passed I heard a scamper. Wilson, like a hunted animal, had made for safety. That was the last I ever saw of him.

He died last year. He had endured that life for six years. He was found one morning on the mountain-side lying quite peacefully as though he had died in his sleep. From where he lay he had been able to see those two great rocks called the Faraglioni which stand out of the sea. It was full moon, and he must have gone to see them by moonlight. Perhaps he died of the beauty of that sight.

The Lion's Skin

A GOOD MANY PEOPLE were shocked when they read
that Captain Forestier had met his death in a forest
fire when trying to save his wife's dog, which had
been accidentally shut up in the house. Some said
they never knew he had it in him; others said it was
exactly what they would have expected of him, but of
these some meant it in one way and some in another.
After the tragic occurrence Mrs. Forestier found
shelter in the villa of some people called Hardy, whose
acquaintance she and her husband had but lately
made. Captain Forestier had not liked them, at any
rate he had not liked Fred Hardy, but she felt that if
he had lived through that terrible night he would
have changed his mind. He would have realized how
much good there was in Hardy notwithstanding his
reputation, and like the great gentleman he was he
would not have hesitated to admit that he had been
mistaken. Mrs. Forestier did not know how she could

ever have kept her reason after the loss of the man who was everything in the world to her but for the Hardys' wonderful kindness. In her immense distress their unfailing sympathy had been her only consolation. They, who had been almost eyewitnesses of her husband's great sacrifice, knew as did no one else how wonderful he had been. She could never forget the words dear Fred Hardy had used when he was breaking the dreadful news to her. It was these words that had enabled her not only to bear the frightful disaster, but to face the desolate future with the courage with which she well knew that brave man, that gallant gentleman, whom she had loved so well, would have wished her to face it.

Mrs. Forestier was a very nice woman. Kindly people often say that of a woman when they can say nothing about her, and it has come to be looked upon as cold praise. I do not mean it as such. Mrs. Forestier was neither charming, beautiful nor intelligent; on the contrary she was absurd, homely and foolish; yet the more you knew her, the more you liked her, and when asked why, you found yourself forced to repeat that she was a very nice woman. She was as tall as the average man; she had a large mouth and a great hooked nose, pale blue short-sighted eyes and big ugly hands. Her skin was lined and weatherbeaten, but she made up heavily, and her hair, which she wore long, was dyed golden, tightly marcelled and elaborately dressed. She did everything she could to counteract the aggressive masculinity of her appearance, and succeeded only in looking like a vaudeville artist doing a female impersonation. Her voice was a woman's voice, but you were always expecting her, at the end of the number as it were, to break into a deep bass, and tearing off that golden wig, discover a man's bald pate. She spent a great deal of money on her clothes, which she got from the most fashionable dressmakers in Paris, but though a woman of fifty she had an unfortunate taste for choosing dresses that looked exquisite on pretty little mannequins in the flower of their youth. She always wore a great quantity of rich jewels. Her movements were awkward and her gestures clumsy. If she went into a drawing room where there was a valuable piece of jade, she managed to sweep it onto the floor; if she lunched with you and you had a set of glasses you treasured, she was almost certain to smash one of them to atoms.

Yet this ungainly exterior sheltered a tender, romantic and idealistic soul. It took you some time to discover this, for when first you knew her you took her for a figure of fun, and then when you knew her better (and had suffered from her clumsiness) she exasperated you; but when you did discover it, you thought yourself very stupid not to have known it all the time, for then it looked out at you through those pale blue near-sighted eyes, rather shyly, but with a sincerity that only a fool could miss. Those dainty muslins and springlike organdies, those virginal silks, clothed not the uncouth body but the fresh, girlish spirit. You forgot that she broke your china and looked like a man dressed up as a woman, you saw her as she saw herself, as indeed she really was if reality were visible, as a dear little thing with a heart of gold. When you came to know her you found her as simple as a child; she was touchingly grateful for any attention you paid her; her own kindness was infinite, you could ask her to do anything for you, however tiresome, and she would do it as though by giving her the opportunity to put herself out you rendered her a service. She had a rare capacity for disinterested love. You knew that never an unkind nor a malicious thought had once passed through her head. And having granted all that, you said over again that Mrs. Forestier was a very nice woman.

Unfortunately she was also a damned fool. This you discovered when you met her husband. Mrs. Forestier was American, and Captain Forestier was English. Mrs. Forestier was born in Portland, Oregon, and had never been to Europe till the war of 1914, when, her first husband having recently died, she joined a hospital unit and came to France. She was not rich by American standards, but by our English ones in affluent circumstances. From the way the Forestiers lived I should guess that she had something like thirty thousand dollars a year. Except that she undoubtedly gave the wrong medicines to the wrong men, put on their bandages so that they were worse than useless, and broke every utensil that was breakable, I am sure that she was an admirable nurse. I do not think she ever found work too revolting for her to do it without hesitation; she certainly never spared herself and was surely never out of temper; I have a notion that many a poor wretch had cause to bless the tenderness of her heart, and it may be that not a few took the last bitter step into the unknown with more courage because of the loving-kindness of her golden soul. It was during the last year of the war that Captain Forestier came under her care, and soon after peace was declared they married. They settled down in a handsome villa on the hills behind Cannes, and in a short time became conspicuous in the social life of the Riviera. Captain Forestier played bridge well and was a keen golfer. He was not a bad tennis player either. He had a sailing boat, and in the summer the Forestiers gave very nice parties between the islands. After seventeen years of marriage Mrs. Forestier still adored her good-looking husband, and you were unlikely to know her long without being told in that slow Western drawl of hers the full story of their courtship.

"It was a case of love at first sight," she said. "He was brought in when I happened to be off duty, and when I came on and found him lying in one of my beds, oh, my dear, I felt such a pang in my heart, for a moment I thought I'd been overworking and had strained it. He was the handsomest man I'd ever seen in my life."

"Was he badly wounded?"

"Well, he wasn't exactly wounded. You know, it's a most extraordinary thing, he went all through the war, he was under fire for months at a time, and of course he risked his life twenty times a day, he's one of those men who simply doesn't know what fear is; but he never even got a scratch. He had carbuncles."

It seemed an unromantic ailment on which to start a passionate attachment. Mrs. Forestier was a trifle prudish, and though Captain Forestier's carbuncles greatly interested her she always found it a little difficult to tell you exactly where they were.

"They were right down at the bottom of his back, even farther really, and he hated to have me dress them. Englishmen are curiously modest, I've noticed that over and over again, and it mortified him terribly. You'd have thought being on those terms, if you know what I mean, from our first acquaintance it would have made us more intimate. But somehow it didn't. He was very standoffish with me. When I used to get to his bed on my round I was so breathless and my heart beat so I couldn't make out what was the matter with me. I'm not naturally a clumsy woman, I never drop things or break anything; but you wouldn't believe it, when I had to give Robert his medicine I used to drop the spoon and break the glass, I couldn't imagine what he must be thinking of me."

It was almost impossible not to laugh when Mrs. Forestier told you this. She smiled rather sweetly.

"I suppose it sounds very absurd to you, but you see I'd never felt that way before. When I married my first husband—well, he was a widower with grown-up children, he was a fine man and one of the most prominent citizens in the state, but somehow it was different."

"And how did you eventually discover that you were in love with Captain Forestier?"

"Well, I don't ask you to believe me, I know it sounds funny, but the fact is that one of the other nurses told me, and as soon as she did of course I knew it was true. I was terribly upset at first. You see, I knew nothing about him. Like all Englishmen he was very reserved, and for all I knew he had a wife and half a dozen children."

"How did you find out he hadn't?"

"I asked him. The moment he told me he was a bachelor I made up my mind that by hook or by crook I was going to marry him. He suffered agonies, poor darling; you see, he had to lie on his face almost all the time, lying on his back was torture, and as to sitting down—well, of course he couldn't even think of that. But I don't believe his agonies were worse than mine. Men like clinging silks and soft, fluffy things, you know what I mean, and I was at such a disadvantage in my nurse's uniform. The matron, one of those New England spinsters, couldn't bear make-up, and in those days I didn't make up anyway; my first husband never liked it; and then my hair wasn't as pretty as it is now. He used to look at me with those wonderful blue eyes of his, and I felt he must be thinking I looked a perfect sight. He was very low, and I thought I ought to do all I could to cheer him up, so whenever I had a few minutes to spare I'd go and talk to him. He said he couldn't bear the thought of a strong, husky chap like he was lying in bed week after week while all his pals were in the trenches. You couldn't talk to him without realizing that he was one of those men who never feel the joy of life so intensely as when the bullets are whistling all round them, and the next moment may be their last. Danger was a stimulant to him. I don't mind telling you that when I used to write down his temperature on the chart I added a point or two so that the doctors should think him a little worse than he was. I knew he was doing his damnedest to get them to discharge him, and I thought it only fair to him to make sure that they wouldn't. He used to look at me thoughtfully while I talked away and I know he

looked forward to our little chats. I told him that I
was a widow and had no one dependent on me, and
I told him that I was thinking of settling down in
Europe after the war. Gradually he thawed a little.
He didn't say much about himself, but he began to
chaff me, he has a great sense of humour, you know,
and sometimes I really began to think he rather liked
me. At last they reported him fit for duty. To my surprise he asked me to dine with him on his last evening.
I managed to get leave from the matron, and we
drove in to Paris. You can't imagine how handsome
he looked in his uniform. I've never seen anyone look
so distinguished. Aristocratic to his finger tips. Somehow or other he wasn't in such good spirits as I'd
expected. He'd been crazy to get back to the front.

"'Why are you so down tonight?' I asked him.
'After all you've got your wish at last.'

"'I know I have,' he said. 'If for all that I'm a bit
blue, can't you guess why?'

"I simply dared not think what he meant. I
thought I'd better make a little joke.

"'I'm not very good at guessing,' I said, with a
laugh. 'If you want me to know you'd better tell me.'

"He looked down, and I could see he was nervous.

"'You've been most awfully good to me,' he said. 'I
can never begin to thank you for all your kindness.
You're the grandest woman I've ever known.'

"It upset me terribly to hear him say that. You know how funny Englishmen are; he'd never paid me a compliment before.

"'I've only done what any competent nurse would have,' I said.

"'Shall I ever see you again?' he said.

"'That's up to you,' I said. I hoped he didn't hear the tremble in my voice.

"'I hate leaving you,' he said.

"I really could hardly speak.

"'Need you?' I said.

"'So long as my king and country want me I am at their service.'"

When Mrs. Forestier reached this point, her pale blue eyes filled with tears.

"'But the war can't last for ever,' I said.

"'When the war ends,' he answered, 'supposing a bullet hasn't put an end to me, I shan't have a penny. I don't even know how I shall set about earning my living. You're a very rich woman; I'm a pauper.'

"'You're an English gentleman,' I said.

"'Will that matter very much when the world has been made safe for democracy?' he said bitterly.

"I was just crying my eyes out by then. Everything he said was so beautiful. Of course I saw what he meant. He didn't think it honourable to ask me to marry him. I felt he'd sooner die than let me think he was after my money. He was a fine man. I knew that I wasn't worthy of him, but I saw that if I wanted him I must go out and get him myself.

"'It's no good pretending I'm not crazy about you, because I am,' I said.

"'Don't make it harder for me,' he said hoarsely.

"I thought I should die, I loved him so much when he said that. It told me all I wanted to know. I stretched out my hand.

"'Will you marry me, Robert?' I said, very simply.

"'Eleanor,' he said.

"It was then he told me that he'd loved me from the first day he ever saw me. At first he hadn't taken it seriously, he thought I was just a nurse and perhaps he'd have an affair with me, and then when he found out that I wasn't that sort of woman and had a certain amount of money, he made up his mind that he must conquer his love. You see, he thought that marriage was quite out of the question."

Probably nothing flattered Mrs. Forestier more than the idea that Captain Forestier had wanted to have a slap and tickle with her. It was certain that no one else had ever made dishonourable proposals to her, and though Forestier hadn't either, the conviction that he had entertained the notion was a never-failing source of satisfaction to her. When they were married Eleanor's relations, hard-bitten Western people, had suggested that her husband should go to work rather than live on her money, and Captain

Forestier was all for it. The only stipulation he made was this:

"There are some things a gentleman can't do, Eleanor. Anything else I'll do gladly. God knows, I don't attach any importance to that sort of thing, but if one's a sahib one can't help it, and damn it all, especially in these days, one does owe something to one's class."

Eleanor thought he had done enough in risking his life for his country in one bloody battle after another during four long years, but she was too proud of him to let it be said that he was a fortune hunter who had married her for her money, and she made up her mind not to object if he found something to do that was worth his while. Unfortunately, the only jobs that offered were not very important. But he did not turn them down on his own responsibility.

"It's up to you, Eleanor," he told her. "You've only got to say the word and I'll take it. It would make my poor old governor turn in his grave to see me do it, but that can't be helped. My first duty is to you."

Eleanor wouldn't hear of it, and gradually the idea of his working was dropped. The Forestiers lived most of the year in their villa on the Riviera. They seldom went to England; Robert said it was no place for a gentleman since the war, and all the good fellows, white men every one of them, that he used to go about with when he was "one of the boys," had been killed. He would have liked to spend his winters in England, three days a week with the Quorn, that was the life for a man, but poor Eleanor, she would be so out of it in that hunting set, he couldn't ask her to make the sacrifice. Eleanor was prepared to make any sacrifice, but Captain Forestier shook his head. He wasn't as young as he had been, and his hunting days were over. He was quite satisfied to breed Sealyhams and raise Buff Orpingtons. They had a good deal of land; the house stood on the top of a hill, on a plateau, surrounded on three sides by forest, and in front they had a garden. Eleanor said he was never so happy as when he was walking round the estate in an old tweed suit with the kennel man, who also looked after the chickens. It was then you saw in him all those generations of country squires that he had behind him. It touched and amused Eleanor to see the long talks he had with the kennel man about the Buff Orpingtons; it was for all the world as if he were discussing the pheasants with his head keeper; and he fussed over the Sealyhams as much as if they had been the pack of hounds you couldn't help feeling he would have been so much more at home with. Captain Forestier's great-grandfather had been one of the bucks of the Regency. It was he who had ruined the family so that the estates had to be sold. They had a wonderful old place in Shropshire, they'd had it for centuries, and Eleanor, even though it no longer belonged to them, would have liked to go and see it; but Captain Forestier said it would be too painful to him and would never take her.

The Forestiers entertained a good deal. Captain Forestier was a connoisseur of wines and was proud of his cellar.

"His father was well known to have the best palate in England," said Eleanor, "and he's inherited it."

Most of their friends were Americans, French and Russians. Robert found them on the whole more interesting than the English, and Eleanor liked everybody he liked. Robert did not think the English quite up to their mark. Most of the people he had known in the old days belonged to the shooting, hunting and fishing set; they, poor devils, were all broke now, and though, thank God, he wasn't a snob, he didn't half like the idea of his wife getting herself mixed up with a lot of *nouveaux riches* no one had ever heard of. Mrs. Forestier was not nearly so particular, but she respected his prejudices and admired his exclusiveness.

"Of course he has his whims and fancies," she said, "but I think it's only loyal on my part to defer to them. When you know the sort of people he comes from you can't help seeing how natural it is he should have them. The only time I've ever seen him vexed in all the years we've been married was when once a gigolo came up to me in the Casino and asked me to dance. Robert nearly knocked him down. I told him the poor little thing was only doing his job, but he said he wasn't going to have a damned swine like that even asking his wife to dance."

Captain Forestier had high moral standards. He thanked God that he wasn't narrow-minded, but one had to draw the line somewhere; and just because he lived on the Riviera he didn't see why he should hob-nob with drunks, wastrels and perverts. He had no indulgence for sexual irregularities and would not allow Eleanor to frequent women of doubtful repu-tation.

"You see," said Eleanor, "he's a man of complete integrity; he's the cleanest man I've ever known; and if sometimes he seems a little intolerant, you must always remember that he never asks of others what he isn't prepared to do himself. After all, one can't help admiring a man whose principles are so high and who's prepared to stick to them at any cost."

When Captain Forestier told Eleanor that such and such a man, whom you met everywhere, and who you thought was rather pleasant, wasn't a pukka sahib, she knew it was no good insisting. She knew that in her husband's judgment that finished him, and she was prepared to abide by it. After nearly twenty years of marriage she was sure of one thing, if of no other, and this was that Robert Forestier was the perfect type of an English gentleman.

"And I don't know that God has ever created any-thing finer than that," she said.

The trouble was that Captain Forestier was almost too perfect a type of the English gentleman. He was at forty-five (he was two or three years younger than Eleanor) still a very handsome man, with his wavy, abundant grey hair and his handsome moustache; he had the weather-beaten, healthy, tanned skin of a man who is much in the open air. He was tall, lean and broad-shouldered. He looked every inch a soldier. He had a bluff, hearty way with him and a loud, frank laugh. In his conversation, in his manner, in his dress he was so typical that you could hardly believe it. He was so much of a country gentleman that he made you think rather of an actor giving a marvellous per-formance of the part. When you saw him walking along the Croisette, a pipe in his mouth, in plus fours and just the sort of tweed coat he would have worn on the moors, he looked so like an English sportsman that it gave you quite a shock. And his conversation, the way he dogmatized, the platitudinous inanity of his statements, his amiable, well-bred stupidity, were all so characteristic of the retired officer that you could hardly help thinking he was putting it on.

When Eleanor heard that the house at the bottom of their hill had been taken by a Sir Frederick and Lady Hardy she was much pleased. It would be nice for Robert to have as a near neighbour someone of his own class. She made enquiries about them from her friends in Cannes. It appeared that Sir Frederick had lately come into the baronetcy on the death of an uncle and was come to the Riviera for two or three years while he was paying off the death duties. He was said to have been very wild in his youth, he was well on in the fifties when he came to Cannes, but now he was respectably married, to a very nice little woman, and had two small boys. It was a pity that Lady Hardy had been an actress, for Robert was apt to be a little stuffy about actresses, but everyone said that she was very well mannered and ladylike, and you would never have guessed she had been on the stage. The Forestiers met her first at a tea party to which Sir Frederick did not go, and Robert acknowledged that she seemed a very decent sort of person; so Eleanor, wishing to be neighbourly, invited them both to luncheon. A day was arranged. The Forestiers had asked a good many people to meet them, and the Hardys were rather late. Eleanor took an immediate fancy to Sir Frederick. He looked much younger than she expected, he hadn't a white hair on his close-cropped head; indeed there was about him something boyish that was rather attractive. He was slightly built, not as tall as she was; and he had bright friendly eyes and a ready smile. She noticed that he wore the same Guards tie that Robert sometimes wore; he was not nearly so well dressed as Robert, who always looked as though he had stepped out of a show window, but he wore his old clothes as though it didn't much matter what one wore. Eleanor could quite believe he had been a trifle wild as a young man. She was not inclined to blame him.

"I must introduce my husband to you," she said.

She called him. Robert was talking to some of the other guests on the terrace, and hadn't noticed the Hardys come in. He came forward and in his affable, hearty way, with a grace that always charmed Eleanor, shook hands with Lady Hardy. Then he turned to Sir Frederick. Sir Frederick gave him a puzzled look.

"Haven't we met before?" he said.

Robert looked at him coolly.

"I don't think so."

"I could have sworn I knew your face."

Eleanor felt her husband stiffen and at once realized that something was going wrong. Robert laughed.

"It sounds terribly rude, but to the best of my belief I've never set eyes on you in my life. We may have run across one another in the war. One met such hosts of fellers, then, didn't one? Will you have a cocktail, Lady Hardy?"

During luncheon Eleanor noticed that Hardy kept looking at Robert. He was evidently trying to place him. Robert was busy with the women on either side of him and did not catch the glances. He was making efforts to entertain his neighbours; and his loud, ringing laugh rang through the room. He was a wonderful host. Eleanor had always admired his sense of social duty; however dull the women were he was sitting next to, he gave them of his best. But when their guests had gone, Robert's gaiety dropped from him like a cloak from his shoulders. She had a feeling that he was upset.

"Was the princess very boring?" she asked kindly.

"She's a malignant old cat, but otherwise she was all right."

"Funny that Sir Frederick thought he knew you."

"I've never set eyes on him in my life. But I know all about him. I wouldn't have more to do with him than you can help if I were you, Eleanor. I don't think he's quite our mark."

"But it's one of the oldest baronetcies in England. We looked it out in *Who's Who*."

"He's a disreputable scamp. I didn't dream that the Captain Hardy," Robert corrected himself, "the Fred Hardy I used to know about in the old days was now Sir Frederick. I would never have allowed you to ask him to my house."

"Why, Robert? I'm bound to tell you that I thought him very attractive."

For once Eleanor thought her husband rather unreasonable.

"A great many women have found him so, and a pretty penny it's cost them."

"You know how people talk. One really can't believe everything one hears."

He took one of her hands in his and looked earnestly into her eyes.

"Eleanor, you know I'm not the sort of chap to say anything against another chap behind his back, and I'd rather not tell you what I know about Hardy; I can only ask you to take my word for it that he isn't a proper person for you to know."

This was an appeal to which Eleanor was incapable of turning a deaf ear. It thrilled her to know that Robert placed such confidence in her; he knew that in a crisis he had only to call on her loyalty and she would not fail him.

"No one can be better aware than I, Robert," she answered gravely, "of your perfect integrity; I know that if you could tell me you would, but even if you wanted to now I wouldn't let you; it would look as if I had less confidence in you than you have in me. I am willing to abide by your judgment. I promise you that the Hardys shall never darken these doors again."

But Eleanor often lunched out without Robert, when he was playing golf, and so frequently met the Hardys. She was very stiff with Sir Frederick, because if Robert disapproved of him, she must too; but he either did not notice or did not care. He went out of his way to be nice to her, and she found him easy to get on with. It was difficult to dislike a man who plainly thought that no woman was better than she should be, but very sweet for all that, and who had such delightful manners. It might be that he was an improper man for her to know, but she couldn't help liking the look in his brown eyes. It was a mocking look, which put you on your guard, and yet so caressing that you could not think he meant you harm. But the more Eleanor heard about him, the more she realized how right Robert was. He was an unprincipled rascal. They mentioned the names of women who had sacrificed everything for his sake and whom he had thrown aside without ceremony the moment he was tired of them. He seemed to have settled down now, and to be devoted to his wife and children; but can the leopard change his spots? It was only too probable that Lady Hardy had more to put up with than anyone suspected.

Fred Hardy was a bad lot. Pretty women, *chemin de fer*, and an unlucky knack for backing the wrong horse had landed him in the bankruptcy court by the time he was twenty-five, and he had been forced to resign his commission. He had seen no shame then in allowing women no longer in their first youth, who found his charm irresistible, to supply his wants. But the war came, he rejoined his regiment, and got a D.S.O. Then he went out to Kenya, where he found occasion to become co-respondent in a notorious divorce case; he left Kenya over some trouble with a cheque. His ideas of honesty were lax. It was unsafe to buy a car or a horse off him, and you did much better to keep away from the champagnes he warmly recommended to you. When with his persuasive charm he put before you a speculation by which you and he would make a fortune, you could only be sure that, whatever he made out of it, you would make nothing. He was in turn a motor salesman, an outside broker, a commission agent and an actor. Were there any justice in the world he should have ended, if not in gaol, at least in the gutter. But by one of fate's monstrous tricks, having at last inherited his baronetcy and an adequate income, having married when well over forty a pretty, clever wife to whom were in due course born two healthy and handsome children, the future offered him affluence, position and respectability. He had never taken life any more seriously than he took women, and life had been as kind to him as women. If he thought of his past it was with complacency; he had had a good time, he had enjoyed his ups and downs; and now, with good health and a clear conscience, he was prepared to settle down as a country gentleman, damn it, bring up the kids as kids should be brought up; and when the old buffer who sat for his constituency pegged out, by George, go into Parliament himself.

"I could tell them a thing or two they don't know," he said.

He was probably right, but he did not stop to reflect that perhaps they were not things they much wanted to know.

One afternoon, about sunset, Fred Hardy went into one of the bars on the Croisette. He was a sociable creature and did not care to drink alone, so he looked around to see if there were anyone he knew. He caught sight of Robert, who had been playing golf and was waiting there for Eleanor.

"Hulloa, Bob, what about having a tiddly?"

Robert gave a start. No one on the Riviera called him Bob. When he saw who it was he answered stiffly.

"I've got a drink, thanks."

"Have another. My old lady don't approve of my drinking between meals, but when I can manage to get away from her I generally slip in and have one about this time. I don't know what you think about it, but my feeling is that God made six o'clock for man to have a drink at."

He flung himself into a great leather armchair next to the one Robert was sitting in and called a waiter. He gave Robert his good-natured, engaging smile.

"A lot of water has passed under the bridges since first we met, old boy, hasn't it?"

Robert, frowning a little, shot a look at him which an observer might have described as wary.

"I don't know exactly what you mean. To the best of my belief we met for the first time three or four weeks ago when you and your wife were good enough to come and have lunch with us."

"Come off it, Bob. I knew I'd seen you before. I was puzzled at first, and then it flashed across me. You were the car washer at that garage off Bruton Street where I used to keep my car."

Captain Forestier gave a hearty laugh.

"I'm sorry, but you've made a mistake. I never heard anything so ridiculous."

"I've got a damned good memory, and I never forget a face. I bet you haven't forgotten me, either. Many's the half-crown I've given you for fetching the car away from my flat when I didn't want to be bothered to bring it round to the garage myself."

"You're talking absolute rot. I'd never seen you in my life till you came to my house."

Hardy grinned cheerfully.

"You know I've always been a Kodak fiend. I've got albums of snaps that I've taken at one time and another. Would it surprise you to learn that I've found a snap of you standing by a two-seater I'd just bought? A damned good-looking fellow you were in those days, even though you had overalls on and your face was none too clean. Of course you've broadened out, your hair's grey and you've got a moustache, but it's the same chap. Unmistakably."

Captain Forestier looked at him coolly.

"You must have been misled by an accidental

resemblance. It was somebody else you gave your half-crowns to."

"Well, where were you then, if you weren't a car washer at the Bruton Garage between 1913 and 1914?"

"I was in India."

"With your regiment?" asked Fred Hardy with another grin.

"I was shooting."

"You liar."

Robert flushed deeply.

"This isn't quite the place to choose for a scrap, but if you think I'm going to stay here to be insulted by a drunken swine like you, you're mistaken."

"Wouldn't you like to hear what else I know about you? You know how things come back to one, and I've remembered quite a lot."

"I'm not in the least interested. I tell you that you're making an absolute mistake. You're confusing me with somebody else."

But he made no attempt to go.

"You were a bit of a slacker even in those days. I remember once, when I was going into the country early, I'd told you to have my car washed by nine, and it wasn't ready, so I kicked up a row and old Thompson told me then your father had been a pal of his and he'd taken you on out of charity because you were down and out. Your father had been a wine waiter at one of the clubs, White's or Brooks's, I forget which, and you'd been a page boy there yourself. You enlisted in the Coldstream Guards, if I remember right, and some chap bought you out and made you his valet."

"It's too fantastic," said Robert scornfully.

"And I remember, when I was home on leave once and went to the garage, old Thompson told me you'd enlisted in the A.S.C. You weren't going to take any more risks than you could help, were you? You've been drawing the longbow a bit, haven't you, with all those stories I hear of your gallantry in the trenches? I suppose you did get a commission, or is that a fake, too?"

"Of course I got a commission."

"Well, a lot of funny people did in those days, but you know, old boy, if it was in the A.S.C. I wouldn't wear a Guards tie if I were you."

Captain Forestier instinctively put his hand up to his tie, and Fred Hardy, watching him with his mocking eyes, was pretty sure that notwithstanding his tan he went white.

"It's no business of yours what tie I wear."

"Don't get snotty, old boy. There's no reason to get up on your hind legs. I've got the goods on you, but I'm not going to give you away, so why don't you come clean?"

"I've got nothing to come clean about. I tell you

it's all an absurd mistake. And I should tell you that if I find that you've been spreading these lying stories about me, I shall immediately start proceedings for slander."

"Stow it, Bob. I'm not going to spread any stories. You don't think I care? I think the whole thing's rather a lark. I've got no ill feeling towards you. I've been a bit of an adventurer myself; I admire you for carrying off such a stupendous bluff. Starting as a page boy and then being a trooper, a valet and a car washer; and there you are a fine gentleman, with a grand house, entertaining all the big bugs of the Riviera, winning golf tournaments, vice-president of the Sailing Club, and I don't know what all. You're It in Cannes and no mistake. It's stupendous. I've done some pretty rum things in my day, but the nerve you must have; old boy, I take off my hat to you."

"I wish I deserved your compliments. I don't. My father was in the Indian cavalry, and I was at least born a gentleman. I may not have had a very distinguished career, but I certainly have nothing to be ashamed of."

"Oh, come off it, Bob. I shan't split, you know, not even to my old lady. I never tell women anything that they don't know already. Believe me, I'd have got into even worse scrapes than I have if I hadn't made a rule of that. I should have thought you'd be glad to have someone around that you could be yourself with. Isn't it a strain never to let up? Silly of you to keep me at arm's length. I haven't got anything on you, old boy. It's true I'm a bart and a landed proprietor now, but I've been in some pretty tight places in my time, and it's a wonder to me that I've kept out of gaol."

"It's a wonder to a good many other people."

Fred Hardy broke into a guffaw.

"That's one on me, old boy. All the same, if you don't mind my saying so, I think it was a bit thick, your telling your wife I wasn't a proper person for her to associate with."

"I never said anything of the sort."

"Oh yes, you did. She's a grand old girl, but a bit garrulous, or am I mistaken?"

"I'm not prepared to discuss my wife with a man like you," said Captain Forestier coldly.

"Oh, don't be so damned gentlemanly with me, Bob. We're a couple of bums and that's all there is to it. We could have some grand times together if you'd only have a little sense. You're a liar, a humbug and a cheat, but you seem to be very decent to your wife, and that's something in your favour. She just dotes upon you, doesn't she? Funny, women are. She's a very nice woman, Bob."

Robert's face grew red, he clenched his fist and half rose from his chair.

"Damn you, stop talking about my wife. If you

mention her name again I swear I'll knock you down."

"Oh no, you won't. You're too great a gentleman to hit a feller smaller than yourself."

Hardy had said these words mockingly, watching Robert, and quite ready to dodge if that great fist struck out; he was astounded at their effect. Robert sank back into his chair and unclenched his fist.

"You're right. But only a mean hound would trade on it."

The reply was so theatrical that Fred Hardy began to chuckle, but then he saw that the man meant it. He was deadly serious. Fred Hardy was no fool; he could hardly have lived for twenty-five years on his wits in tolerable comfort unless he had had them all about him. And now, in amazement, staring at that heavy, powerful man, who looked so like the typical English sportsman, sunk back in the chair, he had a sudden flash of comprehension. He was no common swindler who had got hold of a silly woman to keep him in luxury and idleness. She was only a means to a greater end. He had been captivated by an ideal and in pursuit of it had stuck at nothing. Perhaps the notion had come to him when he was a page boy in a smart club; the members, with their lounging ease, their casual manner, may have seemed very wonderful to him; and afterwards as a trooper, as a valet, as a car washer, the many men he ran across, belonging to a different world and seen through a haze of hero worship, had filled him perhaps with admiration and envy. He wanted to be like them. He wanted to be one of them. That was the ideal that haunted his dreams. He wanted—it was grotesque, it was pathetic —he wanted to be a gentleman. The war, with the commission it brought him, gave him his chance. Eleanor's money provided the means. That wretched fellow had spent twenty years pretending to be something the only value of which was that it wasn't a pretence. That was grotesque too; that was pathetic. Without meaning to, Fred Hardy uttered the thought that passed through his head.

"Poor old chap," he said.

Forestier looked at him quickly. He could not understand what those words meant or the tone in which they were said. He flushed.

"What d'you mean by that?"

"Nothing. Nothing."

"I don't think we need continue this conversation. Apparently there's nothing I can say to persuade you that you're mistaken. I can only repeat that there's not a word of truth in it. I am not the fellow you think I am."

"All right, old boy, have it your own way."

Forestier called the waiter.

"D'you want me to pay for your drink?" he asked icily.

"Yes, old boy."

Forestier somewhat grandly gave the waiter a note and told him to keep the change; then, without a word, without giving Fred Hardy another look, stalked out of the bar.

They did not meet again till the night on which Robert Forestier lost his life.

The winter passed into spring, and the gardens on the Riviera were ablaze with colour. The hillsides were primly gay with wildflowers. The spring passed into summer. In the towns along the Riviera the streets were hot with a bright, eager heat that made the blood run faster; and women walked about in great straw hats and pyjamas. The beaches were crowded. Men in trunks and women almost naked lay in the sun. In the evening the bars on the Croisette were thronged by a restless, chattering crowd as many-coloured as the flowers of spring. It had not rained for weeks. There had been several forest fires along the coast, and Robert Forestier in his hearty, joking way had several times said that they would stand a pretty thin chance if they had a fire in their woods. One or two people had advised him to cut down some of the trees at the back of his house; but he couldn't bear to: they had been in poor condition when the Forestiers bought the place, but now that the deadwood had been cut away year by year, that they had been given air and kept clean of pests, they were magnificent.

"Why, it would be like having my leg chopped off to cut one of 'em down. They must be the best part of a hundred years old."

On the fourteenth of July the Forestiers went over to a gala dinner at Monte Carlo, and they gave their staff leave to go to Cannes. It was the national holiday, and in Cannes they danced in the open air under the plane trees, there were fireworks, and from far and near the people came in to have a good time. The Hardys had sent their servants out too, but they were sitting at home, and their two little boys were in bed. Fred was playing patience, and Lady Hardy was working at a piece of tapestry to cover a chair. Suddenly there was a ring of the bell and a loud knocking on the door.

"Who the devil's that?"

Hardy went to the door and found a boy who told him that fire had broken out in the Forestiers' woods. Some men had gone up from the village and were fighting it, but they needed all the help they could get, and would he come.

"Of course I'll come." He hurried back to his wife and told her. "Wake the kids and let them come up and see the fun. By George, after all this drought it'll be a blaze."

He bolted out. The boy told him they had telephoned to the police station and they were going to send along the soldiers. Someone was trying to get through to Monte Carlo and let Captain Forestier know.

"It'll take him an hour to get here," said Hardy.

As they ran they saw the glow in the sky, and when they came to the top of the hill, the leaping flames. There was no water, and the only thing to do was to try to beat them out. Already a number of men were at work. Hardy joined them. But you had no sooner beat out the flames in one bush than another began to crackle and, before you could look, had turned into a fiery torch. The heat was terrific, and the workers, unable to support it, were slowly driven back. A breeze was blowing, and the sparks were carried from tree to bush. After weeks of drought everything was as dry as tinder, and the moment a spark fell the tree, the bush, went up in flames. If it had not been terrifying, it would have been awe-inspiring to see a great fir tree, sixty feet high, blazing like matchwood. The fire roared like the fire in a factory furnace. The best way to put a stop to it was by cutting down trees and brushwood, but the men were few, and but two or three had axes. The only hope was in the troops, who were used to dealing with the forest fires, and the troops did not come.

"Unless they get here soon we shall never save the house," said Hardy.

He caught sight of his wife, who had come up with the two boys, and waved to them. Already he was black with grime, and the sweat was pouring down his face. Lady Hardy ran up.

"Oh, Fred, the dogs and the chickens."

"By George, yes."

The kennels and the chicken run were at the back of the house, in a clearing that had been cut in the woods, and the wretched animals were already frantic with terror. Hardy let them out, and they rushed to safety. They could only be left to shift for themselves. They must be rounded up later. The blaze could be seen now from far away. But the troops did not come, and the small body of helpers were powerless against the advancing flames.

"If those damned soldiers don't get here soon the house is for it," said Hardy. "I think we'd better get what we can out of it."

It was a stone house, but there were wooden ve-randas all round it, and they would burn like kindling. The Forestiers' servants had come by now. He got them together, his wife gave a hand, and the two boys; they carried out onto the lawn in front such things as were portable, linen and silver, clothes, ornaments, pictures, pieces of furniture. At last the troops came, two lorry-loads of them, and set about systematically digging trenches and felling trees. There was an officer in charge, and Hardy, pointing out the danger to the house, begged him first of all to cut down the trees that surrounded it.

"The house must look after itself," he said. "I've got to prevent the fire spreading beyond the hill."

The lights of a car were seen speeding along the winding road, and a few minutes later Forestier and his wife sprang out of it.

"Where are the dogs?" he cried.

"I've let them out," said Hardy.

"Oh, it's you."

At first in that filthy fellow, his face begrimed with soot and sweat, he had not recognized Fred Hardy. He frowned angrily.

"I thought the house might catch. I've got everything out I could."

Forestier looked at the blazing forest.

"Well, that's the end of my trees," he said.

"The soldiers are working on the side of the hill. They're trying to save the next property. We'd better go along and see if we can save anything."

"I'll go. You needn't," Forestier cried irritably.

On a sudden Eleanor gave an anguished cry.

"Oh, look. The house."

From where they stood they could see a veranda at the back suddenly burst into flames.

"That's all right, Eleanor. The house can't burn. It'll only get the woodwork. Take my coat; I'm going along to help the soldiers."

He took off his dinner jacket and handed it to his wife.

"I'll come with you," said Hardy. "Mrs. Forestier, you'd better go along to where your things are. I think we've got everything out that's valuable."

"Thank heaven, I was wearing most of my jewelry."

Lady Hardy was a woman of sense.

"Mrs. Forestier, let's get the servants together and carry what we can down to our house."

The two men walked towards where the soldiers were at work.

"It's very decent of you to have got that stuff out of my house," said Robert stiffly.

"Not at all," answered Fred Hardy.

They had not gone far when they heard somebody calling. They looked round and vaguely saw a woman running after them.

"*Monsieur, monsieur.*"

They stopped, and the woman, her arms outstretched, rushed up. It was Eleanor's maid. She was distraught.

"*La petite Judy*. Judy. I shut her up when we went out. She's on heat. I put her in the servants' bathroom."

"My God!" cried Forestier.

"What is it?"

"Eleanor's dog. I must save her at any cost."

He turned round and started to run back to the house. Hardy caught hold of his arm to hold him.

"Don't be a damned fool, Bob. The house is burning. You can't go into it."

Forestier struggled to release himself.

"Let me go, damn you. D'you think I'm going to let a dog be burned alive?"

"Oh, shut up. This is no time for play-acting!"

Forestier shook Hardy off, but Hardy sprang on him and seized him round the middle. Forestier with his clenched fist hit Hardy in the face as hard as he could. Hardy staggered, releasing his hold, and Forestier hit him again; Hardy fell to the ground.

"You rotten bounder. I'll show you how a gentleman behaves."

Fred Hardy picked himself up slowly and felt his face. It hurt him.

"God, the black eye I'm going to have tomorrow!" He was shaken and a trifle dazed. The maid suddenly broke into a storm of hysterical tears. "Shut up, you slut," he cried crossly. "And don't say a word to your mistress."

Forestier was nowhere to be seen. It was more than an hour before they were able to get at him. They found him lying on the landing outside the bathroom, dead, with the dead Sealyham in his arms. Hardy looked at him for a long time before speaking.

"You fool," he muttered between his teeth, angrily. "You damned fool!"

That imposture of his had paid him out at last.

Like a man who cherishes a vice till it gets a strangle
hold on him so that he is its helpless slave, he had lied
so long that he had come to believe his own lies. Bob
Forestier had pretended for so many years to be a
gentleman that in the end, forgetting that it was all
a fake, he had found himself driven to act as in that
stupid, conventional brain of his he thought a gentleman must act. No longer knowing the difference
between sham and real, he had sacrificed his life to a
spurious heroism. But Fred Hardy had to break the
news to Mrs. Forestier. She was with his wife, in their
villa at the bottom of the hill, and she still thought
that Robert was with the soldiers cutting down trees
and clearing the brushwood. He told her as gently as
he could, but he had to tell her, and he had to tell her
everything. At first it seemed as though she could
not grasp the sense of what he said.

"Dead?" she cried. "Dead? My Robert?"

Then Fred Hardy, the rip, the cynic, the unscrupulous ruffian, took her hands in his and said the words
that alone enabled her to bear her anguish:

"Mrs. Forestier, he was a very gallant gentleman."

Lord Mountdrago

DR. AUDLIN looked at the clock on his desk. It was twenty minutes to six. He was surprised that his patient was late, for Lord Mountdrago prided himself on his punctuality; he had a sententious way of expressing himself which gave the air of an epigram to a commonplace remark, and he was in the habit of saying that punctuality is a compliment you pay to the intelligent and a rebuke you administer to the stupid. Lord Mountdrago's appointment was for five-thirty.

There was in Dr. Audlin's appearance nothing to attract attention. He was tall and spare, with narrow shoulders and something of a stoop; his hair was grey and thin; his long, sallow face deeply lined. He was not more than fifty, but he looked older. His eyes, pale blue and rather large, were weary. When you had been with him for a while you noticed that they moved very little; they remained fixed on your face,

but so empty of expression were they that it was no
discomfort. They seldom lit up. They gave no clue to
his thoughts nor changed with the words he spoke.
If you were of an observant turn it might have struck
you that he blinked much less often than most of us.
His hands were on the large side, with long, tapering
fingers; they were soft but firm, cool but not clammy.
You could never have said what Dr. Audlin wore
unless you had made a point of looking. His clothes
were dark. His tie was black. His dress made his
sallow lined face paler and his pale eyes more wan. He
gave you the impression of a very sick man.

Dr. Audlin was a psychoanalyst. He had adopted
the profession by accident and practised it with misgiving. When the war broke out he had not been long
qualified and was getting experience at various hos-
pitals; he offered his services to the authorities, and
after a time was sent out to France. It was then that
he discovered his singular gift. He could allay certain
pains by the touch of his cool, firm hands, and by
talking to them often induce sleep in men who were
suffering from sleeplessness. He spoke slowly. His
voice had no particular colour, and its tone did not
alter with the words he uttered, but it was musical,
soft and lulling. He told the men that they must rest,
that they mustn't worry, that they must sleep; and
rest stole into their jaded bones, tranquillity pushed
their anxieties away, like a man finding a place for

himself on a crowded bench, and slumber fell on their
tired eyelids like the light rain of spring upon the
fresh-turned earth. Dr. Audlin found that by speaking to men with that low, monotonous voice of his,
by looking at them with his pale, quiet eyes, by strok-
ing their weary foreheads with his long firm hands,
he could soothe their perturbations, resolve the con-
flicts that distracted them and banish the phobias
that made their lives a torment. Sometimes he effected
cures that seemed miraculous. He restored speech to
a man who, after being buried under the earth by a
bursting shell, had been struck dumb, and he gave
back the use of his limbs to another who had been
paralyzed after a crash in a plane. He could not
understand his powers; he was of a sceptical turn,
and though they say that in circumstances of this
kind the first thing is to believe in yourself, he never
quite succeeded in doing that; and it was only the
outcome of his activities, patent to the most incredu-
lous observer, that obliged him to admit that he had
some faculty, coming from he knew not where, obscure and uncertain, that enabled him to do things
for which he could offer no explanation. When the
war was over he went to Vienna and studied there,
and afterwards to Zurich; and then settled down in
London to practise the art he had so strangely acquired. He had been practising now for fifteen years,
and had attained, in the speciality he followed, a

distinguished reputation. People told one another of the amazing things he had done, and though his fees were high, he had as many patients as he had time to see. Dr. Audlin knew that he had achieved some very extraordinary results; he had saved men from suicide, others from the lunatic asylum, he had assuaged griefs that embittered useful lives, he had turned unhappy marriages into happy ones, he had eradicated abnormal instincts and thus delivered not a few from a hateful bondage, he had given health to the sick in spirit; he had done all this, and yet at the back of his mind remained the suspicion that he was little more than a quack.

It went against his grain to exercise a power that he could not understand, and it offended his honesty to trade on the faith of the people he treated when he had no faith in himself. He was rich enough now to live without working, and the work exhausted him; a dozen times he had been on the point of giving up practice. He knew all that Freud and Jung and the rest of them had written. He was not satisfied; he had an intimate conviction that all their theory was hocus-pocus, and yet there the results were, incomprehensible, but manifest. And what had he not seen of human nature during the fifteen years that patients had been coming to his dingy back room in Wimpole Street? The revelations that had been poured into his ears, sometimes only too willingly, sometimes with shame, with reservations, with anger, had long ceased to surprise him. Nothing could shock him any longer. He knew by now that men were liars, he knew how extravagant was their vanity; he knew far worse than that about them; but he knew that it was not for him to judge or to condemn. But year by year as these terrible confidences were imparted to him his face grew a little greyer, its lines a little more marked and his pale eyes more weary. He seldom laughed, but now and again when for relaxation he read a novel he smiled. Did their authors really think the men and women they wrote of were like that? If they only knew how much more complicated they were, how much more unexpected, what irreconcilable elements coexisted within their souls and what dark and sinister contentions afflicted them!

It was a quarter to six. Of all the strange cases he had been called upon to deal with, Dr. Audlin could remember none stranger than that of Lord Mountdrago. For one thing the personality of his patient made it singular. Lord Mountdrago was an able and a distinguished man. Appointed Secretary for Foreign Affairs when still under forty, now after three years in office he had seen his policy prevail. It was generally acknowledged that he was the ablest politician in the Conservative Party, and only the fact that his father was a peer, on whose death he would no longer be able to sit in the House of Commons, made it impossible for him to aim at the premiership. But if in these democratic times it is out of the question for a Prime Minister of England to be in the House of Lords, there was nothing to prevent Lord Mountdrago from continuing to be Secretary for Foreign Affairs in successive Conservative administrations and so for long directing the foreign policy of his country.

Lord Mountdrago had many good qualities. He had intelligence and industry. He was widely travelled and spoke several languages fluently. From early youth he had specialized in foreign affairs and had conscientiously made himself acquainted with the political and economic circumstances of other countries. He had courage, insight and determination. He was a good speaker, both on the platform and in the House, clear, precise and often witty. He was a brilliant debater and his gift of repartee was celebrated. He had a fine presence: he was a tall, handsome man, rather bald and somewhat too stout, but this gave him solidity and an air of maturity that were of service to him. As a young man he had been something of an athlete and had rowed in the Oxford boat, and he was known to be one of the best shots in England. At twenty-four he had married a girl of eighteen whose father was a duke and her mother a great American heiress, so that she had both position and wealth, and by her he had had two sons. For several years they had lived privately apart, but in public united, so that appearances were saved, and no other attachment on either side had given the gossips occasion to whisper. Lord Mountdrago indeed was too ambitious, too hard-working, and it must be added too patriotic, to be tempted by any pleasures that might interfere with his career. He had in short a great deal to make him a popular and successful figure. He had unfortunately great defects.

He was a fearful snob. You would not have been surprised at this if his father had been the first holder of the title. That the son of an ennobled lawyer, manufacturer or distiller should attach an inordinate importance to his rank is understandable. The earl-dom held by Lord Mountdrago's father was created by Charles II, and the barony held by the first earl dated from the Wars of the Roses. For three hundred years the successive holders of the title had allied themselves with the noblest families of England. But Lord Mountdrago was as conscious of his birth as a *nouveau riche* is conscious of his money. He never missed an opportunity of impressing it upon others. He had beautiful manners when he chose to display them, but this he did only with people whom he re-garded as his equals. He was coldly insolent to those whom he looked upon as his social inferiors. He was rude to his servants and insulting to his secretaries. The subordinate officials in the government offices to which he had been successively attached feared and hated him. His arrogance was horrible. He knew that he was a great deal cleverer than most of the persons he had to do with, and never hesitated to apprise them of the fact. He had no patience with the infirmities of human nature. He felt himself born to command and was irritated with people who expected him to listen to their arguments or wished to hear the reasons for his decisions. He was immeasurably selfish. He looked upon any service that was rendered him as a right due to his rank and intelligence and therefore deserving of no gratitude. It never entered his head that he was called upon to do anything for others. He had many enemies: he despised them. He knew no one who merited his assistance, his sympathy or his compassion. He had no friends. He was distrusted by his chiefs, because they doubted his loyalty; he was unpopular with his party, because he was overbearing and discourteous; and yet his merit was so great, his patriotism so evident, his intelligence so solid and his management of affairs so brilliant, that they had to put up with him. And what made it possible to do this was that on occasion he could be enchanting: when he was with persons whom he considered his equals, or whom he wished to captivate, in the company of foreign dignitaries or women of distinction, he could be gay, witty and debonair; his manners then reminded you that in his veins ran the same blood as had run in the veins of Lord Chesterfield; he could tell a story with point, he could be natural, sensible and even profound. You were surprised at the extent of his knowledge and the sensitiveness of his taste. You thought him the best company in the world; you forgot that he had insulted you the day before and was quite capable of cutting you dead the next.

Lord Mountdrago almost failed to become Dr. Audlin's patient. A secretary rang up the doctor and told him that his lordship, wishing to consult him, would be glad if he would come to his house at ten o'clock on the following morning. Dr. Audlin answered that he was unable to go to Lord Mountdrago's house, but would be pleased to give him an appointment at his consulting room at five o'clock on the next day but one. The secretary took the message and presently rang back to say that Lord Mountdrago insisted on seeing Dr. Audlin in his own house and the doctor could fix his own fee. Dr. Audlin replied that he saw patients only in his consulting room and expressed his regret that unless Lord Mountdrago was prepared to come to him he could not give him his attention. In a quarter of an hour a brief message was delivered to him that his lordship would come not next day but one, but next day, at five.

When Lord Mountdrago was then shown in he did not come forward, but stood at the door and insolently looked the doctor up and down. Dr. Audlin perceived that he was in a rage; he gazed at him, silently, with still eyes. He saw a big heavy man, with greying hair, receding on the forehead so that it gave nobility to his brow, a puffy face with bold regular features and an expression of haughtiness. He had somewhat the look of one of the Bourbon sovereigns of the eighteenth century.

"It seems that it is as difficult to see you as a Prime Minister, Dr. Audlin. I'm an extremely busy man."

"Won't you sit down?" said the doctor.

His face showed no sign that Lord Mountdrago's speech in any way affected him. Dr. Audlin sat in his chair at the desk. Lord Mountdrago still stood, and his frown darkened.

"I think I should tell you that I am His Majesty's Secretary for Foreign Affairs," he said acidly.

"Won't you sit down?" the doctor repeated.

Lord Mountdrago made a gesture, which might have suggested that he was about to turn on his heel and stalk out of the room; but if that was his intention he apparently thought better of it. He seated himself. Dr. Audlin opened a large book and took up his pen. He wrote without looking at his patient.

"How old are you?"

"Forty-two."

"Are you married?"

"Yes."

"How long have you been married?"

"Eighteen years."

"Have you any children?"

"I have two sons."

Dr. Audlin noted down the facts as Lord Mount-drago abruptly answered his questions. Then he leaned back in his chair and looked at him. He did not speak; he just looked, gravely, with pale eyes that did not move.

"Why have you come to see me?" he asked at length.

"I've heard about you. Lady Canute is a patient of yours, I understand. She tells me you've done her a certain amount of good."

Dr. Audlin did not reply. His eyes remained fixed on the other's face, but they were so empty of expression that you might have thought he did not even see him.

"I can't do miracles," he said at length. Not a smile, but the shadow of a smile flickered in his eyes. "The Royal College of Physicians would not approve of it if I did."

Lord Mountdrago gave a brief chuckle. It seemed to lessen his hostility. He spoke more amiably.

"You have a very remarkable reputation. People seem to believe in you."

"Why have you come to me?" repeated Dr. Audlin.

Now it was Lord Mountdrago's turn to be silent.

It looked as though he found it hard to answer. Dr. Audlin waited. At last Lord Mountdrago seemed to make an effort. He spoke.

"I'm in perfect health. Just as a matter of routine I had myself examined by my own doctor the other day, Sir Augustus Fitzherbert, I daresay you've heard of him, and he tells me I have the physique of a man of thirty. I work hard, but I'm never tired, and I enjoy my work. I smoke very little and I'm an extremely moderate drinker. I take a sufficiency of exercise and I lead a regular life. I am a perfectly sound, normal, healthy man. I quite expect you to think it very silly and childish of me to consult you."

Dr. Audlin saw that he must help him.

"I don't know if I can do anything to help you. I'll try. You're distressed?"

Lord Mountdrago frowned.

"The work that I'm engaged in is important. The decisions I am called upon to make can easily affect the welfare of the country and even the peace of the world. It is essential that my judgment should be balanced and my brain clear. I look upon it as my duty to eliminate any cause of worry that may interfere with my usefulness."

Dr. Audlin had never taken his eyes off him. He saw a great deal. He saw behind his patient's pompous manner and arrogant pride an anxiety that he could not dispel.

"I asked you to be good enough to come here because I know by experience that it's easier for someone to speak openly in the dingy surroundings of a doctor's consulting room than in his accustomed environment."

"They're certainly dingy," said Lord Mountdrago acidly. He paused. It was evident that this man who had so much self-assurance, so quick and decided a mind that he was never at a loss, at this moment was embarrassed. He smiled in order to show the doctor that he was at his ease, but his eyes betrayed his disquiet. When he spoke again it was with unnatural heartiness.

"The whole thing's so trivial that I can hardly bring myself to bother you with it. I'm afraid you'll just tell me not to be a fool and waste your valuable time."

"Even things that seem very trivial may have their importance. They can be a symptom of a deep-seated derangement. And my time is entirely at your disposal."

Dr. Audlin's voice was low and grave. The monotone in which he spoke was strangely soothing. Lord Mountdrago at length made up his mind to be frank.

"The fact is I've been having some very tiresome dreams lately. I know it's silly to pay any attention to them, but—well, the honest truth is that I'm afraid they've got on my nerves."

"Can you describe any of them to me?"

Lord Mountdrago smiled, but the smile that tried to be careless was only rueful.

"They're so idiotic, I can hardly bring myself to narrate them."

"Never mind."

"Well, the first I had was about a month ago. I dreamt that I was at a party at Connemara House. It was an official party. The King and Queen were to be there, and of course decorations were worn. I was wearing my ribbon and my star. I went into a sort of cloakroom they have to take off my coat. There was a little man there called Owen Griffiths, who's a Welsh member of Parliament, and to tell you the truth, I was surprised to see him. He's very common, and I said to myself: 'Really, Lydia Connemara is going too far, whom will she ask next?' I thought he looked at me rather curiously, but I didn't take any notice of him; in fact I cut the little bounder and walked upstairs. I suppose you've never been there?"

"Never."

"No, it's not the sort of house you'd ever be likely to go to. It's a rather vulgar house, but it's got a very fine marble staircase, and the Connemaras were at the top receiving their guests. Lady Connemara gave me a look of surprise when I shook hands with her, and began to giggle; I didn't pay much attention—

she's a very silly, ill-bred woman, and her manners
are no better than those of her ancestress whom King
Charles II made a duchess. I must say the reception
rooms at Connemara House are stately. I walked
through, nodding to a number of people and shaking
hands; then I saw the German Ambassador talking
with one of the Austrian archdukes. I particularly
wanted to have a word with him, so I went up and
held out my hand. The moment the Archduke saw
me he burst into a roar of laughter. I was deeply
affronted. I looked him up and down sternly, but he
only laughed the more. I was about to speak to him
rather sharply, when there was a sudden hush, and
I realized that the King and Queen had come. Turning my back on the Archduke, I stepped forward, and
then, quite suddenly, I noticed that I hadn't got any
trousers on. I was in short silk drawers, and I wore
scarlet sock suspenders. No wonder Lady Connemara
had giggled; no wonder the Archduke had laughed!
I can't tell you what that moment was. An agony of
shame. I awoke in a cold sweat. Oh, you don't know
the relief I felt to find it was only a dream."

"It's the kind of dream that's not so very un-
common," said Dr. Audlin.

"I daresay not. But an odd thing happened next
day. I was in the lobby of the House of Commons,
when that fellow Griffiths walked slowly past me.
He deliberately looked down at my legs, and then

he looked me full in the face, and I was almost certain
he winked. A ridiculous thought came to me. He'd
been there the night before and seen me make that
ghastly exhibition of myself and was enjoying the
joke. But of course I knew that was impossible because it was only a dream. I gave him an icy glare,
and he walked on. But he was grinning his head off."

Lord Mountdrago took his handkerchief out of his
pocket and wiped the palms of his hands. He was
making no attempt now to conceal his perturbation.
Dr. Audlin never took his eyes off him.

"Tell me another dream."

"It was the night after, and it was even more
absurd than the first one. I dreamt that I was in the
House. There was a debate on foreign affairs which
not only the country, but the world, had been looking
forward to with the gravest concern. The government
had decided on a change in their policy which vitally
affected the future of the Empire. The occasion was
historic. Of course the House was crowded. All the
ambassadors were there. The galleries were packed.
It fell to me to make the important speech of the
evening. I had prepared it carefully. A man like me
has enemies—there are a lot of people who resent my
having achieved the position I have at an age when
even the cleverest men are content with situations of
relative obscurity—and I was determined that my
speech should not only be worthy of the occasion,

but should silence my detractors. It excited me to
think that the whole world was hanging on my lips.
I rose to my feet. If you've ever been in the House
you'll know how members chat to one another during
a debate, rustle papers and turn over reports. The
silence was the silence of the grave when I began to
speak. Suddenly I caught sight of that odious little
bounder on one of the benches opposite, Griffiths,
the Welsh member; he put out his tongue at me.
I don't know if you've ever heard a vulgar music-hall
song called 'A Bicycle Made for Two.' It was very
popular a great many years ago. To show Griffiths
how completely I despised him I began to sing it. I
sang the first verse right through. There was a moment's surprise, and when I finished they cried 'Hear,
hear,' on the opposite benches. I put up my hand to
silence them and sang the second verse. The House
listened to me in stony silence and I felt the song
wasn't going down very well. I was vexed, for I have a
good baritone voice, and I was determined that they
should do me justice. When I started the third verse
the members began to laugh; in an instant the laughter spread; the ambassadors, the strangers in the
Distinguished Strangers' Gallery, the ladies in the
Ladies' Gallery, the reporters, they shook, they
bellowed, they held their sides, they rolled in their
seats; everyone was overcome with laughter except
the ministers on the Front Bench immediately behind

me. In that incredible, in that unprecedented, uproar they sat petrified. I gave them a glance, and suddenly the enormity of what I had done fell upon me. I had made myself the laughing-stock of the whole world. With misery I realized that I should have to resign. I woke and knew it was only a dream."

Lord Mountdrago's grand manner had deserted him as he narrated this, and now having finished he was pale and trembling. But with an effort he pulled himself together. He forced a laugh to his shaking lips.

"The whole thing was so fantastic that I couldn't help being amused. I didn't give it another thought, and when I went into the House on the following afternoon I was feeling in very good form. The debate was dull, but I had to be there, and I read some documents that required my attention. For some reason I chanced to look up, and I saw that Griffiths was speaking. He has an unpleasant Welsh accent and an unprepossessing appearance. I couldn't imagine that he had anything to say that it was worth my while to listen to, and I was about to return to my papers when he quoted two lines from 'A Bicycle Made for Two.' I couldn't help glancing at him, and I saw that his eyes were fixed on me with a grin of bitter mockery. I faintly shrugged my shoulders. It was comic that a scrubby little Welsh member should look at me like that. It was an odd coincidence that he should quote two lines from that disastrous song that I'd sung all through in my dream. I began to read my papers again, but I don't mind telling you that I found it difficult to concentrate on them. I was a little puzzled. Owen Griffiths had been in my first dream, the one at Connemara House, and I'd received a very definite impression afterwards that he knew the sorry figure I'd cut. Was it a mere coincidence that he had just quoted those two lines? I asked myself if it was possible that he was dreaming the same dreams as I was. But of course the idea was preposterous, and I determined not to give it a second thought."

There was a silence. Dr. Audlin looked at Lord Mountdrago and Lord Mountdrago looked at Dr. Audlin.

"Other people's dreams are very boring. My wife used to dream occasionally and insist on telling me her dreams next day with circumstantial detail. I found it maddening."

Dr. Audlin faintly smiled.

"You're not boring me."

"I'll tell you one more dream I had a few days later. I dreamt that I went into a public house at Limehouse. I've never been to Limehouse in my life and I don't think I've ever been in a public house since I was at Oxford, and yet I saw the street and the place I went into as exactly as if I were at home there. I went into a room—I don't know whether they call it the saloon bar or the private bar; there was a fireplace and a large leather armchair on one side of it, and on the other a small sofa; a bar ran the whole length of the room, and over it you could see into the public bar. Near the door was a round marble-topped table and two armchairs beside it. It was a Saturday night, and the place was packed. It was brightly lit, but the smoke was so thick that it made my eyes smart. I was dressed like a rough, with a cap on my head and a handkerchief round my neck. It seemed to me that most of the people there were drunk. I thought it rather amusing. There was a gramophone going, or the radio, I don't know which, and in front of the fireplace two women were doing a grotesque dance. There was a little crowd round them, laughing, cheering and singing. I went up to have a look, and some man said to me: ''Ave a drink, Bill.' There were glasses on the table full of a dark liquid which I understand is called brown ale. He gave me a glass, and not wishing to be conspicuous I drank it. One of the women who were dancing broke away from the other and took hold of the glass. ''Ere, what's the idea?' she said. 'That's my beer you're putting away.' 'Oh, I'm so sorry,' I said, 'this gentleman offered it me, and I very naturally thought it was his to offer.' 'All right, mate,' she said, 'I don't mind. You come an' 'ave a dance with me.' Before

I could protest she'd caught hold of me and we were
dancing together. And then I found myself sitting in
the armchair with the woman on my lap and we were
sharing a glass of beer. I should tell you that sex has
never played any great part in my life. I married
young because in my position it was desirable that
I should marry, but also in order to settle once for all
the question of sex. I had the two sons I had made up
my mind to have, and then I put the whole matter on
one side. I've always been too busy to give much
thought to that kind of thing, and living so much in
the public eye as I do, it would have been madness
to do anything that might give rise to scandal. The
greatest asset a politician can have is a blameless
record as far as women are concerned. I have no
patience with the men who smash up their careers for
women. I only despise them. The woman I had on my
knees was drunk; she wasn't pretty and she wasn't
young: in fact, she was just a blowsy old prostitute.
She filled me with disgust, and yet when she put her
mouth to mine and kissed me, though her breath
stank of beer and her teeth were decayed, though I
loathed myself, I wanted her—I wanted her with all
my soul. Suddenly I heard a voice: 'That's right, old
boy, have a good time.' I looked up, and there was
Owen Griffiths. I tried to spring out of the chair, but
that horrible woman wouldn't let me. 'Don't you
pay no attention to 'im,' she said, ''e's only one of

them nosy parkers.' 'You go to it,' he said. 'I know Moll. She'll give you your money's worth all right.' You know, I wasn't so much annoyed at his seeing me in that absurd situation as angry that he should address me as old boy. I pushed the woman aside and stood up and faced him. 'I don't know you, and I don't want to know you,' I said. 'I know you all right,' he said. 'And my advice to you, Molly, is, see that you get your money, he'll bilk you if he can.' There was a bottle of beer standing on the table close by. Without a word I seized it by the neck and hit him over the head with it as hard as I could. I made such a violent gesture that it woke me up."

"A dream of that sort is not incomprehensible," said Dr. Audlin. "It is the revenge nature takes on persons of unimpeachable character."

"The story's idiotic. I haven't told it you for its own sake. I've told it you for what happened next day. I wanted to look up something in a hurry, and I went into the library of the House. I got the book and began reading. I hadn't noticed when I sat down that Griffiths was sitting in a chair close by me. Another of the Labour Members came in and went up to him. 'Hullo, Owen,' he said to him, 'you're looking pretty dicky today.' 'I've got an awful headache,' he answered, 'I feel as if I'd been cracked over the head with a bottle.'"

Now Lord Mountdrago's face was grey with anguish.

"I knew then that the idea I'd had and dismissed as preposterous was true. I knew that Griffiths was dreaming my dreams and that he remembered them as well as I did."

"It may also have been a coincidence."

"When he spoke he didn't speak to his friend, he deliberately spoke to me. He looked at me with sullen resentment."

"Can you offer any suggestion why this same man should come into your dreams?"

"None."

Dr. Audlin's eyes had not left his patient's face and he saw that he lied. He had a pencil in his hand, and he drew a straggling line or two on his blotting paper. It often took a long time to get people to tell the truth, and yet they knew that unless they told it he could do nothing for them.

"The dream you've just described to me took place just over three weeks ago. Have you had any since?"

"Every night."

"And does this man Griffiths come into them all?"

"Yes."

The doctor drew more lines on his blotting paper. He wanted the silence, the drabness, the dull light of that little room to have its effect on Lord Mountdrago's sensibility. Lord Mountdrago threw himself back in his chair and turned his head away so that he should not see the other's grave eyes.

"Dr. Audlin, you must do something for me. I'm at the end of my tether. I shall go mad if this goes on. I'm afraid to go to sleep. Two or three nights I haven't. I've sat up reading and when I felt drowsy put on my coat and walked till I was exhausted. But I must have sleep. With all the work I have to do I must be at concert pitch; I must be in complete control of all my faculties. I need rest; sleep brings me none. I no sooner fall asleep than my dreams begin, and he's always there, that vulgar little cad, grinning at me, mocking me, despising me. It's a monstrous persecution. I tell you, Doctor, I'm not the man of my dreams; it's not fair to judge me by them. Ask anyone you like. I'm an honest, upright, decent man. No one can say anything against my moral character either private or public. My whole ambition is to serve my country and maintain its greatness. I have money, I have rank, I'm not exposed to many of the temptations of lesser men, so that it's no credit to me to be incorruptible; but this I can claim, that no honour, no personal advantage, no thought of self would induce me to swerve by a hairsbreadth from my duty. I've sacrificed everything to become the man I am. Greatness is my aim. Greatness is within my reach, and I'm losing my nerve. I'm not that mean, despicable, cowardly, lewd creature that horrible little man sees. I've told you three of my dreams; they're nothing; that man has seen me do things that are so beastly, so horrible, so shameful, that even if my life depended on it I wouldn't tell them. And he remembers them. I can hardly meet the derision and disgust I see in his eyes, and I even hesitate to speak because I know my words can seem to him nothing but utter humbug. He's seen me do things that no man with any self-respect would do, things for which men are driven out of the society of their fellows and sentenced to long terms of imprisonment; he's heard the foulness of my speech; he's seen me not only ridiculous, but revolting. He despises me and he no longer pretends to conceal it. I tell you that if you can't do something to help me I shall either kill myself or kill him."

"I wouldn't kill him if I were you," said Dr. Audlin coolly, in that soothing voice of his. "In this country the consequences of killing a fellow creature are awkward."

"I shouldn't be hanged for it, if that's what you mean. Who would know that I'd killed him? That dream of mine has shown me how. I told you, the day after I'd hit him over the head with a beer bottle he had such a headache that he couldn't see straight. He said so himself. That shows that he can feel with his waking body what happens to his body asleep. It's not with a bottle I shall hit him next time. One night, when I'm dreaming, I shall find myself with a knife in my hand or a revolver in my pocket—I must because I want to so intensely—and then I shall seize my opportunity. I'll stick him like a pig; I'll shoot him like a dog. In the heart. And then I shall be free of this fiendish persecution."

Some people might have thought that Lord Mountdrago was mad; after all the years during which Dr. Audlin had been treating the diseased souls of men he knew how thin a line divides those whom we call sane from those whom we call insane. He knew how often in men who to all appearance were healthy and normal, who were seemingly devoid of imagination, and who fulfilled the duties of common life with credit to themselves and with benefit to their fellows, when you gained their confidence, when you tore away the mask they wore to the world, you found not only hideous abnormality, but kinks so strange, mental extravagances so fantastic, that in that respect you could only call them lunatic. If you put them in an asylum, not all the asylums in the world would be large enough. Anyhow, a man was not certifiable because he had strange dreams and they had shattered his nerve. The case was singular, but it was only an exaggeration of others that had come under Dr. Audlin's observation; he was doubtful, however, whether the methods of treatment that he had so often found efficacious would here avail.

"Have you consulted any other member of my profession?" he asked.

"Only Sir Augustus. I merely told him that I suffered from nightmares. He said I was overworked and recommended me to go for a cruise. That's absurd. I can't leave the Foreign Office just now when the international situation needs constant attention. I'm indispensable, and I know it. On my conduct at the present juncture my whole future depends. He gave me sedatives. They had no effect. He gave me tonics. They were worse than useless. He's an old fool."

"Can you give any reason why it should be this particular man who persists in coming into your dreams?"

"You asked me that question before. I answered it."

That was true. But Dr. Audlin had not been satisfied with the answer.

"Just now you talked of persecution. Why should Owen Griffiths want to persecute you?"

"I don't know."

Lord Mountdrago's eyes shifted a little. Dr. Audlin was sure that he was not speaking the truth.

"Have you ever done him an injury?"

"Never."

Lord Mountdrago made no movement, but Dr. Audlin had a queer feeling that he shrank into his skin. He saw before him a large, proud man who gave the impression that the questions put to him were an insolence, and yet for all that, behind that façade, was something shifting and startled that made you think of a frightened animal in a trap. Dr. Audlin leaned forward and by the power of his eyes forced Lord Mountdrago to meet them.

"Are you quite sure?"

"Quite sure. You don't seem to understand that our ways lead along different paths. I don't wish to harp on it, but I must remind you that I am a Minister of the Crown and Griffiths is an obscure member of the Labour Party. Naturally there's no social connection between us; he's a man of very humble origin, he's not the sort of person I should be likely to meet at any of the houses I go to; and politically our respective stations are so far separated that we could not possibly have anything in common."

"I can do nothing for you unless you tell me the complete truth."

Lord Mountdrago raised his eyebrows. His voice was rasping.

"I'm not accustomed to having my word doubted, Dr. Audlin. If you're going to do that, I think to take up any more of your time can only be a waste of mine. If you will kindly let my secretary know what your fee is, he will see that a cheque is sent to you."

For all the expression that was to be seen on Dr. Audlin's face you might have thought that he simply had not heard what Lord Mountdrago said. He continued to look steadily into his eyes, and his voice was grave and low.

"Have you done anything to this man that *he* might look upon as an injury?"

Lord Mountdrago hesitated. He looked away, and then, as though there were in Dr. Audlin's eyes a compelling force that he could not resist, looked back. He answered sulkily:

"Only if he was a dirty, second-rate little cad."

"But that is exactly what you've described him to be."

Lord Mountdrago sighed. He was beaten. Dr. Audlin knew that the sigh meant he was going at last to say what he had till then held back. Now he had no longer to insist. He dropped his eyes and began again drawing vague geometrical figures on his blotting paper. The silence lasted two or three minutes.

"I'm anxious to tell you everything that can be of any use to you. If I didn't mention this before, it's only because it was so unimportant that I didn't see how it could possibly have anything to do with the case. Griffiths won a seat at the last election, and he began to make a nuisance of himself almost at once. His father's a miner, and he worked in a mine himself when he was a boy; he's been a schoolmaster in the board schools and a journalist. He's that half-baked, conceited intellectual, with inadequate knowledge, ill-considered ideas and impractical plans, that compulsory education has brought forth from the working classes. He's a scrawny, grey-faced man who looks half starved, and he's always very slovenly in appearance; heaven knows members nowadays don't bother much about their dress, but his clothes are an outrage to the dignity of the House. They're ostentatiously shabby, his collar's never clean, and his tie's never tied properly; he looks as if he hadn't had a bath for a month, and his hands are filthy. The Labour Party have two or three fellows on the Front Bench who've got a certain ability, but the rest of them don't amount to much. In the kingdom of the blind the one-eyed man is king: because Griffiths is glib and has a lot of superficial information on a number of subjects, the Whips on his side began to put him up to speak whenever there was a chance. It appeared that he fancied himself on foreign affairs, and he was continually asking me silly, tiresome questions. I don't mind telling you that I made a point of snubbing him as soundly as I thought he deserved. From the beginning I hated the way he talked, his whining voice and his vulgar accent; he had nervous mannerisms that intensely irritated me. He talked rather shyly, hesitatingly, as though it were torture to him to speak and yet he was forced to by some inner passion, and often he used to say some very disconcerting things. I'll admit that now and again he had a sort of tub-thumping eloquence.

It had a certain influence over the ill-regulated minds of the members of his party. They were impressed by his earnestness, and they weren't, as I was, nauseated by his sentimentality. A certain sentimentality is the common coin of political debate. Nations are governed by self-interest, but they prefer to believe that their aims are altruistic, and the politician is justified if with fair words and fine phrases he can persuade the electorate that the hard bargain he is driving for his country's advantage tends to the good of humanity. The mistake people like Griffiths make is to take these fair words and fine phrases at their face value. He's a crank, and a noxious crank. He calls himself an idealist. He has at his tongue's end all the tedious blather that the intelligentsia have been boring us with for years. Nonresistance. The brotherhood of man. You know the hopeless rubbish. The worst of it was that it impressed not only his own party, it even shook some of the sillier, more sloppy-minded members of ours. I heard rumours that Griffiths was likely to get office when a Labour Government came in; I even heard it suggested that he might get the Foreign Office. The notion was grotesque but not impossible. One day I had occasion to wind up a debate on foreign affairs which Griffiths had opened. He'd spoken for an hour. I thought it a very good opportunity to cook his goose, and by God, sir, I cooked it. I tore his speech to pieces. I pointed

out the faultiness of his reasoning and emphasized the
deficiency of his knowledge. In the House of Commons the most devastating weapon is ridicule: I
mocked him; I bantered him; I was in good form that
day and the House rocked with laughter. Their laughter excited me, and I excelled myself. The Opposition
sat glum and silent, but even some of them couldn't
help laughing once or twice; it's not intolerable, you
know, to see a colleague, perhaps a rival, made a fool
of. And if ever a man was made a fool of, I made a
fool of Griffiths. He shrank down in his seat; I saw
his face go white, and presently he buried it in his
hands. When I sat down I'd killed him. I'd destroyed
his prestige for ever; he had no more chance of getting
office when a Labour Government came in than the
policeman at the door. I heard afterwards that his
father, the old miner, and his mother had come up
from Wales, with various supporters of his in the
constituency, to watch the triumph they expected
him to have. They had seen only his utter humiliation.
He'd won the constituency by the narrowest margin.
An incident like that might very easily lose him his
seat. But that was no business of mine."

"Should I be putting it too strongly if I said you
had ruined his career?" asked Dr. Audlin.

"I don't suppose you would."

"That is a very serious injury you've done him."

"He brought it on himself."

"Have you never felt any qualms about it?"

"I think perhaps if I'd known that his father and mother were there I might have let him down a little more gently."

There was nothing further for Dr. Audlin to say, and he set about treating his patient in such a manner as he thought might avail. He sought by suggestion to make him forget his dreams when he awoke; he sought to make him sleep so deeply that he would not dream. He found Lord Mountdrago's resistance impossible to break down. At the end of an hour he dismissed him.

Since then he had seen Lord Mountdrago half a dozen times. He had done him no good. The frightful dreams continued every night to harass the unfortunate man, and it was clear that his general condition was growing rapidly worse. He was worn out. His irritability was uncontrollable. Lord Mountdrago was angry because he received no benefit from his treatment, and yet continued it, not only because it seemed his only hope, but because it was a relief to him to have someone with whom he could talk openly. Dr. Audlin came to the conclusion at last that there was only one way in which Lord Mountdrago could achieve deliverance, but he knew him well enough to be assured that of his own free will he would never, never take it. If Lord Mountdrago was to be saved from the breakdown that was threatening, he must be induced to take a step that must be abhorrent to his pride of birth and his self-complacency. Dr. Audlin was convinced that to delay was impossible. He was treating his patient by suggestion, and after several visits found him more susceptible to it. At length he managed to get him into a condition of somnolence. With his low, soft, monotonous voice he soothed his tortured nerves. He repeated the same words over and over again. Lord Mountdrago lay quite still, his eyes closed; his breathing was regular, and his limbs were relaxed. Then Dr. Audlin in the same quiet tone spoke the words he had prepared.

"You will go to Owen Griffiths and say that you are sorry that you caused him that great injury. You will say that you will do whatever lies in your power to undo the harm that you have done him."

The words acted on Lord Mountdrago like the blow of a whip across his face. He shook himself out of his hypnotic state and sprang to his feet. His eyes blazed with passion, and he poured forth upon Dr. Audlin a stream of angry vituperation such as even he had never heard. He swore at him. He cursed him. He used language of such obscenity that Dr. Audlin, who had heard every sort of foul word, sometimes from the lips of chaste and distinguished women, was surprised that he knew it.

"Apologize to that filthy little Welshman? I'd rather kill myself."

"I believe it to be the only way in which you can regain your balance."

Dr. Audlin had not often seen a man presumably sane in such a condition of uncontrollable fury. Lord Mountdrago grew red in the face, and his eyes bulged out of his head. He did really foam at the mouth. Dr. Audlin watched him coolly, waiting for the storm to wear itself out, and presently he saw that Lord Mountdrago, weakened by the strain to which he had been subjected for so many weeks, was exhausted.

"Sit down," he said then, sharply.

Lord Mountdrago crumpled up into a chair.

"Christ, I feel all in. I must rest a minute and then I'll go."

For five minutes perhaps they sat in complete silence. Lord Mountdrago was a gross, blustering bully, but he was also a gentleman. When he broke the silence he had recovered his self-control.

"I'm afraid I've been very rude to you. I'm ashamed of the things I've said to you, and I can only say you'd be justified if you refused to have anything more to do with me. I hope you won't do that. I feel that my visits to you do help me. I think you're my only chance."

"You mustn't give another thought to what you said. It was of no consequence."

"But there's one thing you mustn't ask me to do, and that is to make excuses to Griffiths."

"I've thought a great deal about your case. I don't pretend to understand it, but I believe that your only chance of release is to do what I proposed. I have a notion that we're none of us one self, but many, and one of the selves in you has risen up against the injury you did Griffiths and has taken on the form of Griffiths in your mind and is punishing you for what you cruelly did. If I were a priest I should tell you that it is your conscience that has adopted the shape and lineaments of this man to scourge you to repentance and persuade you to reparation."

"My conscience is clear. It's not my fault if I smashed the man's career. I crushed him like a slug in my garden. I regret nothing."

It was on these words that Lord Mountdrago had left him. Reading through his notes, while he waited, Dr. Audlin considered how best he could bring his patient to the state of mind that, now that his usual methods of treatment had failed, he thought alone could help him. He glanced at his clock. It was six. It was strange that Lord Mountdrago did not come. He knew he had intended to because a secretary had rung up that morning to say that he would be with him at the usual hour. He must have been detained by pressing work. This notion gave Dr. Audlin something else to think of: Lord Mountdrago was quite unfit to work and in no condition to deal with important matters of state. Dr. Audlin wondered whether it behooved him to get in touch with someone in authority, the Prime Minister or the Permanent Under Secretary for Foreign Affairs, and impart to him his conviction that Lord Mountdrago's mind was so unbalanced that it was dangerous to leave affairs of moment in his hands. It was a ticklish thing to do. He might cause needless trouble and get roundly snubbed for his pains. He shrugged his shoulders.

"After all," he reflected, "the politicians have made such a mess of the world during the last five-and-twenty years, I don't suppose it makes much odds if they're mad or sane."

He rang the bell.

"If Lord Mountdrago comes now, will you tell him that I have another appointment at six-fifteen and so I'm afraid I can't see him."

"Very good, sir."

"Has the evening paper come yet?"

"I'll go and see."

In a moment the servant brought it in. A huge headline ran across the front page: Tragic Death of Foreign Minister.

"My God!" cried Dr. Audlin.

For once he was wrenched out of his wonted calm. He was shocked, horribly shocked, and yet he was not altogether surprised. The possibility that Lord Mountdrago might commit suicide had occurred to him several times, for that it was suicide he could not doubt. The paper said that Lord Mountdrago had been waiting in a tube station, standing on the edge of the platform, and as the train came in was seen to fall on the rail. It was supposed that he had had a sudden attack of faintness. The paper went on to say that Lord Mountdrago had been suffering for some weeks from the effects of overwork, but had felt it impossible to absent himself while the foreign situation demanded his unremitting attention. Lord Mountdrago was another victim of the strain that modern politics placed upon those who played the more important parts in it. There was a neat little piece about the talents and industry, the patriotism and vision, of the deceased statesman, followed by various surmises upon the Prime Minister's choice of his successor. Dr. Audlin read all this. He had not liked Lord Mountdrago. The chief emotion that his death caused in him was dissatisfaction with himself because he had been able to do nothing for him.

Perhaps he had done wrong in not getting into touch with Lord Mountdrago's doctor. He was discouraged, as always when failure frustrated his conscientious efforts, and repulsion seized him for the theory and practice of this empiric doctrine by which he earned his living. He was dealing with dark and mysterious forces that it was perhaps beyond the powers of the human mind to understand. He was like a man blindfold trying to feel his way to he knew not whither. Listlessly he turned the pages of the paper. Suddenly he gave a great start, and an exclamation once more was forced from his lips. His eyes had fallen on a small paragraph near the bottom of a column. Sudden Death of an M.P., he read. Mr. Owen Griffiths, member for so-and-so, had been taken ill in Fleet Street that afternoon and when he was brought to Charing Cross Hospital life was found to be extinct. It was supposed that death was due to natural causes, but an inquest would be held. Dr. Audlin could hardly believe his eyes. Was it possible that the night before Lord Mountdrago had at last in his dream found himself possessed of the weapon, knife or gun, that he had wanted, and had killed his tormentor, and had that ghostly murder, in the same way as the blow with the bottle had given him a racking headache on the following day, taken effect a certain number of hours later on the waking man? Or was it, more mysterious and more frightful, that when Lord Mountdrago sought relief in death, the enemy he had so cruelly wronged, unappeased, escaping from his own mortality, had pursued him to some other sphere, there to torment him still? It was strange. The sensible thing was to look upon it merely as an odd coincidence. Dr. Audlin rang the bell.

"Tell Mrs. Milton that I'm sorry I can't see her this evening, I'm not well."

It was true; he shivered as though of an ague. With some kind of spiritual sense he seemed to envisage a bleak, a horrible void. The dark night of the soul engulfed him, and he felt a strange, primeval terror of he knew not what.

Gigolo and Gigolette

THE BAR WAS CROWDED. Sandy Westcott had had a couple of cocktails, and he was beginning to feel hungry. He looked at his watch. He had been asked to dinner at half past nine, and it was nearly ten. Eva Barrett was always late, and he would be lucky if he got anything to eat by ten-thirty. He turned to the barman to order another cocktail and caught sight of a man who at that moment came up to the bar.

"Hullo, Cotman," he said. "Have a drink."

"I don't mind if I do, sir."

Cotman was a nice-looking fellow, of thirty perhaps, short, but with so good a figure that he did not look it, very smartly dressed in a double-breasted dinner jacket, a little too much waisted, and a butterfly tie a good deal too large. He had a thick mat of black, wavy hair, very sleek and shiny, brushed straight back from his forehead, and large flashing eyes. He spoke with great refinement, but with a Cockney accent.

"How's Stella?" asked Sandy.

"Oh, she's all right. Likes to have a lay-down before the show, you know. Steadies the old nerves, she says."

"I wouldn't do that stunt of hers for a thousand pounds."

"I don't suppose you would. No one can do it but her, not from that height, I mean, and only five foot of water."

"It's the most sick-making thing I've ever seen."

Cotman gave a little laugh. He took this as a compliment. Stella was his wife. Of course she did the trick and took the risk, but it was he who had thought of the flames, and it was the flames that had taken the public fancy and made the turn the huge success it was. Stella dived into a tank from the top of a ladder sixty feet high, and, as he said, there were only five feet of water in the tank. Just before she dived they poured enough petrol on to cover the surface and he set it alight; the flames soared up and she dived straight into them.

"Paco Espinel tells me it's the biggest draw the Casino has ever had," said Sandy.

"I know, he told me they'd served as many dinners in July as they generally do in August. 'And that's you,' he says to me."

"Well, I hope you're making a packet."

"Well, I can't exactly say that. You see, we've got our contract, and naturally we didn't know it was going to be a riot, but Mr. Espinel's talking of booking us for next month, and I don't mind telling you he's not going to get us on the same terms or anything like it. Why, I had a letter from an agent only this morning saying they wanted us to go to Deauville."

"Here are my people," said Sandy.

He nodded to Cotman and left him. Eva Barrett sailed in with the rest of her guests. She had gathered them together downstairs. It was a party of eight.

"I knew we should find you here, Sandy," she said. "I'm not late, am I?"

"Only half an hour."

"Ask them what cocktails they want, and then we'll dine."

While they were standing at the bar, emptying now, for nearly everyone had gone down to the terrace for dinner, Paco Espinel passed through and stopped to shake hands with Eva Barrett. Paco Espinel was a young man who had run through his money and now made his living by arranging the turns with which the Casino sought to attract visitors. It was his duty to be civil to the rich and great. Mrs. Chaloner Barrett was an American widow of vast wealth; she not only entertained expensively, but also gambled. And after all, the dinners and suppers and the two cabaret shows that accompanied them were provided only to induce people to lose their money at the tables.

"Got a good table for me, Paco?" said Eva Barrett.

"The best." His eyes, fine, dark Argentine eyes, expressed his admiration of Mrs. Barrett's opulent, ageing charms. This also was business. "You've seen Stella?"

"Of course. Three times. It's the most terrifying thing I've ever seen."

"Sandy comes every night."

"I want to be in at the death. She's bound to kill herself one of these nights, and I don't want to miss that if I can help it."

Paco laughed.

"She's been such a success, we're going to keep her on another month. All I ask is that she shouldn't kill herself till the end of August. After that she can do as she likes."

"Oh, God, have I got to go on eating trout and roast chicken every night till the end of August?" cried Sandy.

"You brute, Sandy," said Eva Barrett. "Come on, let's go in to dinner. I'm starving."

Paco Espinel asked the barman if he'd seen Cotman. The barman said he'd had a drink with Mr. Westcott.

"Oh, well, if he comes in here again, tell him I want a word with him."

Mrs. Barrett paused at the top of the steps that led down to the terrace long enough for the press representative, a little haggard woman with an untidy head, to come up with her notebook. Sandy whispered the names of the guests. It was a representative Riviera party. There was an English lord and his lady, long and lean both of them, who were prepared to dine with anyone who would give them a free meal. They were certain to be as tight as drums before midnight. There was a gaunt Scotch woman, with a face like a Peruvian mask that has been battered by the storms of ten centuries, and her English husband. Though a broker by profession, he was bluff, military and hearty. He gave you an impression of such integrity that you were almost more sorry for him than for yourself when the good thing he had put you onto as a special favour turned out to be a dud. There was an Italian countess who was neither Italian nor a countess, but played a beautiful game of bridge, and there was a Russian prince who was ready to make Mrs. Barrett a princess and in the meantime sold champagne, motor cars and Old Masters on commission. A dance was in progress, and Mrs. Barrett, waiting for it to end, surveyed, with a look which her short upper lip made scornful, the serried throng on the dance floor. It was a gala night, and the dining tables were crowded together. Beyond the terrace the sea was calm and silent. The music stopped, and the head waiter, affably smiling, came up to guide her to her table. She swept down the steps with majestic gait.

"We shall have quite a good view of the dive," she said as she sat down.

"I like to be next door to the tank," said Sandy, "so that I can see her face."

"Is she pretty?" asked the Countess.

"It's not that. It's the expression of her eyes. She's scared to death every time she does it."

"Oh, I don't believe that," said the City gentleman, Colonel Goodhart by name, though no one had ever discovered how he came by the title. "I mean, the whole bally stunt's only a trick. There's no danger really, I mean."

"You don't know what you're talking about. Diving from that height in as little water as that, she's got to turn like a flash the moment she touches the water. And if she doesn't do it right she's bound to bash her head against the bottom and break her back."

"That's just what I'm telling you, old boy," said the Colonel, "it's a trick. I mean, there's no argument."

"If there's no danger there's nothing to it, anyway," said Eva Barrett. "It's over in a minute. Unless she's risking her life it's the biggest fraud of modern times. Don't say we've come to see this over and over again and it's only a fake."

"Pretty well everything is. You can take my word for that."

"Well, you ought to know," said Sandy.

If it occurred to the Colonel that this might be a nasty dig, he admirably concealed it. He laughed.

"I don't mind saying I know a thing or two," he admitted. "I mean, I've got my eyes peeled all right. You can't put much over on me."

The tank was on the far left of the terrace, and behind it, supported by stays, was an immensely tall ladder at the top of which was a tiny platform. After two or three dances more, when Eva Barrett's party were eating asparagus, the music stopped and the lights were lowered. A spot was turned on the tank. Cotman was visible in the brilliance. He ascended half a dozen steps so that he was on a level with the top of the tank.

"Ladies and gentlemen," he cried out, in a loud clear voice, "you are now going to see the most marvellous feat of the century. Madam Stella, the greatest diver in the world, is about to dive from a height of sixty feet into a lake of flames five foot deep. This is a feat that has never been performed before, and Madam Stella is prepared to give one hundred pounds to anyone who will attempt it. Ladies and gentlemen, I have the honour to present Madam Stella."

A little figure appeared at the top of the steps that

led onto the terrace, ran quickly up to the tank, and bowed to the applauding audience. She wore a man's silk dressing gown and on her head a bathing cap. Her thin face was made up as if for the stage. The Italian countess looked at her through her *face-à-main*.

"Not pretty," she said.

"Good figure," said Eva Barrett. "You'll see."

Stella slipped out of her dressing gown and gave it to Cotman. He went down the steps. She stood for a moment and looked at the crowd. They were in darkness and she could only see vague white faces and white shirt fronts. She was small, beautifully made, with legs long for her body and slim hips. Her bathing costume was very scanty.

"You're quite right about the figure, Eva," said the Colonel. "Bit undeveloped, of course, but I know you girls think that's quite the thing."

Stella began to climb the ladder, and the spotlight followed her. It seemed an incredible height. An attendant poured petrol on the surface of the water. Cotman was handed a flaming torch. He watched Stella reach the top of the ladder and settle herself on the platform.

"Ready?" he cried.

"Yes."

"Go," he shouted.

And as he shouted he seemed to plunge the burning torch into the water. The flames sprang up, leaping

high, and really terrifying to look at. At the same
moment Stella dived. She came down like a streak
of lightning and plunged through the flames, which
subsided a moment after she had reached the water.
A second later she was at the surface and jumped out
to a roar, a storm of applause. Cotman wrapped the
dressing gown round her. She bowed and bowed. The
applause went on. Music struck up. With a final wave
of the hand she ran down the steps and between the
tables to the door. The lights went up, and the waiters hurried along with their neglected service.

Sandy Westcott gave a sigh. He did not know
whether he was disappointed or relieved.

"Top-hole," said the English peer.

"It's a bally fake," said the Colonel, with his
British pertinacity. "I bet you anything you like."

"It's over so quickly," said her English ladyship.
"I mean, you don't get your money's worth really."

Anyhow, it wasn't her money. That it never was.
The Italian countess leaned forward. She spoke fluent
English, but with a strong accent.

"Eva, my darling, who are those extraordinary
people at the table near the door under the balcony?"

"Packet of fun, aren't they?" said Sandy. "I
simply haven't been able to take my eyes off them."

Eva Barrett glanced at the table the Countess indicated, and the Prince, who sat with his back to it,
turned round to look.

"They can't be true," cried Eva. "I must ask Angelo who they are."

Mrs. Barrett was the sort of woman who knew the head waiters of all the principal restaurants in Europe by their first names. She told the waiter who was at that moment filling her glass to send Angelo to her.

It was certainly an odd pair. They were sitting by themselves at a small table. They were very old. The man was big and stout, with a mass of white hair, great bushy white eyebrows and an enormous white moustache. He looked like the late King Humbert of Italy, but much more like a king. He sat bolt upright. He wore full evening dress, with a white tie and a collar that has been out of fashion for hard on thirty years. His companion was a little old lady in a black satin ball dress, cut very low and tight at the waist. Round her neck were several chains of coloured beads. She wore what was obviously a wig, and a very ill-fitting one at that; it was very elaborate, all curls and sausages, and raven black. She was outrageously made up, bright blue under the eyes and on the eyelids, the eyebrows heavily black, a great patch of very pink rouge on each cheek and the lips a livid scarlet. The skin hung loosely on her face in deep wrinkles. She had large bold eyes, and they darted eagerly from table to table. She was taking everything in, and every other minute called the old man's attention to someone or other. The appearance of the couple was so fantastic in that fashionable crowd, the men in dinner jackets, the women in thin, pale-coloured frocks, that many eyes were turned on them. The staring did not seem to incommode the old lady. When she felt certain persons were looking at her she raised her eyebrows archly, smiled and rolled her eyes. She seemed on the point of acknowledging applause.

Angelo hurried up to the good customer that Eva Barrett was.

"You wished to see me, my lady?"

"Oh, Angelo, we're simply dying to know who those absolutely marvellous people are at the table next to the door."

Angelo gave a look and then assumed a deprecating air. The expression of his face, the movement of his shoulders, the turn of his spine, the gesture of his hands, probably even the twiddle of his toes, all indicated a half-humorous apology.

"You must overlook them, my lady." He knew of course that Mrs. Barrett had no right to be thus addressed, just as he knew that the Italian countess was neither Italian nor a countess and that the English lord never paid for a drink if anyone else would pay for it, but he also knew that to be thus addressed did not displease her. "They begged me to give them a table because they wanted to see Madame Stella do her dive. They were in the profession themselves once. I know they're not the sort of people one expects to see dining here, but they made such a point of it I simply hadn't the heart to refuse."

"But I think they're a perfect scream. I adore them."

"I've known them for many years. The man indeed is a compatriot of mine." The head waiter gave a condescending little laugh. "I told them I'd give them a table on the condition that they didn't dance. I wasn't taking any risks, my lady."

"Oh, but I should have loved to see them dance."

"One has to draw the line somewhere, my lady," said Angelo gravely.

He smiled, bowed again and withdrew.

"Look," cried Sandy, "they're going."

The funny old couple were paying their bill. The old man got up and put round his wife's neck a large white, but not too clean, feather boa. She rose. He gave her his arm, holding himself very erect, and she, small in comparison, tripped out beside him. Her black satin dress had a long train, and Eva Barrett (who was well over fifty) screamed with joy.

"Look, I remember my mother wearing a dress like that when I was in the schoolroom."

The comic pair walked, still arm in arm, through the spacious rooms of the Casino till they came to the door. The old man addressed a commissionaire.

"Be so good as to direct me to the artistes' dressing

rooms. We wish to pay our respects to Madame Stella."

The commissionaire gave them a look and summed them up. They were not people with whom it was necessary to be very polite.

"You won't find her there."

"She has not gone? I thought she gave a second performance at two."

"That's true. They might be in the bar."

"It won't 'urt us just to go an' 'ave a look, Carlo," said the old lady.

"Right-o, my love," he answered with a great roll of the R.

They walked slowly up the great stairs and entered the bar. It was empty but for the deputy barman and a couple sitting in two armchairs in the corner. The old lady released her husband's arm and tripped up with outstretched hands.

"'Ow are you, dear? I felt I just 'ad to come and congratulate you, bein' English same as you are. And in the profession meself. It's a grand turn, my dear, it deserves to be a success." She turned to Cotman. "And is this your 'usband?"

Stella got out of her armchair and a shy smile broke on her lips as she listened with some confusion to the voluble old lady.

"Yes, that's Syd."

"Pleased to meet you," he said.

"And this is mine," said the old lady, with a little

dig of the elbow in the direction of the tall, white-haired man. "Mr. Penezzi. 'E's a count really, and I'm the Countess Penezzi by rights, but when we retired from the profession we dropped the title."

"Will you have a drink?" said Cotman.

"No, you 'ave one with us," said Mrs. Penezzi, sinking into an armchair. "Carlo, you order."

The barman came, and after some discussion three bottles of beer were ordered. Stella would not have anything.

"She never has anything till after the second show," explained Cotman.

Stella was slight and small, about twenty-six, with light brown hair, cut short and waved, and grey eyes. She had reddened her lips, but wore little rouge on her face. Her skin was pale. She was not very pretty, but she had a neat little face. She wore a very simple evening frock of white silk. The beer was brought, and Mr. Penezzi, evidently not very talkative, took a long swig.

"What was your line?" asked Syd Cotman politely.

Mrs. Penezzi gave him a rolling glance of her flashing, made-up eyes and turned to her husband.

"Tell 'em who I am, Carlo," she said.

"The 'uman cannon ball," he announced.

Mrs. Penezzi smiled brightly and with a quick, birdlike glance looked from one to the other. They stared at her in dismay.

"Flora," she said. "The 'uman cannon ball."

She so obviously expected them to be impressed that they did not quite know what to do. Stella gave her Syd a puzzled look. He came to the rescue.

"It must have been before our time."

"Naturally it was before your time. Why, we retired from the profession definitely the year poor Queen Victoria died. It made quite a sensation when we did, too. But you've 'eard of me, of course." She saw the blank look on their faces; her tone changed a little. "But I was the biggest draw in London. At the Old Aquarium, that was. All the swells came to see me. The Prince of Wales and I don't know who all. I was the talk of the town. Isn't that true, Carlo?"

"She crowded the Aquarium for a year."

"It was the most spectacular turn they'd ever 'ad there. Why, only a few years ago I went up and introduced meself to Lady de Bathe. Lily Langtry, you know. She used to live down 'ere. She remembered me perfectly. She told me she'd seen me ten times."

"What did you do?" asked Stella.

"I was fired out of a cannon. Believe me, it was a sensation. And after London I went all over the world with it. Yes, my dear, I'm an old woman now and I won't deny it. Seventy-eight Mr. Penezzi is, and I shall never see seventy again, but I've 'ad me portrait on every 'oardin' in London. Lady de Bathe said to me: 'My dear, you was as celebrated as I was.' But you know what the public is, give 'em a good thing and they go mad over it, only they want change; 'owever good it is, they get sick of it, and then they won't go and see it any more. It'll 'appen to you, my dear, same as it 'appened to me. It comes to all of us. But Mr. Penezzi always 'ad 'is 'ead screwed on 'is shoulders the right way. Been in the business since 'e was so 'igh. Circus, you know. Ringmaster. That's 'ow I first knew 'im. I was in a troupe of acrobacks. Trapeze act, you know. 'E's a fine-lookin' man now, but you should 'ave seen 'im then, in 'is Russian boots, and ridin' breeches, and a tight-fittin' coat with frogs all down the front of it, crackin' 'is long whip as 'is 'orses galloped round the ring, the 'and-somest man I ever see in my life."

Mr. Penezzi did not make any remark, but thought-fully twisted his immense white moustache.

"Well, as I was tellin' you, 'e was never one to throw money about and when the agents couldn't get us bookin's any more 'e said, 'Let's retire.' And 'e was quite right, after 'avin' been the biggest star in London, we couldn't go back to circus work any more, I mean, Mr. Penezzi bein' a count really, 'e 'ad 'is dignity to think of, so we come down 'ere and we bought a 'ouse and started a pension. It always 'ad been Mr. Penezzi's ambition to do something like that. Thirty-five years we been 'ere now. We 'aven't done so badly, not until the last two or three years,

and the slump came, though visitors are very different from what they was when we first started, the
things they want, electric light and runnin' water in
their bedrooms and I don't know what all. Give them
a card, Carlo. Mr. Penezzi does the cookin' 'imself,
and if ever you want a real 'ome from 'ome, you'll
know where to find it. I like professional people, and
we'd 'ave a rare lot to talk about, you and me, dearie.
Once a professional always a professional, I say."

At that moment the head barman came back from
his supper. He caught sight of Syd.

"Oh, Mr. Cotman, Mr. Espinel was looking for
you, wants to see you particularly."

"Oh, where is he?"

"You'll find him around somewhere."

"We'll be going," said Mrs. Penezzi, getting up.
"Come and 'ave lunch with us one day, will you? I'd
like to show you my old photographs and me press
cuttin's. Fancy you not 'avin' 'eard of the 'uman
cannon ball. Why, I was as well known as the Tower
of London."

Mrs. Penezzi was not vexed at finding that these
young people had never even heard of her. She was
simply amused.

They bade one another good-bye, and Stella sank
back again into her chair.

"I'll just finish my beer," said Syd, "and then I'll
go and see what Paco wants. Will you stay here,

ducky, or would you like to go to your dressing room?"

Stella's hands were tightly clenched. She did not answer. Syd gave her a look and then quickly glanced away.

"Perfect riot, that old girl," he went on, in his hearty way. "Real figure of fun. I suppose it's true what she said. It's difficult to believe, I must say. Fancy 'er drawing all London, what, forty years ago? And the funny thing is, her thinking anybody remembered. Seemed as though she simply couldn't understand us not having heard of her even."

He gave Stella another glance, from the corner of his eye so that she should not see he was looking at her, and he saw she was crying. He faltered. The tears were rolling down her pale face. She made no sound.

"What's the matter, darling?"

"Syd, I can't do it again tonight," she sobbed.

"Why on earth not?"

"I'm afraid."

He took her hand.

"I know you better than that," he said. "You're the bravest little woman in the world. Have a brandy, that'll pull you together."

"No, that'd only make it worse."

"You can't disappoint your public like that."

"That filthy public. Swine who eat too much and drink too much. A pack of chattering fools with more money than they know what to do with. I can't stick them. What do they care if I risk my life?"

"Of course it's the thrill they come for, there's no denying that," he replied uneasily. "But you know and I know, there's no risk, not if you keep your nerve."

"But I've lost my nerve, Syd. I shall kill myself."

She had raised her voice a little, and he looked round quickly at the barman. But the barman was reading the *Eclaireur de Nice* and paying no attention.

"You don't know what it looks like from up there, the top of the ladder, when I look down at the tank. I give you my word, tonight I thought I was going to faint. I tell you I can't do it again tonight, you've got to get me out of it, Syd."

"If you funk it tonight it'll be worse tomorrow."

"No, it won't. It's having to do it twice kills me. The long wait and all that. You go and see Mr. Espinel and tell him I can't give two shows a night. It's more than my nerves'll stand."

"He'll never stand for that. The whole supper trade depends on you. It's only to see you they come in then at all."

"I can't help it, I tell you I can't go on."

He was silent for a moment. The tears still streamed down her pale little face, and he saw that she was quickly losing control of herself. He had felt for some days that something was up, and he had been anxious. He had tried not to give her an opportunity to talk. He knew obscurely that it was better for her not to put into words what she felt. But he had been worried. For he loved her.

"Anyhow, Espinel wants to see me," he said.

"What about?"

"I don't know. I'll tell him you can't give the show more than once a night and see what he says. Will you wait here?"

"No, I'll go along to the dressing room."

Ten minutes later he found her there. He was in great spirits and his step was jaunty. He burst open the door.

"I've got grand news for you, honey. They're keeping us on next month at twice the money."

He sprang forward to take her in his arms and kiss her, but she pushed him away.

"Have I got to go on again tonight?"

"I'm afraid you must. I tried to make it only one show a night, but he wouldn't hear of it. He says it's quite essential you should do the supper turn. And after all, for double the money, it's worth it."

She flung herself down on the floor and this time burst into a storm of tears.

"I can't, Syd, I can't. I shall kill myself."

He sat down on the floor and raised her head and took her in his arms and petted her.

"Buck up, darling. You can't refuse a sum like that. Why, it'll keep us all the winter, and we shan't have to do a thing. After all there are only four more days to the end of July, and then it's only August."

"No, no, no. I'm frightened. I don't want to die, Syd. I love you."

"I know you do, darling, and I love you. Why, since we married I've never looked at another woman. We've never had money like this before, and we shall never get it again. You know what these things are, we're a riot now, but we can't expect it to go on forever. We've got to strike while the iron's hot."

"D'you want me to die, Syd?"

"Don't talk so silly. Why, where should I be without you? You mustn't give way like this. You've got your self-respect to think of. You're famous all over the world."

"Like the human cannon ball was," she cried with a laugh of fury.

"That damned old woman," he thought.

He knew that was the last straw. Bad luck, Stella taking it like that.

"That was an eye-opener to me," she went on. "What do they come and see me over and over again for? On the chance they'll see me kill myself. And a week after I'm dead they'll have forgotten even my name. That's what the public is. When I looked at that painted old hag I saw it all. Oh, Syd, I'm so miserable." She threw her arms round his neck and pressed her face to his. "Syd, it's no good, I can't do it again."

"Tonight, d'you mean? If you really feel like that about it, I'll tell Espinel you've had a fainting fit. I daresay it'll be all right just for once."

"I don't mean tonight, I mean never."

She felt him stiffen a little.

"Syd dear, don't think I'm being silly. It's not just today, it's been growing on me. I can't sleep at night thinking of it, and when I do drop off I see myself standing at the top of the ladder and looking down. Tonight I could hardly get up it, I was trembling so, and when you lit the flames and said go, something seemed to be holding me back. I didn't even know I'd jumped. My mind was a blank till I found myself on the platform and heard them clapping. Syd, if you loved me you wouldn't want me to go through such torture."

He sighed. His own eyes were wet with tears. For he loved her devotedly.

"You know what it means," he said. "The old life. Marathons and all."

"Anything's better than this."

The old life. They both remembered it. Syd had been a dancing gigolo since he was eighteen. He was very good-looking in his dark Spanish way and full of life. Old women and middle-aged women were glad to pay to dance with him, and he was never out of work. He had drifted from England to the Continent, and there he had stayed, going from hotel to hotel, to the Riviera in the winter, to watering places in France in the summer. It wasn't a bad life they led. There were generally two or three of them together, the men, and they shared a room in cheap lodgings. They didn't have to get up till late, and they only dressed in time to go to the hotel at twelve to dance with stout women who wanted to get their weight down. Then they were free till five, when they went to the hotel again and sat at a table, the three of them together, keeping a sharp eye open for anyone who looked a likely client. They had their regular customers. At night they went to the restaurant, and the house provided them with quite a decent meal.

Between the courses they danced. It was good money. They generally got fifty or a hundred francs from anyone they danced with. Sometimes a rich woman, after dancing a good deal with one of them for two or three nights, would give him as much as a thousand francs. Sometimes a middle-aged woman would ask one to spend a night with her, and he would get two hundred and fifty francs for that. There was always the chance of a silly old fool losing her head, and then there were platinum and sapphire rings, cigarette cases, clothes and a wrist watch to be got. One of Syd's friends had married one of them who was old enough to be his mother, but she gave him a car and money to gamble with, and they lived in a beautiful villa at Biarritz. Those were the good days when everybody had money to burn. The slump came and hit the gigolos hard. The hotels were empty, and the clients didn't seem to want to pay for the pleasure of dancing with a nice-looking young fellow. Often and often Syd passed a whole day without earning the price of a drink, and more than once a fat old girl who weighed a ton had had the nerve to give him ten francs. His expenses didn't go down, for he had to be smartly dressed or the manager of the hotel made remarks, washing cost a packet, and you'd be surprised the amount of linen he needed; then shoes, those floors were terribly hard on shoes, and they had to look new. He had his room to pay for and his lunch.

It was then he met Stella. It was at Evian, and the season was disastrous. She was a swimming instructress. She was Australian and a beautiful diver. She gave exhibitions every morning and afternoon. At night she was engaged to dance at the hotel. They dined together at a little table in the restaurant apart from the guests, and when the band began to play they danced together to induce the customers to come onto the floor. But often no one followed them and they danced by themselves. Neither of them got anything much in the way of paying partners. They

fell in love with one another, and at the end of the
season got married.

They had never regretted it. They had gone through
hard times. Even though for business reasons (elderly
ladies didn't so much like the idea of dancing with
a married man when his wife was there), they concealed their marriage, it was not so easy to get a
hotel job for the pair of them, and Syd was far from
being able to earn enough to keep Stella, even in the
most modest pension, without working. The gigolo
business had gone to pot. They went to Paris and
learnt a dancing act, but the competition was fearful
and cabaret engagements were very hard to get.
Stella was a good ballroom dancer, but the rage was
for acrobatics, and however much they practised she
never managed to do anything startling. The public
was sick of the apache turn. They were out of a job
for weeks at a time. Syd's wrist watch, his gold
cigarette case, his platinum ring, all went up the
spout. At last they found themselves in Nice reduced
to such straits that Syd had to pawn his evening
clothes. It was a catastrophe. They were forced to
enter for the Marathon that an enterprising manager
was starting. Twenty-four hours a day they danced,
resting every hour for fifteen minutes. It was frightful. Their legs ached, their feet were numb. For long
periods they were unconscious of what they were
doing. They just kept time to the music, exerting

themselves as little as possible. They made a little money, people gave them sums of a hundred francs, or two hundred, to encourage them, and sometimes to attract attention they roused themselves to give an exhibition dance. If the public was in a good humour, this might bring in a decent sum. They grew terribly tired. On the eleventh day Stella fainted and had to give up. Syd went on by himself, moving, moving without pause, grotesquely, without a partner. That was the worst time they had ever had. It was the final degradation. It had left with them a recollection of horror and misery.

But it was then that Syd had his inspiration. It had come to him while he was slowly going round the hall by himself. Stella always said she could dive in a saucer. It was just a trick.

"Funny how ideas come," he said afterwards. "Like a flash of lightning."

He suddenly remembered having seen a boy set fire to some petrol that had been spilt on the pavement, and the sudden blaze-up. For of course it was the flames on the water and the spectacular dive into them that had caught the public fancy. He stopped dancing there and then; he was too excited to go on. He talked it over with Stella, and she was enthusiastic. He wrote to an agent who was a friend of his—everyone liked Syd, he was a nice little man—and the agent put up the money for the apparatus. He got

them an engagement at a circus in Paris, and the turn
was a success. They were made. Engagements followed here and there. Syd bought himself an entire
outfit of new clothes, and the climax came when they
got a booking for the summer casino on the coast. It
was no exaggeration of Syd's when he said that Stella
was a riot.

"All our troubles are over, old girl," he said fondly.
"We can put a bit by now for a rainy day, and when
the public's sick of this I'll just think of something
else."

And now, without warning, at the top of their
boom, Stella wanted to chuck it. He didn't know
what to say to her. It broke his heart to see her so
unhappy. He loved her more now even than when he
had married her. He loved her because of all they'd
gone through together—after all, for five days once
they'd had nothing to eat but a hunk of bread each
and a glass of milk—and he loved her because she'd
taken him out of all that; he had good clothes to wear
again and his three meals a day. He couldn't look
at her; the anguish in her dear grey eyes was more
than he could bear. Timidly she stretched out her
hand and touched his. He gave a deep sigh.

"You know what it means, honey. Our connection
in the hotels has gone west, and the business is finished, anyway. What there is'll go to people younger
than us. You know what these old women are as well

as I do, it's a boy they want, and besides, I'm not tall enough really. It didn't matter so much when I was a kid. It's no good saying I don't look my age, because I do."

"Perhaps we can get into pictures."

He shrugged his shoulders. They'd tried that before when they were down and out.

"I wouldn't mind what I did. I'd serve in a shop."

"D'you think jobs can be had for the asking?"

She began to cry again.

"Don't, honey. It breaks my heart."

"We've got a bit put by."

"I know we have. Enough to last us six months. And then it'll mean starvation. First popping the bits and pieces, and then the clothes'll have to go, same as they did before. And then dancing in low-down joints for our supper and fifty francs a night. Out of a job for weeks together. And Marathons whenever we hear of one. And how long will the public stand for them?"

"I know you think I'm unreasonable, Syd."

He turned and looked at her now. There were tears in her eyes. He smiled, and the smile he gave her was charming and tender.

"No, I don't, ducky. I want to make you happy. After all, you're all I've got. I love you."

He took her in his arms and held her. He could feel the beating of her heart. If Stella felt like that about it, well, he must just make the best of it. After all, supposing she were killed? No, no, let her chuck it and be damned to the money. She made a little movement.

"What is it, honey?"

She released herself and stood up. She went over to the dressing table.

"I expect it's about time for me to be getting ready," she said.

He started to his feet.

"You're not going to do a show tonight?"

"Tonight, and every night till I kill myself. What else is there? I know you're right, Syd. I can't go back to all that other, stinking rooms in fifth-rate hotels and not enough to eat. Oh, that Marathon. Why did you bring that up? Being tired and dirty for days at a time and then having to give up because flesh and blood just couldn't stand it. Perhaps I can go on another month and then there'll be enough to give you a chance of looking round."

"No, darling, I can't stand for that. Chuck it. We'll manage somehow. We starved before; we can starve again."

She slipped out of her clothes, and for a moment stood naked but for her stockings, looking at herself in the glass. She gave her reflection a hard smile.

"I mustn't disappoint my public," she sniggered.

The Voice of the Turtle

FOR SOME TIME I could not make up my mind if I
liked Peter Melrose or not. He had had a novel published that had caused some stir among the rather
dreary but worthy people who are always on the look-
out for new talent. Elderly gentlemen with nothing
much to do but go to luncheon parties praised it with
girlish enthusiasm, and wiry little women who didn't
get on with their husbands thought it showed promise. I read a few reviews. They contradicted one another freely. Some of the critics claimed that with this
first novel the author had sprung into the front rank
of English novelists: others reviled it. I did not read
it. I have learnt by experience that when a book
makes a sensation it is just as well to wait a year before you read it. It is astonishing how many books
then you need not read at all. But it chanced that one
day I met Peter Melrose. With some misgiving I had
accepted an invitation to a sherry party. It was in the

top flat of a converted house in Bloomsbury, and I was a trifle out of breath when I had climbed four flights of stairs. My hostesses were two women, much over life size, in early middle life, the sort of women who know all about the insides of motor cars and like a good tramp in the rain, but very feminine for all that, fond of eating out of paper bags. The drawing room, which they called "our workshop," though being of independent means neither had ever done a stroke of work in her life, was large and bare, furnished with rustless-steel chairs, which looked as though they could with difficulty support the very substantial weight of their owners, glass-topped tables and a vast divan covered with zebra skin. On the walls were bookshelves, and pictures by the better-known English imitators of Cézanne, Braque and Picasso. In the shelves, besides a number of "curious" books of the eighteenth century (for pornography is ageless) there were only the works of living authors, mostly first editions, and it was indeed to sign some of my own that I had been asked to the party.

It was quite small. There was but one other woman, who might have been a younger sister of my hostesses, for, though stout, she was not quite so stout, though tall, not quite so tall, and though hearty, not quite so hearty. I did not catch her name, but she answered to that of Boofuls. The only man besides myself was Peter Melrose. He was quite young, twenty-two or twenty-three, of the middle height, but with an ungainly figure that made him look squat. He had a reddish skin that seemed to fit over the bones of his face too tightly, a rather large Semitic nose, though he was not a Jew, and alert green eyes under bushy eyebrows. His brown hair, cut very short, was scurfy. He was dressed in the brown Norfolk jacket and grey flannel trousers that are worn by the art students who wander hatless along King's Road, Chelsea. An uncouth young man. Nor was there much to attract in his manner. He was self-assertive, disputatious and intolerant. He had a hearty contempt for his fellow writers which he expressed with zest. The satisfaction he gave me by his breezy attacks on reputations which for my part I considered exaggerated, but prudently held my tongue about, was only lessened by the conviction that no sooner would my back be turned than he would tear my own to shreds. He talked well. He was amusing and sometimes witty. I should have laughed at his sallies more easily if those three ladies had not been so unreasonably convulsed by them. They roared with laughter at what he said, whether it was funny or whether it was inept. He said many silly things, for he talked without stopping, but he also said some very clever ones. He had a point of view, crude and not so original as he thought, but sincere. But the most striking thing about him was his eager, impetuous vitality; it was like a hot flame that burnt him with an unendurable fury. It even shed a glow on those about him. He had something, if only that, and when I left it was with a slight sense of curiosity at what would come of him. I did not know if he had talent; so many young things can write a clever novel —that means nothing; but it seemed to me that as a man he was not quite like everybody else. He was the sort of person who at thirty, when time had softened his asperity and experience had taught him that he was not quite so intelligent as he thought, would turn into an interesting and agreeable fellow. But I never expected to see him again.

It was with surprise that I received two or three days later a copy of his novel with a very flattering dedication. I read it. It was obviously autobiographical. The scene was a small town in Sussex, and the characters of the upper middle class that strives to keep up appearances on an inadequate income. The humour was rather brutal and rather vulgar. It grated on me, for it consisted chiefly of mockery at people because they were old and poor. Peter Melrose did not know how hard those misfortunes are to bear, and that the efforts made to cope with them are more deserving of sympathy than of derision. But there were descriptions of places, little pictures of a room or impressions of the countryside, which were excellently done. They showed tenderness and a sense of the spiritual beauty of material things. The book was written easily, without affectation, and with a pleasant feeling for the sound of words. But what made it indeed somewhat remarkable, so that I understood why it had attracted attention, was the passion that quivered in the love story of which the plot, such as it was, consisted. It was, as is the modern fashion, more than a trifle coarse and, again in the modern fashion, it tailed off vaguely, without any particular result, so that everything was left in the end pretty much as it had been in the beginning; but you did get the impression of young love, idealistic and yet vehemently sexual; it was so vivid and so deeply felt that it took your breath away. It seemed to throb on the printed page like the pulse of life. It had no reticence. It was absurd, scandalous and beautiful. It was like a force of nature. That was passion all right. There is nothing, anywhere, so moving and so awe-inspiring.

I wrote to Peter Melrose and told him what I thought of his book, then suggested that we might lunch together. He rang me up next day, and we made a date.

I found him unaccountably shy when we sat down opposite one another at a table in a restaurant. I gave him a cocktail. He talked glibly enough, but I could not help seeing that he was ill at ease. I gained the impression that his self-assurance was a pose assumed to conceal, from himself maybe, a diffidence that tortured him. His manners were brusque and awkward. He would say a rude thing and then laugh nervously to cover his own embarrassment. Though he pretended to be so sure of himself, he wanted all the time to be reassured by you. By irritating you, by saying the things he thought would annoy, he tried to force from you some admission, tacit it might be, that he was as wonderful as he longed to think himself. He wanted to despise the opinion of his fellows, and nothing was more important to him. I thought him rather an odious young man, but I did not mind that. It is very natural that clever young men should be rather odious. They are conscious of gifts that they do not know how to use. They are exasperated with the world that will not recognize their merit. They have something to give, and no hand is stretched out to receive it. They are impatient for the fame they regard as their due. No, I do not mind odious young men; it is when they are charming that I button up the pockets of my sympathy.

Peter Melrose was extremely modest about his book. He blushed through his reddish skin when I praised what I liked in it, and accepted my strictures with a humility that was almost embarrassing. He had made very little money out of it, and his publishers were giving him a small monthly allowance in advance of royalties on the next one. This he had just started, but he wanted to get away to write it in peace, and knowing I lived on the Riviera he asked me if I could tell him of a quiet place where he could bathe and live cheaply. I suggested that he should come and spend a few days with me so that he could look about till he found something to suit him. His green eyes sparkled when I proposed this, and he flushed.

"Shouldn't I be an awful nuisance?"

"No. I shall be working. All I can offer you is three meals a day and a room to sleep in. It'll be very dull, but you can do exactly what you like."

"It sounds grand. May I let you know if I decide to come?"

"Of course."

We separated, and a week or two later I went home. This was in May. Early in June I received a letter from Peter Melrose asking, if I had really meant what I said when I invited him to spend a few days with me, whether he might arrive on such and such a date. Well, at the time I had meant it, but now, a month later, I remembered that he was an arrogant and ill-bred youth, whom I had seen but twice and wasn't in the least interested in, and I didn't mean it any longer. It seemed to me very likely that he would be bored stiff. I lived a very quiet life and saw few people. And I thought it would be a great strain on my nerves if he were as rude as I knew he could be and I as his host felt it behooved me to keep my temper. I saw myself driven beyond endurance and ringing the bell to have his clothes packed and the car brought round to take him away within half an hour. But there was nothing to do about it. It would save him the cost of board and lodging to spend a short period with me, and if he was tired and unhappy, as he said in his letter, it might be that it would do him good. I sent him a wire, and shortly afterwards he arrived.

He looked very hot and grubby in his grey flannel trousers and brown tweed coat when I met him at the station, but after a swim in the pool he changed into white shorts and a Cochet shirt. He looked then quite absurdly young. He had never been out of England before. He was excited. It was touching to see his delight. He seemed, amid those unaccustomed surroundings, to lose his sense of himself, and he was simple, boyish and modest. I was agreeably surprised. In the evening, after dinner, sitting in the garden, with only the croaking of the little green frogs to break the silence, he began talking to me of his novel. It was a romantic story about a young writer and a celebrated prima donna. The theme was reminiscent of Ouida, the last thing I should have expected this hard-boiled youth to write, and I was tickled; it was odd how the fashion completed the circle and returned generation after generation to the same themes. I had no doubt that Peter Melrose would treat it in a very modern way, but there it was, the same old story as had entranced sentimental readers in the three-volume novels of the eighties. He proposed to set it in the beginning of the Edwardian era, which to the young has already acquired the fantastic, far-away feeling of a past age. He talked and talked. He was not unpleasant to listen to. He had no notion that he was putting into fiction his own daydreams, the comic and touching daydreams of a rather unattractive, obscure young man who sees himself beloved, to the admiration of the whole world, by an incredibly beautiful, celebrated and magnificent woman. I always enjoyed the novels of Ouida, and Peter's idea did not at all displease me. With his charming gift of description, his vivid, ingenuous way of looking at material things, fabrics, pieces of furniture, walls, trees, flowers, and his power of representing the passion of life, the passion of love, that thrilled every fibre of his own uncouth body, I had a notion that he might well produce something exuberant, absurd and poetical. But I asked him a question.

"Have you ever known a prima donna?"

"No, but I've read all the autobiographies and memoirs that I could find. I've gone into it pretty thoroughly. Not only the obvious things, you know, but I've hunted around in all sorts of byways to get the revealing touch or the suggestive anecdote."

"And have you got what you wanted?"

"I think so."

He began to describe his heroine to me. She was young and beautiful, wilful it is true and with a quick temper, but magnanimous. A woman on the grand scale. Music was her passion; there was music not only in her voice, but in her gestures and in her inmost thoughts. She was devoid of envy, and her appreciation of art was such that when another singer had done her an injury she forgave her when she heard her sing a role beautifully. She was of a wonderful generosity, and would give away everything she possessed when a story of misfortune touched her soft heart. She was a great lover, prepared to sacrifice the world for the man she loved. She was intelligent and well read. She was tender, unselfish and disinterested. In fact she was much too good to be true.

"I think you'd better meet a prima donna," I said at last.

"How can I?"

"Have you ever heard of La Falterona?"

"Of course I have. I've read her memoirs."

"She lives just along the coast. I'll ring her up and ask her to dinner."

"Will you really? It would be wonderful."

"Don't blame me if you don't find her quite what you expect."

"It's the truth I want."

Everyone has heard of La Falterona. Not even

Melba had a greater reputation. She had ceased now to sing in opera, but her voice was still lovely, and she could fill a concert hall in any part of the world. She went for long tours every winter, and in summer rested in a villa by the sea. On the Riviera people are neighbours if they live thirty miles from one another, and for some years I had seen a good deal of La Falterona. She was a woman of ardent temperament, and she was celebrated not only for her singing, but for her love affairs: she never minded talking about them, and I had often sat entranced for hours while, with the humour which to me was her most astonishing characteristic, she regaled me with lurid tales of royal or very opulent adorers. I was satisfied that there was at least a measure of truth in them. She had been married, for short periods, three or four times, and in one of these unions had annexed a Neapolitan prince. Thinking that to be known as La Falterona was grander than any title, she did not use his name (to which indeed she had no right, since after divorcing him she had married somebody else); but her silver, her cutlery and her dinner service were heavily decorated with a coat of arms and a crown, and her servants invariably addressed her as *madame la princesse*. She claimed to be a Hungarian, but her English was perfect, she spoke it with a slight accent (when she remembered), but with an intonation suggestive, I had been told, of Kansas City. This she explained by saying that her father was a political exile who had fled to America when she was no more than a child; but she did not seem quite sure whether he was a distinguished scientist who had got into trouble for his liberal views, or a Magyar of high rank who had brought down on his head the imperial wrath because he had had a love affair with an archduchess. It depended on whether she was just an artist among artists, or a great lady among persons of noble birth.

With me she was, not natural, for that she could never have been if she had tried, but franker than with anyone else. She had a natural and healthy contempt for the arts. She genuinely looked upon the whole thing as a gigantic bluff, and deep down in her heart was an amused sympathy for all the people who were able to put it over on the public. I will admit that I looked forward to the encounter between Peter Melrose and La Falterona with a good deal of sardonic amusement.

She liked coming to dine with me because she knew the food was good. It was the only meal she ate in the day, for she took great care of her figure, but she liked that one to be succulent and ample. I asked her to come at nine, knowing that was the earliest hour she dreamt of eating, and ordered dinner for half past. She turned up at a quarter to ten. She was dressed in apple-green satin, cut very low in front, with no back at all, and she wore a string of huge pearls, a number of expensive-looking rings, and on her left arm diamond and emerald bracelets from the wrist to the elbow. Two or three of them were certainly real. On her raven black hair was a thin circlet of diamonds. She could not have looked more splendid if she had been going to a ball at Stafford House in the old days. We were in white ducks.

"How grand you are," I said. "I told you it wasn't a party."

She flashed a look of her magnificent black eyes at Peter.

"Of course it's a party. You told me your friend was a writer of talent. I am only an interpreter." She ran one finger down her flashing bracelets. "This is the homage I pay to the creative artist."

I did not utter the vulgar monosyllable that rose to my lips, but offered her what I knew was her favourite cocktail. I was privileged to call her Maria, and she always called me Master. This she did, first because she knew it made me feel a perfect fool, and secondly because, though she was in point of fact not more than two or three years younger than me, it made it quite clear that we belonged to different generations. Sometimes, however, she also called me "you dirty swine." This evening she certainly might very well have passed for thirty-five. She had those rather large features which somehow do not seem to betray age. On the stage she was a beautiful woman, and even in private life, notwithstanding her big nose, large mouth and fleshy face, a good-looking one. She wore a brown make-up, with dark rouge, and her lips were vividly scarlet. She looked very Spanish and, I suspected, felt it, for her accent at the beginning of dinner was quite Sevillian. I wanted her to talk so that Peter should get his money's worth, and I knew there was but one subject in the world that she could talk about. She was in point of fact a stupid woman who had acquired a line of glib chatter which made people on first meeting her think she was as brilliant as she looked; but it was merely a performance she gave, and you soon discovered that she not only did not know what she was talking about, but was not in the least interested in it. I do not think she had ever read a book in her life. Her knowledge of what was going on in the world was confined to what she was able to gather by looking at the pictures in the illustrated press. Her passion for music was complete bunkum. Once at a concert to which I went with her she slept all through the Fifth Symphony, and I was charmed to hear her during the interval telling people that Beethoven stirred her so much that she hesitated to come and hear him, for with those glorious themes singing through her head, it meant that she wouldn't sleep a wink all night. I could well believe she would lie awake, for she had had so sound a nap during the Symphony that it could not but interfere with her night's rest.

But there was one subject in which her interest never failed. She pursued it with indefatigable energy. No obstacle prevented her from returning to it; no chance word was so remote that she could not use it as a stepping-stone to come back to it, and in effecting this she displayed a cleverness of which one would never have thought her capable. On this subject she could be witty, vivacious, philosophic, tragic and inventive. It enabled her to exhibit all the resources of her ingenuity. There was no end to its ramifications, and no limit to its variety. This subject was herself. I gave her an opening at once, and then all I had to do was to make suitable interjections. She was in great form. We were dining on the terrace, and a full moon was obligingly shining on the sea in front of us. Nature, as though she knew what was proper to the occasion, had set just the right scene. The view was framed by two tall black cypresses, and all round us on the terrace the orange trees in full flower exhaled their heady perfume. There was no wind, and the candles on the table flamed with a steady softness. It was a light that exactly suited La Falterona. She sat between us, eating heartily and thoroughly appreciating the champagne, and she was enjoying herself. She gave the moon a glance. On the sea was a broad pathway of silver.

"How beautiful nature is," she said. "My God, the scenery one has to play in. How can they expect one to sing? You know, really, the sets at Covent Garden are a disgrace. The last time I sang Juliet I just told them I wouldn't go on unless they did something about the moon."

Peter listened to her in silence. He ate her words. She was better value than I had dared to hope. She got a little tight not only on the champagne but on her own loquaciousness. To listen to her you would have thought she was a meek and docile creature against whom the whole world was in conspiracy. Her life had been one long bitter struggle against desperate odds. Managers treated her vilely, impresarios played foul tricks on her, singers combined to ruin her, critics bought by the money of her enemies wrote scandalous things about her, lovers for whom she had sacrificed everything used her with base ingratitude; and yet, by the miracle of her genius and her quick wits, she had discomfited them all. With joyous glee, her eyes flashing, she told us how she had defeated their machinations and what disaster had befallen the wretches who had stood in her way. I wondered how she had the nerve to tell the disgraceful stories she told. Without the smallest consciousness of what she was doing she showed herself vindictive and envious, hard as nails, incredibly vain, cruel, selfish, scheming and mercenary. I stole a glance now and then at Peter. I was tickled at the confusion he must be experiencing when he compared his ideal picture of the prima donna with the ruthless reality. She was a woman without a heart. When at last she left us, I turned to Peter with a smile.

"Well," I said, "at all events you've got some good material."

"I know, and it all fits in so beautifully," he said with enthusiasm.

"Does it?" I exclaimed, taken aback.

"She's exactly like my woman. She'll never believe that I'd sketched out the main lines of the character before I'd ever seen her."

I stared at him in amazement.

"The passion for art. The disinterestedness. She has that same nobility of soul that I saw in my mind's eye. The small-minded, the curious, the vulgar put every obstacle in her way, and she sweeps them all aside by the greatness of her purpose and the purity of her ends." He gave a little happy laugh. "Isn't it wonderful how nature copies art? I swear to you, I've got her to the life."

I was about to speak; I held my tongue; though I shrugged a spiritual shoulder, I was touched. Peter had seen in her what he was determined to see. There was something very like beauty in his illusion. In his own way he was a poet. We went to bed, and two or three days later, having found a pension to his liking, he left me.

In course of time his book appeared, and like most second novels by young people it had but a very moderate success. The critics had overpraised his first effort and now were unduly censorious. It is of course a very different thing to write a novel about yourself and the people you have known from childhood and to write one about persons of your own invention. Peter's was too long. He had allowed his gift for word painting to run away with him, the humour was still rather vulgar; but he had reconstructed the period with skill, and the romantic story had that same thrill of real passion which in his first book had so much impressed me.

After the dinner at my house I did not see La Falterona for more than a year. She went for a long tour in South America and did not come down to the Riviera till late in the summer. One night she asked me to dine with her. We were alone but for her companion-secretary, an Englishwoman, Miss Glaser by name, whom La Falterona bullied and ill treated, hit and swore at, but whom she could not do without. Miss Glaser was a haggard person of fifty, with grey hair and a sallow, wrinkled face. She was a queer creature. She knew everything there was to be known about La Falterona. She both adored and hated her. Behind her back she could be extremely funny at her expense, and the imitation she gave in secret of the great singer with her admirers was the most richly comic thing I have ever heard. But she watched over her like a mother. It was she who, sometimes by wheedling, sometimes by sheer plainness of speech, caused La Falterona to behave herself something like a human being. It was she who had written the singer's exceedingly inaccurate memoirs.

La Falterona wore pale blue satin pyjamas (she liked satin) and, presumably to rest her hair, a green silk wig; except for a few rings, a pearl necklace, a couple of bracelets and a diamond brooch at her waist, she wore no jewelry. She had much to tell me of her triumphs in South America. She talked on and on. She had never been in more superb voice, and the ovations she had received were unparalleled. The concert halls were sold out for every performance, and she had made a packet.

"Is it true or it it not true, Glaser?" cried Maria with a strong South American accent.

"Most of it," said Miss Glaser.

La Falterona had the objectionable habit of addressing her companion by her surname. But it must long since have ceased to annoy the poor woman, so there was not much point in it.

"Who was that man we met in Buenos Aires?"

"Which man?"

"You fool, Glaser. You remember perfectly. The man I was married to once."

"Pepe Zapata," Miss Glaser replied without a smile.

"He was broke. He had the impudence to ask me to give him back a diamond necklace he'd given me. He said it had belonged to his mother."

"It wouldn't have hurt you to give it him," said Miss Glaser. "You never wear it."

"Give it him back?" cried La Falterona, and her astonishment was such that she spoke the purest English. "Give it him back? You're crazy."

She looked at Miss Glaser as though she expected her there and then to have an attack of acute mania. She got up from the table, for we had finished our dinner.

"Let us go outside," she said. "If I hadn't the patience of an angel I'd have sacked that woman long ago."

La Falterona and I went out, but Miss Glaser did not come with us. We sat on the veranda. There was a magnificent cedar in the garden, and its dark branches were silhouetted against the starry sky. The sea, almost at our feet, was marvellously still. Suddenly La Falterona gave a start.

"I almost forgot. Glaser, you fool," she shouted, "why didn't you remind me?" And then again to me: "I'm furious with you."

"I'm glad you didn't remember till after dinner," I answered.

"That friend of yours and his book."

I didn't immediately grasp what she was talking about.

"What friend and what book?"

"Don't be so stupid. An ugly little man with a shiny face and a bad figure. He wrote a book about me."

"Oh! Peter Melrose. But it's not about you."

"Of course it is. Do you take me for a fool? He had the impudence to send it me."

"I hope you had the decency to acknowledge it."

"Do you think I have the time to acknowledge all the books twopenny-halfpenny authors send me? I expect Glaser wrote to him. You had no right to ask me to dinner to meet him. I came to oblige you, because I thought you liked me for myself, I didn't know I was just being made use of. It's awful that one can't trust one's oldest friends to behave like gentlemen. I'll never dine with you again so long as I live. Never, never, never."

She was working herself into one of her tantrums, so I interrupted her before it was too late.

"Come off it, my dear," I said. "In the first place the character of the singer in that book, which I suppose is the one you're referring to——"

"You don't suppose I'm referring to the charwoman, do you?"

"Well, the character of the singer was roughed out before he'd even seen you, and besides it isn't in the least like you."

"How d'you mean, it's not like me? All my friends have recognized me. I mean, it's the most obvious portrait."

"Mary," I expostulated.

"My name is Maria, and no one knows it better than you, and if you can't call me Maria you can call me Madame Falterona or Princess."

I paid no attention to this.

"Did you read the book?"

"Of course I read it. When everyone told me it was about me."

"But the boy's heroine, the prima donna, is twenty-five."

"A woman like me is ageless."

"She's musical to her finger tips, gentle as a dove, and a miracle of unselfishness; she's frank, loyal and disinterested. Is that the opinion you have of yourself?"

"And what is *your* opinion of me?"

"Hard as nails, absolutely ruthless, a born intriguer and as self-centred as they make 'em."

She then called me a name which a lady does not habitually apply to a gentleman who, whatever his faults, has never had his legitimacy called in question. But though her eyes flashed I could see that she was not in the least angry. She accepted my description of her as complimentary.

"And what about the emerald ring? Are you going to deny that I told him that?"

The story of the emerald ring was this: La Falterona was having a passionate love affair with the Crown Prince of a powerful state, and he had made her a present of an emerald of immense value. One night they had a quarrel, high words passed, and some reference being made to the ring she tore it off her finger and flung it in the fire. The Crown Prince, being a man of thrifty habit, with a cry of consternation, threw himself on his knees and began raking out the coals till he recovered the ring. The Falterona watched him scornfully as he grovelled on the floor. She didn't give much away herself, but she could not bear economy in others. She finished the story with these splendid words:

"After that I *couldn't* love him."

The incident was picturesque and had taken Peter's fancy. He had used it very neatly.

"I told you both about that in the greatest confidence and I've never told it to a soul before. It's a scandalous breach of confidence to have put it into a book. There are no excuses either for him or for you."

"But I've heard you tell the story dozens of times. And it was told me by Florence Montgomerie about herself and the Crown Prince Rudolf. It was one of her favourite stories, too. Lola Montez used to tell it about herself and the King of Bavaria. I have little doubt that Nell Gwyn told it about herself and Charles II. It's one of the oldest stories in the world."

She was taken aback, but only for an instant.

"I don't see anything strange in its having happened more than once. Everyone knows that women are passionate and that men are as mean as cat's meat. I could show you the emerald if you liked. I had to have it reset of course."

"With Lola Montez it was pearls," I said ironically. "I believe they were considerably damaged."

"Pearls?" She gave that brilliant smile of hers. "Have I ever told you about Benjy Riesenbaum and the pearls? You might make a story out of it."

Benjy Riesenbaum was a person of great wealth, and it was common knowledge that for a long time he had been the Falterona's lover. In fact it was he who had bought her the luxurious little villa in which we were now sitting.

"He'd given me a very handsome string in New York. I was singing at the Metropolitan, and at the end of the season we travelled back to Europe together. You never knew him, did you?"

"No."

"Well, he wasn't bad in some ways, but he was insanely jealous. We had a row on the boat because a young Italian officer was paying me a good deal of attention. Heaven knows, I'm the easiest woman in the world to get on with, but I will not be bullied by any man. After all, I have my self-respect to think of. I told him where he got off, if you understand what I mean, and he slapped my face. On deck if you please. I don't mind telling you I was mad. I tore the string of pearls off my neck and flung it in the sea. 'They cost fifty thousand dollars,' he gasped. He went white. I drew myself up to my full height. 'I only valued them because I loved you,' I said. And I turned on my heel."

"You were a fool," I said.

"I wouldn't speak to him for twenty-four hours. At the end of that time I had him eating out of my hand. When we got to Paris the first thing he did was to go to Cartier's and buy me another just as good."

She began to giggle.

"Did you say I was a fool? I'd left the real string in the bank in New York, because I knew I was going back next season. It was an imitation one that I threw in the sea."

She started to laugh, and her laugh was rich and joyous and like a child's. That was the sort of trick that thoroughly appealed to her. She chortled with glee.

"What fools men are," she gasped. "And you, you thought I'd throw a real string into the sea."

She laughed and laughed. At last she stopped. She was excited.

"I want to sing. Glaser, play an accompaniment."
A voice came from the drawing room.

"You can't sing after all that food you walloped down."

"Shut up, you old cow. Play something, I tell you."

There was no reply, but in a moment Miss Glaser began to play the opening bars of one of Schumann's songs. It was no strain on the voice, and I guessed that Miss Glaser knew what she was doing when she chose it. La Falterona began to sing, in an undertone, but as she heard the sounds come from her lips and found that they were clear and pure, she let herself go. The song finished. There was silence. Miss Glaser had heard that La Falterona was in magnificent voice, and she sensed that she wished to sing again. The prima donna was standing in the window, with her back to the lighted room, and she looked out at the darkly shining sea. The cedar made a lovely pattern against the sky. The night was soft and balmy. Miss Glaser played a couple of bars. A cold shiver ran down my spine. La Falterona gave a little start as she recognized the music, and I felt her gather herself together.

> "*Mild und leise wie er lächelt*
> *Wie das Auge hold er öffnet.*"

It was Isolde's death song. She had never sung in Wagner, fearing the strain on her voice, but this, I suppose, she had often sung in concerts. It did not matter now that instead of an orchestral accompaniment she had only the thin tinkle of a piano. The notes of the heavenly melody fell upon the still air and travelled over the water. In that too-romantic scene, in that lovely night, the effect was shattering. La Falterona's voice, even now, was exquisite in its quality, mellow and crystalline; and she sang with wonderful emotion, so tenderly, with such tragic, beautiful anguish that my heart melted within me. I had a most awkward lump in my throat when she finished, and looking at her I saw that tears were streaming down her face. I did not want to speak. She stood quite still, looking out at that ageless sea.

What a strange woman! I thought then that I would sooner have her as she was, with her monstrous faults, than as Peter Melrose saw her, a pattern of all the virtues. But then people blame me because I rather like people who are a little worse than is reasonable. She was hateful, of course, but she was irresistible.

An Official Position

He was a sturdy broad-shouldered fellow, of the middle height; though his bones were well covered as became his age, which was fifty, he was not fat; he had a ruddy complexion which neither the heat of the sun nor the unwholesomeness of the climate had affected. It was good rich blood that ran through his veins. His hair was brown and thick, and only at the temples touched with grey; he was very proud of his fair, handsome moustache, and he kept it carefully brushed. There was a pleasant twinkle in his blue eyes. You would have said that this was a man whom life had treated well. There was in his appearance an air of good nature and in his vigour a glow of health that gave you confidence. He reminded you of one of those well-fed, rubicund burghers in an old Dutch picture, with their pink-cheeked wives, who made money and enjoyed the good things with which their industry provided them. He was, however, a widower. His name was Louis Remire, and his number 68763.

He was serving a twelve-year sentence at St. Laurent de Maroni, the great penal settlement of French Guiana, for killing his wife, but partly because he had served in the police force at Lyons, his native town, and partly on account of his good character, he had been given an official position. He had been chosen among nearly two hundred applicants to be the public executioner.

That was why he was allowed to sport the handsome moustache of which he took so much care. He was the only convict who wore one. It was in a manner of speaking his badge of office. That also was why he was allowed to wear his own clothes. The convicts wear pyjamas in pink-and-white stripes, round straw hats and clumsy boots with wooden soles and leather tops. Louis Remire wore espadrilles on his bare feet, blue cotton trousers, and a khaki shirt the open neck of which exposed to view his hairy and virile chest. When you saw him strolling about the public garden, with a kindly eye looking at the children, black or half-caste, who played there, you would have taken him for a respectable shopkeeper who was enjoying an hour's leisure. He had his own house. That was not only one of the perquisites of his office, but it was a necessity, since if he had lodged in the prison camp the convicts would have made short work of him. One morning he would have been found with his belly ripped open. It was true that the house was small, it was just a wooden shack of one room, with a lean-to that served as a kitchen; but it was surrounded by a tiny garden, within a palisade, and in the garden grew bananas, papayas and such vegetables as the climate allowed him to raise. The garden faced the sea and was surrounded by a coconut grove. The situation was charming. It was only a quarter of a mile from the prison, which was convenient for his rations. They were fetched by his assistant who lived with him. The assistant, a tall, gawky, ungainly fellow, with deep-set, staring eyes and cavernous jaws, was serving a life sentence for rape and murder; he was not very intelligent, but in civil life he had been a cook, and it was wonderful what, with the help of the vegetables they grew and such condiments as Louis Remire could afford to buy at the Chinese grocer's, he managed to do with the soup, potatoes and cabbage and eternal beef, beef for three hundred and sixty-five days of the year, which the prison kitchens provided. It was on this account that Louis Remire had pressed his claim on the commandant when it had been found necessary to get a new assistant. The last one's nerves had given way and, absurdly enough, thought Louis Remire with a good-natured laugh, he had developed scruples about capital punishment; now, suffering from neurasthenia, he was on the Ile St. Joseph, where the insane were confined.

His present assistant happened to be ill. He had

high fever and looked very much as if he were going to die. It had been necessary to send him to hospital. Louis Remire was sorry; he would not easily find so good a cook again. It was bad luck that this should have happened just now, for next day there was a job of work to be done. Six men were to be executed. Two were Algerians, one was a Pole, another a Spaniard from the mainland, and only two were French. They had escaped from prison in a band and gone up the river. For nearly twelve months, stealing, raping and killing, they had spread terror through the colony. People scarcely dared move from their homesteads. Recaptured at last, they had all been sentenced to death, but the sentence had to be confirmed by the Minister of the Colonies, and the confirmation had only just arrived. Louis Remire could not manage without help, and besides there was a lot to arrange beforehand; it was particularly unfortunate that on this occasion of all others he should have to depend on an inexperienced man. The commandant had assigned to him one of the turnkeys. The turnkeys are convicts like the others, but they have been given their places for good behaviour and they live in separate quarters. They are on the side of the authorities and so are disliked by the other prisoners. Louis Remire was a conscientious fellow, and he was anxious that everything next day should go without a hitch. He arranged that his temporary assistant should come that afternoon to the place where the guillotine was kept so that he might explain to him thoroughly how it worked and show him exactly what he would have to do.

The guillotine, when not in use, stood in a small room which was part of the prison building, but which was entered by a separate door from the outside. When he sauntered along there at the appointed hour he found the man already waiting. He was a large-limbed, coarse-faced fellow. He was dressed in the pink-and-white stripes of the prison garb, but as turn-key he wore a felt hat instead of the straw of common convicts.

"What are you here for?"

The man shrugged his shoulders.

"I killed a farmer and his wife."

"H'm. How long have you got?"

"Life."

He looked a brute, but you could never be sure of people. He had himself seen a warder, a big, powerful man, faint dead away at an execution. He did not want his assistant to have an attack of nerves at the wrong moment. He gave him a friendly smile, and with his thumb pointed to the closed door behind which stood the guillotine.

"This is another sort of job," he said. "There are six of them, you know. They're a bad lot. The sooner they're out of the way the better."

"Oh, that's all right. After what I've seen in this place I'm scared of nothing. It means no more to me than cutting the head off a chicken."

Louis Remire unlocked the door and walked in. His assistant followed him. The guillotine in that small room, hardly larger than a cell, seemed to take up a great deal of space. It stood grim and sinister. Louis Remire heard a slight gasp and, turning round, saw that the turnkey was staring at the instrument with terrified eyes. His face was sallow and drawn from the fever and the hookworm from which all the convicts intermittently suffered, but now its pallor was ghastly. The executioner smiled good-naturedly.

"Gives you a turn, does it? Have you never seen it before?"

"Never."

Louis Remire gave a little throaty chuckle.

"If you had, I suppose you wouldn't have survived to tell the tale. How did you escape it?"

"I was starving when I did my job. I'd asked for something to eat, and they set the dogs on me. I was condemned to death. My lawyer went to Paris, and he got the President to reprieve me."

"It's better to be alive than dead, there's no denying that," said Louis Remire, with that agreeable twinkle in his eyes.

He always kept his guillotine in perfect order. The wood, a dark hard native wood somewhat like mahogany, was highly polished; but there was a certain amount of brass, and it was Louis Remire's pride that this should be as bright and clean as the brasswork on a yacht. The knife shone as though it had just come out of the workshop. It was necessary not only to see that everything functioned properly, but to show his assistant how it functioned. It was part of the assistant's duty to refix the rope when the knife had dropped, and to do this he had to climb a short ladder.

It was with the satisfaction of a competent workman who knows his job from A to Z that Remire entered upon the necessary explanations. It gave him a certain quiet pleasure to point out the ingenuity of the apparatus. The condemned man was strapped to the bascule, a sort of shelf, and this by a simple mechanism was precipitated down and forwards so that the man's neck was conveniently under the knife. The conscientious fellow had brought with him a banana stem, about five feet long, and the turnkey had wondered why. He was now to learn. The stem was of about the same circumference and consistency as the human neck, so that it afforded a very good way, not only of showing a novice how the apparatus worked, but of making sure beforehand that it was in perfect order. Louis Remire placed the banana stem in position. He released the knife. It fell with incredible speed and with a great bang. From the time the man was attached to the bascule to the time his head was off only thirty seconds elapsed. The head fell in the basket. The executioner took it up by the ears and exhibited it to those whose duty it was to watch the execution. He uttered the solemn words:

"*Au nom de peuple français justice est faite*. In the name of the French people justice is done."

Then he dropped the head back into the basket. Tomorrow, with six to be dispatched, the trunk would have to be unstrapped from the bascule and placed with the head on a stretcher, and the next man brought forward. They were taken in the order of their guilt. The least guilty, executed first, were spared the horror of seeing the death of their mates.

"We shall have to be careful that the right head goes with the right body," said Louis Remire, in that rather jovial manner of his, "or there may be no end of confusion at the Resurrection."

He let down the knife two or three times in order to make quite sure that the assistant understood how to fix it, and then getting his cleaning materials from the shelf on which he kept them, set him to work on the brass. Though it was spotless, he thought that a final polish would do no harm. He leaned against the wall and idly smoked cigarettes.

Finally everything was in order and Louis Remire dismissed the assistant till midnight. At midnight they were moving the guillotine from the room in which it stood to the prison yard. It was always a bit of a job to set it up again, but it had to be in place an hour before dawn, at which time the execution took place. Louis Remire strolled slowly home to his shack. The afternoon was drawing to its close, and as he walked along he passed a working party who were returning to the prison. They spoke to one another in undertones, and he guessed that they spoke of him; some looked down, two or three threw him a glance of hatred, and one spat on the ground. Louis Remire, the end of a cigarette sticking to his lip, looked at them with irony. He was indifferent to the loathing, mingled with fear, with which they regarded him. It did not matter to him that not one of them would speak to him, and it only amused him to think that there was hardly one who would not gladly have thrust a knife into his guts. He had a supreme contempt for them all. He could take care of himself. He could use a knife as well as any of them, and he had confidence in his strength. The convicts knew that men were to be executed next day, and as always before an execution they were depressed and nervous. They went about their work in sullen silence, and the warders had to be more than usually on the alert.

"They'll settle down when it's all over," said Louis Remire as he let himself into his little compound.

The dogs barked as he came along, and brave though he was, he listened to their uproar with satisfaction. With his own assistant ill, so that he was alone in the house, he was not sorry that he had the protection of those two savage mongrels. They prowled about the coconut grove outside his compound all night, and they would give him good warning if anyone lurked there. They could be relied on to spring at the throat of any stranger who ventured too near. If his predecessor had had these dogs he wouldn't have come to his end.

The man who had been executioner before Louis Remire had only held the job a couple of years when one day he disappeared. The authorities thought he had run away; he was known to have a bit of money, and it was very probable that he had managed to make arrangements with the captain of a schooner to take him to Brazil. His nerves had given way. He had gone two or three times to the governor of the prison and told him that he feared for his life. He was convinced that the convicts were out to kill him. The governor felt pretty sure that his fears were groundless and paid no attention, but when the man was nowhere to be found he concluded that his terror had got the better of him and he had preferred to run the danger of escape, and the danger of being recaptured and put back into prison, rather than face the risk of an avenging convict's knife. About three weeks later the warder in charge of a working party in the jungle noticed a great flock of vultures clustered round a tree. These vultures, called urubus, are large black birds, of a horrible aspect, and they fly about the market place of St. Laurent, picking up the offal that is left there by the starving liberated convicts, and flit heavily from tree to tree in the neat, well-kept streets of the town. They fly in the prison yard to remind the convicts that if they attempt an escape into the jungle their end, ten to one, will be to have their bones picked clean by these loathsome creatures. They were fighting and screaming in such a mass round the tree that the warder thought there was something strange there. He reported it, and the commandant sent a party to see. They found a man hanging by the neck from one of the branches, and when they cut him down discovered that he was the executioner. It was given out that he had committed suicide, but there was a knife thrust in his back, and the convicts knew that he had been stabbed and then, still alive, taken to the jungle and hanged.

Louis Remire had no fear that anything of that sort would happen to him. He knew how his predecessor had been caught. The job had not been done by the convicts. By the French law when a man is sentenced to hard labour for a certain number of years he has at the expiration of his sentence to remain in the colony for the same number of years. He is free, but he may not stir from the spot that is assigned to him as a residence. In certain circumstances he can get a concession, and if he works hard he manages to scrape a bare living from it, but after a long term of penal servitude, during which he has lost all power of initiative, what with the debilitating effect of fever, hookworm and so on, he is unfit for heavy and continuous labour, and so most of the liberated men subsist on begging, larceny, smuggling tobacco or money to the prisoners, and loading and unloading cargoes when two or three times a month a steamer comes into the harbour. It was the wife of one of these freed men that had been the means of the undoing of Louis Remire's predecessor. She was a coloured woman, young and pretty, with a neat little figure and mischievous eyes. The plot was well considered. The executioner was a burly, sanguine man, of ardent passions. She had thrown herself in his way, and when she caught his approving glance, had cast him a saucy look. He saw her a day or two later in the public garden. He did not venture to speak to her (no one, man, woman or child, would be seen speaking to him), but when he winked at her she smiled. One evening he met her walking through the coconut grove that surrounded his compound. No one was about. He got into conversation with her. They only exchanged a few words, for she was evidently terrified of being seen with him. But she came again to the coconut grove. She played him carefully till his suspicions were allayed; she teased his desires; she made

him give her little presents, and at last on the promise
of what was for both of them quite a sum of money
she agreed to come one dark night to the compound.
A ship had just come in, and her husband would be
working till dawn. It was when he opened the door
for her and she hesitated to come in, as though at the
last moment she could not make up her mind, that he
stepped outside to draw her in, and fell to the ground
with the violence of the knife thrust in his back.

"The fool," muttered Louis Remire. "He only got
what he deserved. He should have smelt a rat. The
eternal vanity of man."

For his part he was through with women. It was on
account of women that he found himself in the situation he was in now, at least on account of one woman;
and besides, at his time of life, his passions were assuaged. There were other things in life, and after a
certain age a man, if he was sensible, turned his attention to them. He had always been a great fisherman.
In the old days, at home in France before he had had
his misfortune, as soon as he came off duty, he took
his rod and line and went down to the Rhone. He got
a lot of fishing now. Every morning, till the sun grew
hot, he sat on his favourite rock and generally managed to get enough for the prison governor's table.
The governor's wife knew the value of things and beat
him down on the price he asked, but he did not blame
her for that; she knew that he had to take what she

was prepared to give, and it would have been stupid
of her to pay a penny more than she had to. In any
case it brought in a little money useful for tobacco
and rum and other odds and ends. But this evening
he was going to fish for himself. He got his bait from
the lean-to, and his rod, and settled down on his rock.
No fish was so good as the fish you caught yourself,
and by now he knew which were those that were good
to eat and which were so tough and flavourless that
you could only throw them back into the sea. There
was one sort that, fried in real olive oil, was as good
as mullet. He had not been sitting there five minutes
when his float gave a sudden jerk, and when he pulled
up his line, there, like an answer to prayer, was one of
those very fish wriggling on the hook. He took it off,
banged its head on the rock, and putting it down, replaced his bait. Four of them would make a good
supper, the best a man could have, and with a night's
hard work before him he needed a hearty meal. He
would not have time to fish tomorrow morning. First
of all the scaffold would have to be taken down and
the pieces brought back to the room in which it was
kept, and there would be a lot of cleaning to do. It
was a bloody business; last time he had had his pants
so soaked that he had been able to do nothing with
them and had had to throw them away. The brass
would have to be polished, the knife would have to be
honed. He was not a man to leave a job half finished,

and by the time it was through he would be pretty peckish. It would be worth while to catch a few more fish and put them in a cool place so that he could have a substantial breakfast. A cup of coffee, a couple of eggs and a bit of fried fish; he could do with that. Then he would have a good sleep; after a night on his feet, the anxiety of an inexperienced assistant, and the clearing away of all the mess, God knew he would deserve it.

In front of him was spread the bay in a noble sweep, and in the distance was a little island green with trees. The afternoon was exquisitely still. Peace descended on the fisherman's soul. He watched his float idly. When you came to think of it, he reflected, he might be a great deal worse off; some of them, the convicts he meant, the convicts who swarmed in the prison a few hundred yards away from him, some of them had such a nostalgia for France that they went mad with melancholy; but he was a bit of a philosopher, so long as he could fish he was content; and did it really matter if he watched his float on the southern sea or in the Rhone? His thoughts wandered back to the past. His wife was an intolerable woman, and he did not regret that he had killed her. He had never meant to marry her. She was a dressmaker, and he had taken a fancy to her because she was always neatly and smartly dressed. She seemed respectable and ladylike. He would not have been surprised if she had looked upon herself as a cut above a policeman. But he had a way with him. She soon gave him to understand that she was no snob, and when he made the customary advances he discovered to his relief, for he was not a man who considered that resistance added a flavour to conquest, that she was no prude. He liked to be seen with her when he took her out to dinner. She talked intelligently, and she was economical. She knew where they could dine well at the cheapest price. His situation was enviable. It added to his satisfaction that he could gratify the sexual desires natural to his healthy temperament at so moderate an expense. When she came to him and said she was going to have a baby, it seemed natural enough that they should get married. He was earning good wages, and it was time that he should settle down. He often grew tired of eating, *en pension*, at a restaurant, and he looked forward to having his own home and home cooking. Well, it turned out that it had been a mistake about the baby, but Louis Remire was a good-natured fellow, and he didn't hold it up against Adèle. But he found, as many men have found before, that the wife was a very different woman from the mistress. She was jealous and possessive. She seemed to think that on a Sunday afternoon he ought to take her for a walk instead of going out fishing, and she made it a grievance that, on coming off duty, he would go to the café. There was one café he frequented where other fishermen went and where he met men with whom he had a lot in common. He found it much pleasanter to spend his free evenings there over a glass or two of beer, whiling away the time with a game of cards, than to sit at home with his wife. She began to make scenes. Though sociable and jovial by nature, he had a quick temper. There was a rough crowd at Lyons, and sometimes you could not manage them unless you were prepared to show a certain amount of firmness. When his wife began to make a nuisance of herself, it never occurred to him that there was any other way of dealing with her than that he adopted. He let her know the strength of his hand. If she had been a sensible woman she would have learnt her lesson, but she was not a sensible woman. He found occasion more and more often to apply a necessary correction; she revenged herself by screaming the place down and by telling the neighbours— they lived in a two-roomed apartment on the fifth floor of a big house—what a brute he was. She told them that she was sure he would kill her one day. And yet never was there a more good-natured man than Louis Remire; she blamed him for the money he spent at the café, she accused him of wasting it on other women; well, in his position he had opportunities now and then, and as any man would he took them, and he was easy with his money, he never minded paying a round of drinks for his friends, and when a girl who had been nice to him wanted a new hat or a pair of silk stockings he wasn't the man to say no. His wife looked upon money that he did not spend on her as money stolen from her; she tried to make him account for every penny he spent, and when in his jovial way he told her he had thrown it out of the window, she was infuriated. Her tongue grew bitter, and her voice was rasping. She was in a sullen rage with him all the time. She could not speak without saying something disagreeable. They led a cat-and-dog life. Louis Remire used to tell his friends what a harridan she was, he used to tell them that he wished ten times a day that he had never married her, and sometimes he would add that if an epidemic of influenza did not carry her off he would really have to kill her.

It was these remarks, made merely in jest, and the fact that she had so often told the neighbours that she knew he would murder her, that had sent him to St. Laurent de Maroni with a twelve-year sentence. Otherwise he might very well have got off with three or four years in a French prison. The end had come one hot summer's day. He was, which was rare for him, in a bad temper. There was a strike in progress, and the strikers had been violent. The police had had to make a good many arrests, and the men had not submitted to this peaceably. Louis Remire had got a nasty blow on the jaw, and he had had to make free

use of his truncheon. To get the arrested men to the
station had been a hot and tiring job. On coming off
duty he had gone home to get out of his uniform and
was intending to go to the café and have a glass of
beer and a pleasant game of cards. His jaw was hurt-
ing him. His wife chose that moment to ask him for
money, and when he told her that he had none to give
her she made a scene. He had plenty of money to go
to the café, but none for her to buy a scrap of food
with, she could starve for all he cared. He told her to
shut up, and then the row began. She got in front of
the door and swore that he should not pass till he gave
her money. He told her to get out of the way and took
a step towards her. She whipped out his service revolver which he had taken off when he removed his
uniform and threatened that she would shoot him if
he moved a step. He was used to dealing with dangerous criminals, and the words were hardly out of her
mouth before he had sprung upon her and snatched
the revolver out of her hand. She screamed and hit
him in the face. She hit him exactly where his jaw
most hurt him. Blind with rage and mad with pain,
he fired, he fired twice and she fell to the floor. For a
moment he stood and stared at her. He was dazed.
She looked as if she were dead. His first feeling was
one of indescribable relief. He listened. No one seemed
to have heard the sound of the shot. The neighbours
must be out. That was a bit of luck, for it gave him

time to do what he had to do in his own way. He changed back into his uniform, went out, locking the door behind him and putting the key in his pocket; he stopped for five minutes at his familiar café to have a glass of beer and then returned to the police station he had lately left. On account of the day's disturbances the chief inspector was still there. Louis Remire went to his room and told him what had happened. He spent the night in a cell adjoining those of the strikers he had so recently himself arrested. Even at that tragic moment he was struck by the irony of the situation.

Louis Remire had on frequent occasions appeared as a police witness in criminal cases, and he knew how eager are a man's companions to give any information that may damage him when he gets into trouble. It had caused him a certain grim amusement to realize how often it happened that a conviction was obtained only by the testimony of a prisoner's best friends. But notwithstanding his experience he was amazed, when his own case came up for trial, to listen to the evidence given by the proprietor of the little café he had so much frequented, and to that of the men who for years had fished with him, played cards with him and drunk with him. They seemed to have treasured every careless word he had ever uttered, the complaints he had made about his wife and the joking threats he had from time to time made that he would get even with her. He knew that at the time they had taken them no more seriously than he meant them. If he was able to do them a small service—and a man in the force often has it in his power to do one—he never hesitated. He had never been ungenerous with his money. You would have thought as you listened to them in the witness box that it gave them the most intense satisfaction to disclose every trivial detail that could damage him.

From what appeared at the trial you would have thought that he was a bad man, dissolute, of violent temper, extravagant, idle and corrupt. He knew that he was nothing of the kind. He was just an ordinary, good-natured, easy-going fellow, who was willing to let you go your way if you would let him go his. It was true that he liked his game of cards and his glass of beer, it was true that he liked a pretty girl, but what of it? When he looked at the jury he wondered how many of them would come out of it any better than he if all their errors, all their rash words, all their follies, were thus laid bare. He did not resent the long term of penal servitude to which he was sentenced. He was an officer of the law; he had committed a crime and it was right that he should be punished. But he was not a criminal; he was the victim of an unfortunate accident.

At St. Laurent de Maroni, in the prison camp, wearing the pink-and-white stripes of the prison garb and the ugly straw hat, he remembered still that he had been a policeman and that the convicts with whom he must now consort had always been his natural enemies. He despised and disliked them. He had as little to do with them as he could. And he was not frightened of them. He knew them too well. Like all the rest he had a knife, and he showed that he was prepared to use it. He did not want to interfere with anybody, but he was not going to allow anyone to interfere with him.

The chief of the Lyons police had liked him, his character while in the force had been exemplary, and the *fiche* which accompanied every prisoner spoke well of him. He knew that what officials like is a prisoner who gives no trouble, who accepts his position with cheerfulness and who is willing. He got a soft job; very soon he got a cell of his own and so escaped the horrible promiscuity of the dormitories; he got on well with the warders, they were decent chaps, most of them, and knowing that he had formerly been in the police they treated him more as a comrade than as a convict. The commandant of the prison trusted him. Presently he got the job of servant to one of the prison officials. He slept in the prison, but otherwise enjoyed complete freedom. He took the children of his master to school every day and fetched them at the end of their school hours. He made toys for them. He accompanied his mistress to market and carried back the provisions she bought. He spent long hours gossiping with her. The family liked him. They liked his chaffing manner and his good-natured smile. He was industrious and trustworthy. Life once more was tolerable.

But after three years his master was transferred to Cayenne. It was a blow. But it happened just then that the post of executioner fell free, and he obtained it. Now once more he was in the service of the state. He was an official. However humble his residence it was his own. He need no longer wear the prison uniform. He could grow his hair and his moustache. He cared little if the convicts looked upon him with horror and contempt. That was how he looked upon them. Scum. When he took the bleeding head of an executed man from the basket and, holding it by the ears, pronounced those solemn words: *Au nom du peuple français justice est faite*, he felt that he did represent the republic. He stood for law and order. He was the protector of society against that vast horde of ruthless criminals.

He got a hundred francs for each execution. That and what the governor's wife paid him for his fish provided him with many a pleasant comfort and not a few luxuries. And now as he sat on his rock in the peace of eventide he considered what he would do with the money he would earn next day. Occasionally he got a bite, now and then a fish; he drew it out of the water, took it off the hook and put on fresh bait; but he did this mechanically, and it did not disturb the current of his thoughts. Six hundred francs. It was a respectable sum. He scarcely knew what to do with it. He had everything he wanted in his little house, he had a good store of groceries, and plenty of rum for one who was as little of a drinker as he was; he needed no fishing tackle; his clothes were good enough. The only thing was to put it aside. He already had a tidy little sum hidden in the ground at the root of a papaya tree. He chuckled when he thought how Adèle would have stared had she known that he was actually saving. It would have been balm to her avaricious soul. He was saving up gradually for when he was released. That was the difficult moment for the convicts. So long as they were in prison they had a roof over their heads and food to eat, but when they were released, with the obligation of staying for so many years more in the colony, they had to shift for themselves. They all said the same thing: it was at the expiration of their term that their real punishment began. They could not get work. Employers mistrusted them. Contractors would not engage them because the prison authorities hired out convict labour at a price that defied competition. They slept in the open, in the market place, and for food were often glad to go to the Salvation Army. But the Salvation Army made them work hard for what they gave and

besides forced them to listen to their services. Sometimes they committed a violent crime merely to get
back to the safety of prison. Louis Remire was not
going to take any risks. He meant to amass a sufficient capital to start in business. He ought to be able
to get permission to settle in Cayenne, and there he
might open a bar. People might hesitate to come at
first because he had been the executioner, but if he
provided good liquor they would get over their preju-
dice, and with his jovial manner, with his experience
in keeping order, he ought to be able to make a go
of it. Visitors came to Cayenne now and then, and
they would come out of curiosity. It would be something interesting to tell their friends when they got
home that the best rum punch they had had in
Cayenne was at the executioner's. But he had a good
many years to go yet, and if there really was something he needed there was no reason why he shouldn't
get it. He racked his brains. No, there wasn't a thing
in the world he wanted. He was surprised. He allowed
his eyes to wander from his float. The sea was wonderfully calm, and now it was rich with all the colour of
the setting sun. In the sky already a solitary star
twinkled. A thought came to him that filled him with
an extraordinary sensation.

"But if there's nothing in the world you want,
surely that's happiness." He stroked his handsome
moustache and his blue eyes shone softly. "There are

no two ways about it. I'm a happy man and till this moment I never knew it."

The notion was so unexpected that he did not know what to make of it. It was certainly a very odd one. But there it was, as obvious to anyone with a logical mind as a proposition of Euclid.

"Happy, that's what I am. How many men can say the same? In St. Laurent de Maroni of all places, and for the first time in my life."

The sun was setting. He had caught enough fish for his supper and enough for his breakfast. He drew in his line, gathered up his fish, and went back to his house. It stood but a few yards from the sea. It did not take him long to light his fire, and in a little while he had four little fish cheerfully frizzling in a pan. He was always very particular about the oil he used. The best olive oil was expensive, but it was worth the money. The prison bread was good, and after he had fried his fish, he fried a couple of pieces of bread in the rest of the oil. He sniffed the savoury smell with satisfaction. He lit a lamp, washed a lettuce grown in his own garden, and mixed himself a salad. He had a notion that no one in the world could mix a salad better than he. He drank a glass of rum and ate his supper with appetite. He gave a few odds and ends to the two mongrel dogs who were lying at his feet, and then, having washed up—for he was by nature a tidy man, and when he came in to breakfast next morning

did not want to find things in a mess—let the dogs
out of the compound to wander about the coconut
grove. He took the lamp into the house, made himself
comfortable in his deck chair, and smoking a cigar
smuggled in from the neighbouring Dutch colony settled down to read one of the French papers that had
arrived by the last mail. Replete, his mind at ease, he
could not but feel that life, with all its disadvantages,
was good to live. He was still affected by the amused
surprise that had overcome him when it suddenly
occurred to him that he was a happy man. When you
considered that men spent their lives seeking for
happiness, it seemed hardly believable that he had
found it. Yet the fact stared him in the face. A man
who has everything he wants is happy. He had everything he wanted; therefore he was happy. He chuckled
as a new thought crossed his mind.

"There's no denying it, I owe it to Adèle."

Old Adèle. What a foul woman!

Presently he decided that he had better have a nap;
he set his alarm clock for a quarter to twelve and,
lying down on his bed, in a few minutes was fast
asleep. He slept soundly, and no dreams troubled
him. He woke with a start when the alarm sounded,
but in a moment remembered why he had set it. He
yawned and stretched himself lazily.

"Ah, well, I suppose I must get to work. Every job
has its inconveniences."

He slipped from under his mosquito net and relit his lamp. To freshen himself he washed his hands and face, and then as a protection against the night air drank a glass of rum. He thought for a moment of his inexperienced assistant and wondered whether it would be wise to take some rum in a flask with him.

"It would be a pretty business if his nerves went back on him."

It was unfortunate that so many as six men had to be executed. If there had been only one, it wouldn't have mattered so much his assistant being new to the game; but with five others waiting there, it would be awkward if there were a hitch. He shrugged his shoulders. They would just have to do the best they could. He passed a comb through his tousled hair and carefully brushed his handsome moustache. He lit a cigarette. He walked through his compound, unlocked the door in the stout palisade that surrounded it, and locked it again behind him. There was no moon. He whistled for his dogs. He was surprised that they did not come. He whistled again. The brutes. They'd probably caught a rat and were fighting over it. He'd give them a good hiding for that; he'd teach them not to come when he whistled! He set out to walk in the direction of the prison. It was dark under the coconut trees, and he would just as soon have had the dogs with him. Still there were only fifty yards to go, and then he would be out in the open. There were lights

in the governor's house, and it gave him confidence
to see them. He smiled, for he guessed what those
lights at that late hour meant; the governor, with the
execution before him at dawn, was finding it hard to
sleep. The anxiety, the malaise, that affected convicts
and ex-convicts alike on the eve of an execution, had
got on his nerves. It was true that there was always
the chance of an outbreak then, and the warders went
around with their eyes skinned and their hands ready
to draw their guns at a suspicious movement.

Louis Remire whistled for his dogs once more, but
they did not come. He could not understand it. It
was a trifle disquieting. He was a man who habitually
walked slowly, strolling along with a sort of roll, but
now he hastened his pace. He spat the cigarette out
of his mouth. It had struck him that it was prudent
not to betray his whereabouts by the light it gave.
Suddenly he stumbled against something. He stopped
dead. He was a brave man, with nerves of steel, but
on a sudden he felt sick with terror. It was something
soft and rather large that he had stumbled against,
and he was pretty sure what it was. He wore espadrilles, and with one foot he cautiously felt the object
on the ground before him. Yes, he was right. It was
one of his dogs. It was dead. He took a step backwards and drew his knife. He knew it was no good to
shout. The only house in the neighbourhood was the
prison governor's—it faced the clearing just beyond

the coconut grove; but they would not hear him, or if they did would not stir. St. Laurent de Maroni was not a place where you went out in the dead of night when you heard a man calling for help. If next day one of the freed convicts was found lying dead, well, it was no great loss. Louis Remire saw in a flash what had happened.

He thought rapidly. They had killed his dogs while he was sleeping. They must have got them when he had put them out of his compound after supper. They must have thrown them some poisoned meat and the brutes had snatched at it. If the one he had stumbled over was near his house, it was because it had tried to crawl home to die. Louis Remire strained his eyes. He could see nothing. The night was pitch black. He could hardly see the trunks of the coconut trees a yard away from him. His first thought was to make a rush for his shack. If he got back to the safety of that, he could wait till the prison people, wondering why he did not come, sent to fetch him. But he knew he could never get back. He knew they were there in the darkness, the men who had killed his dogs; he would have to fumble with the key to find the lock, and before he found it he would have a knife plunged in his back. He listened intently. There was not a sound. And yet he felt that there were men there, lurking behind the trees, and they were there to kill him. They would kill him as they had killed his dogs. And

he would die like a dog. There was more than one
certainly. He knew them, there were three or four of
them at least, there might be more, convicts in service in private houses who were not obliged to get
back to the camp till a late hour, or desperate and
starving freed men who had nothing to lose. For a
moment he hesitated what to do. He dared not make
a run for it, they might easily have put a rope across
the pathway that led from his house to the open, and
if he tripped he was done for. The coconut trees were
loosely planted, and among them his enemies would
see him as little as he saw them. He stepped over the
dead dog and plunged into the grove. He stood with
his back to a tree to decide how he should proceed.
The silence was terrifying. Suddenly he heard a whisper, and the horror of it was frightful. Again a dead
silence. He felt he must move on, but his feet seemed
rooted to the ground. He felt that they were peering
at him out of the darkness, and it seemed to him that
he was as visible to them as though he stood in the
broad light of day. Then from the other side was a
little cough. It came as such a shock that Louis
Remire nearly screamed. He was conscious now that
they were all round him. He could expect no mercy
from those robbers and murderers. He remembered
the other executioner, his predecessor, whom they had
carried still alive into the jungle, whose eyes they had
gouged out, and whom they had left hanging for the

vultures to devour. His knees began to tremble. What a fool he had been to take on the job! There were soft jobs he could have found in which you ran no risk. It was too late to think of that. He pulled himself together. He had no chance of getting out of the coconut grove alive, he knew that; he wanted to be sure that he would be dead. He tightened his grip on his knife. The awful part was that he could hear no one, he could see no one, and yet he knew that they were lurking there waiting to strike. For one moment he had a mad idea: he would throw his knife away and shout out to them that he was unarmed and they could come and kill him in safety. But he knew them; they would never be satisfied merely to kill him. Rage seized him. He was not the man to surrender tamely to a pack of criminals. He was an honest man and an official of the state; it was his duty to defend himself. He could not stay there all night. It was better to get it over quickly. Yet that tree at his back seemed to offer a sort of security; he could not bring himself to move. He stared at the trunk of a tree in front of him, and suddenly it moved and he realized with horror that it was a man. That made up his mind for him, and with a huge effort he stepped forwards. He advanced slowly and cautiously. He could hear nothing, he could see nothing. But he knew that as he advanced they advanced too. It was as though he were accompanied by an invisible bodyguard. He thought he could hear the sound of their naked feet on the ground. His fear had left him. He walked on, keeping as close to the trees as he could, so that they should have less chance of attacking him from behind; a wild hope sprang up in his breast that they would be afraid to strike, they knew him, they all knew him, and whoever struck the first blow would be lucky if he escaped a knife in his own guts; he had only another thirty yards to go, and once in the open, able to see, he could make a fight for it. A few yards more and then he would run for his life. Suddenly something happened that made him start out of his skin, and he stopped dead. A light was flashed, and in that heavy darkness the sudden glare was terrifying. It was an electric torch. Instinctively he sprang to a tree and stood with his back to it. He could not see who held the light. He was blinded by it. He did not speak. He held his knife low; he knew that when they struck it was in the belly, and if someone flung himself at him he was prepared to strike back. He was going to sell his life dearly. For half a minute perhaps the light shone on his face, but it seemed to him an eternity. He thought now that he discerned dimly the faces of men. Then a word broke the horrible silence.

"Throw."

At the same instant a knife came flying through the air and struck him on the breastbone. He threw up his hands and as he did so someone sprang at him and with a great sweep of the knife ripped up his belly. The light was switched off. Louis Remire sank to the ground with a groan, a terrible groan of pain. Five, six men gathered out of the gloom and stood over him. With his fall the knife that had stuck in his breastbone was dislodged. It lay on the ground. A quick flash of the torch showed where it was. One of the men took it and with a single, swift motion cut Remire's throat from ear to ear.

"*Au nom du peuple français justice est faite,*" he said.

They vanished into the darkness, and in the coconut grove was the immense silence of death.

The Facts of Life

It was Henry Garnet's habit on leaving the city of an afternoon to drop in at his club and play bridge before going home to dinner. He was a pleasant man to play with. He knew the game well, and you could be sure that he would make the best of his cards. He was a good loser; and when he won was more inclined to ascribe his success to his luck than to his skill. He was indulgent, and if his partner made a mistake, could be trusted to find an excuse for him. It was surprising then on this occasion to hear him telling his partner with unnecessary sharpness that he had never seen a hand worse played; and it was more surprising still to see him not only make a grave error himself, an error of which you would never have thought him capable, but when his partner, not unwilling to get a little of his own back, pointed it out, insist against all reason and with considerable heat that he was perfectly right. But they were all old friends, the men he was playing with, and none of them took his ill humour very seriously. Henry Garnet was a broker, a partner in a firm of repute, and it occurred to one of them that something had gone wrong with some stock he was interested in.

"How's the market today?" he asked.

"Booming. Even the suckers are making money."

It was evident that stocks and shares had nothing to do with Henry Garnet's vexation; but something was the matter; that was evident, too. He was a hearty fellow who enjoyed excellent health; he had plenty of money; he was fond of his wife and devoted to his children. As a rule he had high spirits, and he laughed easily at the nonsense they were apt to talk while they played; but today he sat glum and silent. His brows were crossly puckered, and there was a sulky look about his mouth. Presently, to ease the tension, one of the others mentioned a subject upon which they all knew Henry Garnet was glad to speak.

"How's your boy, Henry? I see he's done pretty well in the tournament."

Henry Garnet's frown grew darker.

"He's done no better than I expected him to."

"When does he come back from Monte?"

"He got back last night."

"Did he enjoy himself?"

"I suppose so; all I know is that he made a damned fool of himself."

"Oh. How?"

"I'd rather not talk about it if you don't mind."

The three men looked at him with curiosity. Henry Garnet scowled at the green baize.

"Sorry, old boy. Your call."

The game proceeded in a strained silence. Garnet got his bid, and when he played his cards so badly that he went three down not a word was said. Another rubber was begun, and in the second game Garnet denied a suit.

"Having none?" his partner asked him.

Garnet's irritability was such that he did not even reply, and when at the end of the hand it appeared that he had revoked, and that his revoke cost the rubber, it was not to be expected that his partner should let his carelessness go without remark.

"What the devil's the matter with you, Henry?" he said. "You're playing like a fool."

Garnet was disconcerted. He did not so much mind losing a big rubber himself, but he was sore that his inattention should have made his partner lose too. He pulled himself together.

"I'd better not play any more. I thought a few rubbers would calm me, but the fact is I can't give my mind to the game. To tell you the truth I'm in a hell of a temper."

They all burst out laughing.

"You don't have to tell us that, old boy. It's obvious."

Garnet gave them a rueful smile.

"Well, I bet you'd be in a temper if what's happened to me had happened to you. As a matter of fact I'm in a damned awkward situation, and if any of you fellows can give me any advice how to deal with it I'd be grateful."

"Let's have a drink and you tell us all about it. With a K.C., a Home Office official and an eminent surgeon—if we can't tell you how to deal with a situation, nobody can."

The K.C. got up and rang the bell for a waiter.

"It's about that damned boy of mine," said Henry Garnet.

Drinks were ordered and brought. And this is the story that Henry Garnet told them.

The boy of whom he spoke was his only son. His name was Nicholas, and of course he was called Nicky. He was eighteen. The Garnets had two daughters besides, one of sixteen and the other of twelve, but however unreasonable it seemed, for a father is generally supposed to like his daughters best, and though he did all he could not to show his preference, there was no doubt that the greater share of Henry Garnet's affection was given to his son. He was kind, in a chaffing, casual way, to his daughters, and gave them handsome presents on their birthdays and at Christmas; but he doted on Nicky. Nothing was too good for him. He thought the world of him. He could

hardly take his eyes off him. You could not blame
him, for Nicky was a son that any parent might have
been proud of. He was six foot two, lithe but muscu-
lar, with broad shoulders and a slim waist, and he
held himself gallantly erect; he had a charming head,
well placed on the shoulders, with pale brown hair
that waved slightly, blue eyes with long dark lashes
under well-marked eyebrows, a full red mouth and
a tanned, clean skin. When he smiled he showed very
regular and very white teeth. He was not shy, but
there was a modesty in his demeanour that was
attractive. In social intercourse he was easy, polite
and quietly gay. He was the offspring of nice, healthy,
decent parents, he had been well brought up in a good
home, he had been sent to a good school, and the
general result was as engaging a specimen of young
manhood as you were likely to find in a long time.
You felt that he was as honest, open and virtuous as
he looked. He had never given his parents a moment's
uneasiness. As a child he was seldom ill and never
naughty. As a boy he did everything that was expected of him. His school reports were excellent. He
was wonderfully popular, and he ended his career,
with a creditable number of prizes, as head of the
school and captain of the football team. But this was
not all. At the age of fourteen Nicky had developed
an unexpected gift for lawn tennis. This was a game
that his father not only was fond of, but played very

well, and when he discerned in the boy the promise of a tennis player he fostered it. During the holidays he had him taught by the best professionals, and by the time he was sixteen he had won a number of tournaments for boys of his age. He could beat his father so badly that only parental affection reconciled the older player to the poor show he put up. At eighteen Nicky went to Cambridge and Henry Garnet conceived the ambition that before he was through with the university he should play for it. Nicky had all the qualifications for becoming a great tennis player. He was tall, he had a long reach, he was quick on his feet and his timing was perfect. He realized instinctively where the ball was coming and, seemingly without hurry, was there to take it. He had a powerful serve, with a nasty break that made it difficult to return, and his forehand drive, low, long and accurate, was deadly. He was not so good on the backhand and his volleying was wild, but all through the summer before he went to Cambridge Henry Garnet made him work on these points under the best teacher in England. At the back of his mind, though he did not even mention it to Nicky, he cherished a further ambition, to see his son play at Wimbledon, and who could tell, perhaps be chosen to represent his country in the Davis Cup. A great lump came into Henry Garnet's throat as he saw in fancy his son leap over the net to shake hands with the American champion whom he had just defeated, and walk off the court to the deafening plaudits of the multitude.

As an assiduous frequenter of Wimbledon, Henry Garnet had a good many friends in the tennis world, and one evening he found himself at a city dinner sitting next to one of them, a Colonel Brabazon, and in due course began talking to him of Nicky and what chance there might be of his being chosen to play for his university during the following season.

"Why don't you let him go down to Monte Carlo and play in the spring tournament there?" said the Colonel suddenly.

"Oh, I don't think he's good enough for that. He's not nineteen yet, he only went up to Cambridge last October; he wouldn't stand a chance against all those cracks."

"Of course, Austin and Von Cramm and so on would knock spots off him, but he might snatch a game or two; and if he got up against some of the smaller fry there's no reason why he shouldn't win two or three matches. He's never been up against any of the first-rate players, and it would be wonderful practice for him. He'd learn a lot more than he'll ever learn in the seaside tournaments you enter him for."

"I wouldn't dream of it. I'm not going to let him leave Cambridge in the middle of a term. I've always impressed upon him that tennis is only a game and it mustn't interfere with work."

Colonel Brabazon asked Garnet when the term ended.

"That's all right. He'd only have to cut about three days. Surely that could be arranged. You see, two of the men we were depending on have let us down, and we're in a hole. We want to send as good a team as we can. The Germans are sending their best players, and so are the Americans."

"Nothing doing, old boy. In the first place Nicky's not good enough, and secondly, I don't fancy the idea of sending a kid like that to Monte Carlo without anyone to look after him. If I could get away myself I might think of it, but that's out of the question."

"I shall be there. I'm going as the nonplaying captain of the English team. I'll keep an eye on him."

"You'll be busy, and besides, it's not a responsibility I'd like to ask you to take. He's never been abroad in his life, and to tell you the truth, I shouldn't have a moment's peace all the time he was there."

They left it at that, and presently Henry Garnet went home. He was so flattered by Colonel Brabazon's suggestion that he could not help telling his wife.

"Fancy his thinking Nicky's as good as that. He told me he'd seen him play and his style was fine. He only wants more practice to get into the first flight.

We shall see the kid playing in the semifinals at Wimbledon yet, old girl."

To his surprise Mrs. Garnet was not so much opposed to the notion as he would have expected.

"After all the boy's eighteen. Nicky's never got into mischief yet, and there's no reason to suppose he will now."

"There's his work to be considered; don't forget that. I think it would be a very bad precedent to let him cut the end of term."

"But what can three days matter? It seems a shame to rob him of a chance like that. I'm sure he'd jump at it if you asked him."

"Well, I'm not going to. I haven't sent him to Cambridge just to play tennis. I know he's steady, but it's silly to put temptation in his way. He's much too young to go to Monte Carlo by himself."

"You say he won't have a chance against these crack players, but you can't tell."

Henry Garnet sighed a little. On the way home in the car it had struck him that Austin's health was uncertain and that Von Cramm had his off days. Supposing, just for the sake of argument, that Nicky had a bit of luck like that—then there would be no doubt that he would be chosen to play for Cambridge. But of course that was all nonsense.

"Nothing doing, my dear. I've made up my mind, and I'm not going to change it."

Mrs. Garnet held her peace. But next day she wrote to Nicky, telling him what had happened, and suggested to him what she would do in his place if, wanting to go, he wished to get his father's consent. A day or two later Henry Garnet received a letter from his son. He was bubbling over with excitement. He had seen his tutor, who was a tennis player himself, and the Provost of his college, who happened to know Colonel Brabazon, and no objection would be made to his leaving before the end of term; they both thought it an opportunity that shouldn't be missed. He didn't see what harm he could come to, and if only, just this once, his father would stretch a point, well, next term, he promised faithfully, he'd work like blazes. It was a very pretty letter. Mrs. Garnet watched her husband read it at the breakfast table; she was undisturbed by the frown on his face. He threw it over to her.

"I don't know why you thought it necessary to tell Nicky something I told you in confidence. It's too bad of you. Now you've thoroughly unsettled him."

"I'm so sorry. I thought it would please him to know that Colonel Brabazon had such a high opinion of him. I don't see why one should only tell people the disagreeable things that are said about them. Of course I made it quite clear that there could be no question of his going."

"You've put me in an odious position. If there's

anything I hate it's for the boy to look upon me as a spoilsport and a tyrant."

"Oh, he'll never do that. He may think you rather silly and unreasonable, but I'm sure he'll understand that it's only for his own good that you're being so unkind."

"Christ," said Henry Garnet.

His wife had a great inclination to laugh. She knew the battle was won. Dear, oh dear, how easy it was to get men to do what you wanted. For appearance' sake Henry Garnet held out for forty-eight hours, but then he yielded, and a fortnight later Nicky came to London. He was to start for Monte Carlo next morning, and after dinner, when Mrs. Garnet and her elder daughter had left them, Henry took the opportunity to give his son some good advice.

"I don't feel quite comfortable about letting you go off to a place like Monte Carlo at your age practically by yourself," he finished, "but there it is, and I can only hope you'll be sensible. I don't want to play the heavy father, but there are three things especially that I want to warn you against: one is gambling, don't gamble; the second is money, don't lend anyone money; and the third is women, don't have anything to do with women. If you don't do any of those three things you can't come to much harm, so remember them well."

"All right, Father," Nicky smiled.

"That's my last word to you. I know the world pretty well, and believe me, my advice is sound."

"I won't forget it. I promise you."

"That's a good chap. Now let's go up and join the ladies."

Nicky beat neither Austin nor Von Cramm in the Monte Carlo tournament, but he did not disgrace himself. He snatched an unexpected victory over a Spanish player and gave one of the Austrians a closer match than anyone had thought possible. In the mixed doubles he got into the semifinals. His charm conquered everyone, and he vastly enjoyed himself. It was generally allowed that he showed promise, and Colonel Brabazon told him that when he was a little older and had had more practice with first-class players he would be a credit to his father. The tournament came to an end, and the day following he was to fly back to London. Anxious to play his best, he had lived very carefully, smoking little and drinking nothing, and going to bed early; but on his last evening he thought he would like to see something of the life in Monte Carlo of which he had heard so much. An official dinner was given to the tennis players, and after dinner with the rest of them he went into the Sporting Club. It was the first time he had been there. Monte Carlo was very full, and the rooms were crowded. Nicky had never before seen roulette played except in the pictures; in a maze he stopped at the first table he came to; chips of different sizes were scattered over the green cloth in what looked like a hopeless muddle; the croupier gave the wheel a sharp turn and with a flick threw in the little white ball. After what seemed an endless time the ball stopped and another croupier with a broad, indifferent gesture raked in the chips of those who had lost.

Presently Nicky wandered over to where they were playing *trente et quarante*, but he couldn't understand what it was all about, and he thought it dull. He saw a crowd in another room and sauntered in. A big game of baccara was in progress, and he was immediately conscious of the tension. The players were protected from the thronging bystanders by a brass rail; they sat round the table, nine on each side, with the dealer in the middle and the croupier facing him. Big money was changing hands. The dealer was a member of the Greek Syndicate. Nicky looked at his impassive face. His eyes were watchful, but his expression never changed whether he won or lost. It was a terrifying, strangely impressive sight. It gave Nicky, who had been thriftily brought up, a peculiar thrill to see someone risk a thousand pounds on the turn of a card and when he lost make a little joke and laugh. It was all terribly exciting. An acquaintance came up to him.

"Been doing any good?" he asked.

"I haven't been playing."

"Wise of you. Rotten game. Come and have a drink."

"All right."

While they were having it Nicky told his friend that this was the first time he had ever been in the rooms.

"Oh, but you must have one little flutter before you go. It's idiotic to leave Monte without having tried your luck. After all it won't hurt you to lose a hundred francs or so."

"I don't suppose it will, but my father wasn't any too keen on my coming at all, and one of the three things he particularly advised me not to do was to gamble."

But when Nicky left his companion he strolled back to one of the tables where they were playing roulette. He stood for a while looking at the losers' money being raked in by the croupier and the money that was won paid out to the winners. It was impossible to deny that it was thrilling. His friend was right, it did seem silly to leave Monte without putting something on the table just once. It would be an experience, and at his age you had to have all the experience you could get. He reflected that he hadn't promised his father not to gamble, he'd promised him not to forget his advice. It wasn't quite the

same, was it? He took a hundred-franc note out of
his pocket and rather shyly put it on number eighteen.
He chose it because that was his age. With a wildly
beating heart he watched the wheel turn; the little
white ball whizzed about like a small demon of mischief; the wheel went round more slowly, the little
white ball hesitated, it seemed about to stop, it went
on again; Nicky could hardly believe his eyes when
it fell into number eighteen. A lot of chips were passed
over to him, and his hands trembled as he took them.
It seemed to amount to a lot of money. He was so
confused that he never thought of putting anything
on the following round; in fact he had no intention
of playing any more, once was enough; and he was
surprised when eighteen again came up. There was
only one chip on it.

"By George, you've won again," said a man who
was standing near to him.

"Me? I hadn't got anything on."

"Yes, you had. Your original stake. They always
leave it on unless you ask for it back. Didn't you
know?"

Another packet of chips was handed over to him.
Nicky's head reeled. He counted his gains: seven
thousand francs. A queer sense of power seized him;
he felt wonderfully clever. This was the easiest way
of making money that he had ever heard of. His
frank, charming face was wreathed in smiles. His

bright eyes met those of a woman standing by his side. She smiled.

"You're in luck," she said.

She spoke English, but with a foreign accent.

"I can hardly believe it. It's the first time I've ever played."

"That explains it. Lend me a thousand francs, will you? I've lost everything I've got. I'll give it you back in half an hour."

"All right."

She took a large red chip from his pile and with a word of thanks disappeared. The man who had spoken to him before grunted.

"You'll never see that again."

Nicky was dashed. His father had particularly advised him not to lend anyone money. What a silly thing to do! And to somebody he'd never seen in his life. But the fact was, he felt at that moment such a love for the human race that it had never occurred to him to refuse. And that big red chip, it was almost impossible to realize that it had any value. Oh, well, it didn't matter, he still had six thousand francs, he'd just try his luck once or twice more, and if he didn't win he'd go home. He put a chip on sixteen, which was his elder sister's age, but it didn't come up; then on twelve, which was his younger sister's, and that didn't come up either; he tried various numbers at random, but without success. It was funny, he seemed to have lost his knack. He thought he would try just once more and then stop; he won. He had made up all his losses and had something over. At the end of an hour, after various ups and downs, having experienced such thrills as he had never known in his life, he found himself with so many chips that they would hardly go in his pockets. He decided to go. He went to the changers' office, and he gasped when twenty thousand-franc notes were spread out before him. He had never had so much money in his life. He put it in his pocket and was turning away when the woman to whom he had lent the thousand francs came up to him.

"I've been looking for you everywhere," she said. "I was afraid you'd gone. I was in a fever, I didn't know what you'd think of me. Here's your thousand francs and thank you so much for the loan."

Nicky, blushing scarlet, stared at her with amazement. How he had misjudged her! His father had said, don't gamble; well, he had, and he'd made twenty thousand francs; and his father had said, don't lend anyone money; well, he had, he'd lent quite a lot to a total stranger, and she'd returned it. The fact was that he wasn't nearly such a fool as his father thought: he'd had an instinct that he could lend her the money with safety, and you see, his instinct was right. But he was so obviously taken aback that the little lady was forced to laugh.

"What is the matter with you?" she asked.

"To tell you the truth I never expected to see the money back."

"What did you take me for? Did you think I was a—cocotte?"

Nicky reddened to the roots of his wavy hair.

"No, of course not."

"Do I look like one?"

"Not a bit."

She was dressed very quietly, in black, with a string of gold beads round her neck; her simple frock showed off a neat, slight figure; she had a pretty little face and a trim head. She was made up, but not excessively, and Nicky supposed that she was not more than three or four years older than himself. She gave him a friendly smile.

"My husband is in the administration in Morocco, and I've come to Monte Carlo for a few weeks because he thought I wanted a change."

"I was just going," said Nicky because he couldn't think of anything else to say.

"Already!"

"Well, I've got to get up early tomorrow. I'm going back to London by air."

"Of course. The tournament ended today, didn't it? I saw you play, you know, two or three times."

"Did you? I don't know why you should have noticed me."

"You've got a beautiful style. And you looked very sweet in your shorts."

Nicky was not an immodest youth, but it did cross his mind that perhaps she had borrowed that thousand francs in order to scrape acquaintance with him.

"Do you ever go to the Knickerbocker?" she asked.

"No. I never have."

"Oh, but you mustn't leave Monte without having been there. Why don't you come and dance a little? To tell you the truth, I'm starving with hunger, and I should adore some bacon and eggs."

Nicky remembered his father's advice not to have anything to do with women, but this was different; you had only to look at the pretty little thing to know at once that she was perfectly respectable. Her husband was in what corresponded, he supposed, to the civil service. His father and mother had friends who were civil servants, and they and their wives sometimes came to dinner. It was true that the wives were neither so young nor so pretty as this one, but she was just as ladylike as they were. And after winning twenty thousand francs he thought it wouldn't be a bad idea to have a little fun.

"I'd love to go with you," he said. "But you won't mind if I don't stay very long. I've left instructions at my hotel that I'm to be called at seven."

"We'll leave as soon as ever you like."

Nicky found it very pleasant at the Knickerbocker.

He ate his bacon and eggs with appetite. They shared a bottle of champagne. They danced, and the little lady told him he danced beautifully. He knew he danced pretty well, and of course she was easy to dance with. As light as a feather. She laid her cheek against his and when their eyes met there was in hers a smile that made his heart go pit-a-pat. A coloured woman sang in a throaty, sensual voice. The floor was crowded.

"Have you ever been told that you're very good-looking?" she asked.

"I don't think so," he laughed. "Gosh," he thought, "I believe she's fallen for me."

Nicky was not such a fool as to be unaware that women often liked him, and when she made that remark he pressed her to him a little more closely. She closed her eyes, and a faint sigh escaped her lips.

"I suppose it wouldn't be quite nice if I kissed you before all these people," he said.

"What do you think they would take me for?"

It began to grow late, and Nicky said that really he thought he ought to be going.

"I shall go too," she said. "Will you drop me at my hotel on your way?"

Nicky paid the bill. He was rather surprised at its amount, but with all that money he had in his pocket he could afford not to care, and they got into a taxi.

She snuggled up to him, and he kissed her. She seemed to like it.

"By Jove," he thought, "I wonder if there's anything doing."

It was true that she was a married woman, but her husband was in Morocco, and it certainly did look as if she'd fallen for him. Good and proper. It was true also that his father had warned him to have nothing to do with women, but, he reflected again, he hadn't actually promised he wouldn't, he'd only promised not to forget his advice. Well, he hadn't; he was bearing it in mind that very minute. But circumstances alter cases. She was a sweet little thing; it seemed silly to miss the chance of an adventure when it was handed to you like that on a tray. When they reached the hotel he paid off the taxi.

"I'll walk home," he said. "The air will do me good after the stuffy atmosphere of that place."

"Come up a moment," she said. "I'd like to show you the photo of my little boy."

"Oh, have you got a little boy?" he exclaimed, a trifle dashed.

"Yes, a sweet little boy."

He walked upstairs after her. He didn't in the least want to see the photograph of her little boy, but he thought it only civil to pretend he did. He was afraid he'd made a fool of himself; it occurred to him that she was taking him up to look at the photograph in order to show him in a nice way that he'd made a mistake. He'd told her he was eighteen.

"I suppose she thinks I'm just a kid."

He began to wish he hadn't spent all that money on champagne at the night club.

But she didn't show him the photograph of her little boy after all. They had no sooner got into her room than she turned to him, flung her arms round his neck, and kissed him full on the lips. He had never in all his life been kissed so passionately.

"Darling," she said.

For a brief moment his father's advice once more crossed Nicky's mind, and then he forgot it.

Nicky was a light sleeper, and the least sound was apt to wake him. Two or three hours later he awoke and for a moment could not imagine where he was. The room was not quite dark, for the door of the bathroom was ajar, and the light in it had been left on. Suddenly he was conscious that someone was moving about the room. Then he remembered. He saw that it was his little friend, and he was on the point of speaking when something in the way she was behaving stopped him. She was walking very cautiously, as though she were afraid of waking him; she stopped once or twice and looked over at the bed. He wondered what she was after. He soon saw. She went over to the chair on which he had placed his clothes and once more looked in his direction. She waited for what seemed to him an interminable time. The silence was so intense that Nicky thought he could hear his own heart beating. Then, very slowly, very quietly, she took up his coat, slipped her hand into the inside pocket and drew out all those beautiful thousand-franc notes that Nicky had been so proud to win. She put the coat back and placed some other clothes on it so that it should look as though it had not been disturbed, then, with the bundle of notes in her hand, for an appreciable time stood once more stock-still. Nicky had repressed an instinctive impulse to jump up and grab her; it was partly surprise that had kept him quiet, partly the notion that he was in a strange hotel, in a foreign country, and if he made a row he didn't know what might happen. She looked at him. His eyes were partly closed, and he was sure that she thought he was asleep. In the silence she could hardly fail to hear his regular breathing. When she had reassured herself that her movements had not disturbed him, she stepped, with infinite caution, across the room. On a small table in the window a cineraria was growing in a pot. Nicky watched her now with his eyes wide open. The plant was evidently placed quite loosely in the pot, for, taking it by the stalks, she lifted it out; she put the bank notes in the bottom of the pot and replaced the plant. It was an excellent hiding place.

No one could have guessed that anything was concealed under that richly flowering plant. She pressed the earth down with her fingers and then, very slowly, taking care not to make the smallest noise, crept across the room and slipped back into bed.

"Chéri," she said, in a caressing voice.

Nicky breathed steadily, like a man immersed in deep sleep. The little lady turned over on her side and disposed herself to slumber. But though Nicky lay so still, his thoughts worked busily. He was extremely indignant at the scene he had just witnessed, and to himself he spoke his thoughts with vigour.

"She's nothing but a damned tart. She and her dear little boy and her husband in Morocco. My eye! She's a rotten thief, that's what she is. Took me for a mug. If she thinks she's going to get away with anything like that, she's mistaken."

He had already made up his mind what he was going to do with the money he had so cleverly won. He had long wanted a car of his own and had thought it rather mean of his father not to have given him one. After all, a feller doesn't always want to drive about in the family bus. Well, he'd just teach the old man a lesson and buy one himself. For twenty thousand francs, two hundred pounds roughly, he could get a very decent second-hand car. He meant to get the money back, but just then he didn't quite know how. He didn't like the idea of kicking up a row, he was a stranger, in a hotel he knew nothing of; it might very well be that the beastly woman had friends there; he didn't mind facing anyone in a fair fight, but he'd look pretty foolish if someone pulled a gun on him. He reflected besides, very sensibly, that he had no proof the money was his. If it came to a show-down and she swore it was hers, he might very easily find himself hauled off to a police station. He really didn't know what to do. Presently by her regular breathing he knew that the little lady was asleep. She must have fallen asleep with an easy mind, for she had done her job without a hitch. It infuriated Nicky that she should rest so peacefully while he lay awake, worried to death. Suddenly an idea occurred to him. It was such a good one that it was only by the exercise of all his self-control that he prevented him-self from jumping out of bed and carrying it out at once. Two could play at her game. She'd stolen his money; well, he'd steal it back again, and they'd be all square. He made up his mind to wait quite quietly until he was sure that deceitful woman was sound asleep. He waited for what seemed to him a very long time. She did not stir. Her breathing was as regular as a child's.

"Darling," he said at last.

No answer. No movement. She was dead to the world. Very slowly, pausing after every movement, very silently, he slipped out of bed. He stood still for a while, looking at her to see whether he had disturbed her. Her breathing was as regular as before. During the time he was waiting he had taken note carefully of the furniture in the room so that in crossing it he should not knock against a chair or a table and make a noise. He took a couple of steps and waited; he took a couple of steps more; he was very light on his feet and made no sound as he walked; he took fully five minutes to get to the window, and here he waited again. He started, for the bed slightly creaked, but it was only because the sleeper turned in her sleep. He forced himself to wait till he had counted one hundred. She was sleeping like a log. With infinite care he seized the cineraria by the stalks and gently pulled it out of the pot; he put his other hand in, his heart beat nineteen to the dozen as his fingers touched the notes, his hand closed on them and he slowly drew them out. He replaced the plant and in his turn carefully pressed down the earth. While he was doing all this he had kept one eye on the form lying in the bed. It remained still. After another pause he crept softly to the chair on which his clothes were lying. He first put the bundle of notes in his coat pocket and then proceeded to dress. It took him a good quarter of an hour, because he could afford to make no sound. He had been wearing a soft shirt with his dinner jacket, and he congratulated himself on this because it was easier to put on silently than a stiff one. He had some difficulty in tying his tie without a looking glass, but he very wisely reflected that it didn't really matter if it wasn't tied very well. His spirits were rising. The whole thing now began to seem rather a lark. At length he was completely dressed except for his shoes, which he took in his hand; he thought he would put them on when he got into the passage. Now he had to cross the room to get to the door. He reached it so quietly that he could not have disturbed the lightest sleeper. But the door had to be unlocked. He turned the key very slowly; it creaked.

"Who's that?"

The little woman suddenly sat up in bed. Nicky's heart jumped to his mouth. He made a great effort to keep his head.

"It's only me. It's six o'clock and I've got to go. I was trying not to wake you."

"Oh, I forgot."

She sank back onto the pillow.

"Now that you're awake I'll put on my shoes."

He sat down on the edge of the bed and did this.

"Don't make a noise when you go out. The hotel people don't like it. Oh, I'm so sleepy."

"You go right off to sleep again."

"Kiss me before you go." He bent down and kissed her. "You're a sweet boy and a wonderful lover. *Bon voyage*."

Nicky did not feel quite safe till he got out of the hotel. The dawn had broken. The sky was unclouded, and in the harbour the yachts and the fishing boats lay motionless on the still water. On the quay fishermen were getting ready to start on their day's work. The streets were deserted. Nicky took a long breath of the sweet morning air. He felt alert and well. He also felt as pleased as Punch. With a swinging stride, his shoulders well thrown back, he walked up the hill and along the gardens in front of the Casino—the flowers in that clear light had a dewy brilliance that was delicious—till he came to his hotel. Here the day had already begun. In the hall porters with mufflers round their necks and berets on their heads were busy sweeping. Nicky went up to his room and had a hot bath. He lay in it and thought with satisfaction that he was not such a mug as some people might think. After his bath he did his exercises, dressed, packed and went down to breakfast. He had a grand appetite. No continental breakfast for him! He had grapefruit, porridge, bacon and eggs, rolls fresh from the oven, so crisp and delicious they melted in your mouth, marmalade and three cups of coffee. Though feeling perfectly well before, he felt better after that. He lit the pipe he had recently learnt to smoke, paid his bill and stepped into the car that was waiting to take him to the aerodrome on the other side of Cannes. The road as far as Nice ran over the hills, and below him

was the blue sea and the coast line. He couldn't help
thinking it damned pretty. They passed through
Nice, so gay and friendly in the early morning, and
presently they came to a long stretch of straight road
that ran by the sea. Nicky had paid his bill, not with
the money he had won the night before, but with
the money his father had given him; he had changed
a thousand francs to pay for supper at the Knickerbocker, but that deceitful little woman had returned
him the thousand francs he had lent her, so that he
still had twenty thousand-franc notes in his pocket.
He thought he would like to have a look at them. He
had so nearly lost them that they had a double value
for him. He took them out of his hip pocket into
which for safety's sake he had stuffed them when he
put on the suit he was travelling in, and counted
them one by one. Something very strange had happened to them. Instead of there being twenty notes,
as there should have been, there were twenty-six.
He couldn't understand it at all. He counted them
twice more. There was no doubt about it; somehow
or other he had twenty-six thousand francs instead
of the twenty he should have had. He couldn't make
it out. He asked himself if it was possible that he had
won more at the Sporting Club than he had realized.
But no, that was out of the question; he distinctly
remembered the man at the desk laying the notes
out in four rows of five, and he had counted them

himself. Suddenly the explanation occurred to him; when he had put his hand into the flower pot, after taking out the cineraria, he had grabbed everything he felt there. The flower pot was the little hussy's money box, and he had taken out not only his own money, but her savings as well. Nicky leant back in the car and burst into a roar of laughter. It was the funniest thing he had ever heard in his life. And when he thought of her going to the flower pot sometime later in the morning when she awoke, expecting to find the money she had so cleverly got away with, and finding, not only that it wasn't there, but that her own had gone too, he laughed more than ever. And so far as he was concerned there was nothing to do about it, he knew neither her name nor the name of the hotel to which she had taken him. He couldn't return her money even if he wanted to.

"It serves her damned well right," he said.

This then was the story that Henry Garnet told his friends over the bridge table, for the night before, after dinner when his wife and daughter had left them to their port, Nicky had narrated it in full.

"And you know what infuriated me is that he's so damned pleased with himself. Talk of a cat swallowing a canary. And d'you know what he said to me when he'd finished? He looked at me with those innocent eyes of his and said: 'You know, Father, I can't help thinking there was something wrong about the advice you gave me. You said, don't gamble; well, I did, and I made a packet; you said, don't lend money; well, I did, and I got it back; and you said, don't have anything to do with women; well, I did, and I made six thousand francs on the deal.'"

It didn't make it any better for Henry Garnet that his three companions burst out laughing.

"It's all very well for you fellows to laugh, but you know, I'm in a damned awkward position. The boy looked up to me, he respected me, he took whatever I said as gospel truth, and now, I saw it in his eyes, he just looks upon me as a drivelling old fool. It's no good my saying one swallow doesn't make a summer; he doesn't see that it was just a fluke, he thinks the whole thing was due to his own cleverness. It may ruin him."

"You do look a bit of a damned fool, old man," said one of the others. "There's no denying that, is there?"

"I know I do, and I don't like it. It's so dashed unfair. Fate has no right to play one tricks like that. After all, you must admit that my advice was good."

"Very good."

"And the wretched boy ought to have burnt his fingers. Well, he hasn't. You're all men of the world, you tell me how I'm to deal with the situation now."

But they none of them could.

"Well, Henry, if I were you I wouldn't worry," said the lawyer. "My belief is that your boy's born lucky, and in the long run that's better than to be born clever or rich."